THE WHITE PRIORY MURDERS

THE WHITE PRIORY MURDERS

A MYSTERY FOR CHRISTMAS

CARTER DICKSON

With an Introduction by
Martin Edwards

Introduction © 2022, 2023 by Martin Edwards
The White Priory Murders © 1934 by The Estate of Clarice M. Carr
Cover and internal design © 2023 by Sourcebooks
Cover image © NRM/Pictorial Collection/Science & Society Picture Library

Published by Poisoned Pen Press, an imprint of Sourcebooks,
in association with the British Library
P.O. Box 4410, Naperville, Illinois 60567-4410
(630) 961-3900
sourcebooks.com

The White Priory Murders was originally published in the
UK in 1935 by William Heinemann, London.

Cataloging-in-Publication Data is on file with the Library of Congress.

Printed and bound in the United States of America.
KP 10 9 8 7 6 5 4 3 2 1

Contents

Introduction

The White Priory Murders is an "impossible crime" novel by the master of the locked-room mystery, John Dickson Carr, masquerading as Carter Dickson, the name associated with his stories featuring Sir Henry Merrivale. Originally published in 1934, this was Merrivale's second recorded case, written with youthful verve at a time when the author was still in his twenties.

This is a mystery set in the run-up to Christmas, and the presence of snow on the ground provides the scenario for the paradox at the heart of the book. How could someone be beaten to death in the Queen's Mirror pavilion, when it is surrounded by snow, and there is just one set of footprints leading to the pavilion, and none leading away?

The first edition of the novel listed the key characters on the flap of the dust jacket:

"*Marcia Tait*, glamorous film star, who has broken her Hollywood contract to open in a London play, *The Private Life of Charles II;*

The eccentric *Maurice Bohun*, author of the play, and
　　Master of the White Priory;
John Bohun, his brother, in love with Marcia Tait;
Emery (publicity) and *Rainger* (production), who have
　　rushed after Marcia Tait from Hollywood, trying to
　　persuade her to return;
Mouthy old *Lord Canifest*, backer of the play, and his
　　subdued daughter, Louise;
The lovely niece of the Bohuns, *Katharine Bohun*; Young
　　James Bennett, American, nephew of *Sir Henry
　　Merrivale*; and *Chief Inspector Masters*.

　　*Two of these people are murdered.
　　And one of them is the murderer."*

This is, therefore, not only an impossible crime story, but a "closed circle" mystery in the "fair play" tradition, in which the culprit is a member of a tightly defined group. The device of revealing that group in a "cast list" at the start of a detective novel was later developed into something of a fine art by Carr's friend and fellow Detection Club member Christianna Brand.

In an admiring review in the *Sunday Times*, Dorothy L. Sayers praised the way the author kept "the equilibrium between his plot and his writing," adding: "Mr. Dickson has handled this classic material very capably, using scrupulous fairness in deduction and concealing the identity of his criminal with considerable cunning. His group of characters contains a number of oddities, but the oddities are both interesting and believable, and he uses his skill in suggesting queerness, both of psychology and atmosphere, for the legitimate double purpose of distracting attention from the material clues and preparing our minds to accept his solution."

Sir Henry Merrivale, often called "H.M." or "the old man," had made his debut in a locked-room-mystery novel published earlier in 1934, *The Plague Court Murders*. When writing that book, Carr envisaged the official police detective Masters would take centre stage. Merrivale only enters the story half-way through. The novel was published under a pseudonym partly (in effect) as a matter of branding, so as to differentiate it from his stories about Henri Bencolin and Dr. Gideon Fell; he'd already published a non-series mystery, *The Bowstring Murders*, under the even more transparent pen-name, Carr Dickson.

Merrivale is a larger than life individual, with a personality so vivid that Carr soon realised that he, rather than the Scotland Yard man, should take centre stage in the books. Ultimately, Sir Henry appeared in twenty-two novels and two short stories, including "The House in Goblin Wood," one of the finest of all detective puzzles in the short form.

Carr (1906–77) published his last Merrivale novel, *The Cavalier's Cup*, in 1953, but the appeal of the character was such that for many years readers begged his creator to revive him. Among these fans was Francis Wilford Smith, who began to correspond with Carr after trying to put together a comprehensive chronology of Merrivale's adventures. He calculated, for instance, that the events recorded in *The White Priory Murders* take place in December 1931.

Sir Henry Merrivale was a baronet and a man of varied

accomplishments. A qualified physician, he was also a barrister, as we see to dramatic effect in *The Judas Window* (1938), widely acknowledged as one of the finest locked-room mysteries ever written. Initially characterized as "a fighting socialist," he eventually shifts his political affiliations to fall in line with Carr's conservative worldview. During the First World War he served as head of the British counter-espionage operations (earning the nickname "Mycroft"), and he continued to hold this post in the post-war era. Secret service work plays a part in three of his recorded adventures, *The Unicorn Murders* (1935), *The Punch and Judy Murders* (1936), and *And So To Murder* (1940), but his greatest gift is for detecting ingenious crimes and unravelling the puzzles which arise from what he calls "the blinkin' awful cussedness of things in general."

Carr took a great deal of care when constructing his intricate plots, but like most crime writers responsible for a long series, he proved fallible on matters of detail about his protagonist. He admitted in a letter to Smith that: "Errors or contradictions...abound in H.M.'s saga... During the nineteen-thirties, being young and full of beans, I was grinding out four novels a year." As for bringing Merrivale back to life, he said: "Many readers seem fond of...the old gentleman... I also am fond of him. But that's just the trouble. For many years certain critics...have been bewailing my 'schoolboy' sense of humour. H.M. usually enters the story with a rush and a crash, heels in the air. Once, in an unwise moment, I gave the date of his birth: February 6th, 1871. If he were alive today he would be ninety-six years old. His customary antics at so venerable an age would be as inadvisable for him to perform as for me to chronicle."

Carr flirted with the idea of setting a new story "back to a time when he [Merrivale] was a mere stripling… In that case…even so deplorable a sense of humour might be pardoned for one or two books more." In discussion with his literary agents, he contemplated titles such as *Commander Sir Henry Merrivale, Enter Three Poisoners,* and *The Nine Black Reasons.* Ultimately, he decided against writing more stories about the old man. Nevertheless, the Merrivale canon includes some outstanding examples of the impossible crime scenario, and *The White Priory Murders* is an entertaining illustration of Carr's skill as a literary conjuror.

—Martin Edwards
www.martinedwardsbooks.com

A Note from the Publisher

The original novels and short stories reprinted in the British Library Crime Classics series were written and published in a period ranging, for the most part, from the 1890s to the 1960s. There are many elements of these stories which continue to entertain modern readers; however, in some cases there are also uses of language, instances of stereotyping and some attitudes expressed by narrators or characters which may not be endorsed by the publishing standards of today. We acknowledge therefore that some elements in the works selected for reprinting may continue to make uncomfortable reading for some of our audience. With this series, British Library Publishing and Poisoned Pen Press aim to offer a new readership a chance to read some of the rare books of the British Library's collections in an affordable paperback format, to enjoy their merits, and to look back into the world of the twentieth century as portrayed by its writers. It is not possible to separate these stories from the history of their writing and as such the following stories are presented as they were originally published with the inclusion of minor edits made for consistency of style and sense, and with pejorative terms of an extremely offensive nature partly obscured. We welcome feedback from our readers.

I

CERTAIN REFLECTIONS
IN THE MIRROR

'Humph,' said H.M., 'so you're my nephew, hey?' He continued to peer morosely over the tops of his glasses, his mouth turned down sourly and his big hands folded over his big stomach. His swivel chair squeaked behind the desk. He sniffed. 'Well, have a cigar, then. And some whisky.—What's so blasted funny, hey? You got a cheek, you have. What're you grinnin' at, curse you?'

The nephew of Sir Henry Merrivale had come very close to laughing in Sir Henry Merrivale's face. It was, unfortunately, the way nearly everybody treated the great H.M., including all his subordinates at the War Office, and this was a very sore point with him. Mr. James Boynton Bennett could not help knowing it. When you are a young man just arrived from over the water, and you sit for the first time in the office of an eminent uncle who once managed all the sleight-of-hand known as the British Military Intelligence Department, then some little tact is indicated. H.M., although largely ornamental in these slack days, still worked a few wires. There was sport, and often danger, that came out of an unsettled Europe. Bennett's father, who was H.M.'s brother-in-law and enough of a somebody at Washington to know, had given him some extra-family hints before Bennett sailed.

'Don't,' said the elder Bennett, 'don't, under any circumstances, use any ceremony with him. He wouldn't understand it. He has frequently got into trouble at political meetings by making speeches in which he absent-mindedly refers to their Home Secretary as Boko and their Premier as Horse-face. You will probably find him asleep, although he will pretend he is very busy. His favourite delusion is that he is being persecuted, and that nobody appreciates him. His baronetcy is two or three hundred years old, and he is also a fighting Socialist. He is a qualified barrister and physician, and he speaks the world's most slovenly grammar. His mind is scurrilous; he shocks lady typists, wears white socks, and appears in public without his necktie. Don't be deceived by his looks; he likes to think he is as expressionless as a Buddha and as sour-faced as Scrooge. I may add,' said the elder Bennett, 'that at criminal investigation he is a good deal of a genius.'

What surprised Sir Henry Merrivale's nephew was that he fulfilled the description exactly. Two hundred pounds of him were piled into a chair behind the big untidy desk, wheezing and grumbling. His big bald head showed against the window of the dingy room, high up and quiet above the bustle of the War Office. H.M.'s room, spacious in decayed finery, is in the most ancient part of the damp old rabbit-warren, once a part of Whitehall Palace: it looks down over a bleak strip of garden, the Victoria Embankment, and the river. A smoky blue twilight—the frosty twilight of Christmas week—blurred the window now. Bennett could see reflections from the lamps along the parapet of the Embankment; he could hear the window rattle to the pelting and hooting of buses, and the stir of the fire under the battered white-marble mantelpiece. Except for the fire, there was no light. H.M. sat morosely, his glasses pulled down on his thick nose, blinking. Just over his head there hung from the chandelier a large red-paper Christmas bell.

'Ah!' growled H.M., peering at him with sudden suspicion. 'I see you lookin' at it, young man. Don't think *I* hang things like that all around my room. But *I* never count for anything. That's the way they treat me around here. That's Lollypop's work.'

'Lollypop?' said Bennett.

'Secretary,' growled H.M. 'Good girl, but a pest. She's always got me talkin' on the telephone when I give her strict orders I'm busy. I'm always busy. Bah. But she puts flowers on my desk, and hangs bells all about…'

'Well, sir,' observed Bennett reasonably, 'if you don't like it, why don't you take it down?'

H.M.'s heavy eyelids raised. He began to make violent noises like 'Rrrr!' and rumble and glare. Then he changed the subject abruptly.

'Fine way for a nephew to talk,' he said. 'Humph. You're like all the others. Let's see—you're Kitty's son, hey? The one that married the Yank? Yes. Do anything for a livin'? Yanks are hell on people working.'

'I do something,' admitted Bennett. 'But I'm not certain

what it is. Sort of international errand-boy for my father: that's the reason for my crossing the ocean in December.'

'Hey!' wheezed H.M., peering up. 'Don't tell me they've got you in this business too? Bad. Keep out of it! Mug's game. Dull. And they pester you to death. Home Office is always gettin' a scare about protecting the battleships we haven't got.—*Are* you in it?'

Bennett took a cigar from the box that was thrust at him across the desk. He said:

'No, sir. I only wish I were. All I ever do is shake cocktails for visiting celebrities to my father's department; or else carry messages full of platitudes from the old man to the Foreign Offices of smaller governments. You know the sort of thing. "The Secretary presents his compliments, and assures His Excellency that the matter suggested will receive the fullest attention—" and so on. It was only a freak of luck that I came to London at all.' He hesitated, wondering whether he dared broach the subject on his mind. 'It was because of Canifest. A certain Lord Canifest; maybe you know of him? He's the one who owns the string of newspapers.'

H.M. knew everybody. His slovenly figure bumped everywhere through the crush; and even Mayfair hostesses had long since ceased to apologize for him. 'Canifest, hey?' he inquired, as though the smoke of the cigar were unpleasant to his nostrils. 'Sure I know him. He's the one that's whooping for an Anglo-American alliance, and damn the Japanese with their evil eye? Uh, yes. Big fella, with Prime-Ministerish airs and a manner like the world's grandpapa—buttery voice—likes to talk on every possible occasion, hey? Uh-huh. Gay dog, too.'

Bennett was startled.

'Well,' he said feelingly, 'I can tell you that's news to me, sir. I wish he had been; it would have been easier. You see, he came to the States on a semi-political mission, I gather. Goodwill tour and all that. How about an Anglo-American alliance? Of course nobody could do anything, but it made a good impression. They gave him dinners,' said Bennett, with dreary recollections of the platitudes that flowed; of Canifest standing impressively bland and white-haired above a microphone and a table of roses. 'And he spoke over the radio and everybody said what a wonderful thing brotherly love was. Part of my job as errand-boy was to go with his party and help conduct him round New York. But as to his being a gay dog—'

He paused, with a few uncomfortable half-memories that made him wonder. But he saw H.M. regarding him curiously, and went on:

'I'll admit you never know quite what to do in those circumstances, because you have to know your man. The distinguished foreigner says he wants to see American life. All right. You arrange a lot of cocktail parties. And then it turns out that the distinguished foreigner wants to see Grant's Tomb and the Statue of Liberty. All Canifest wanted to do was ask a million questions about the state of America, which nobody can ever answer anyway. It's true, though, that when Marcia Tait arrived—'

H.M. took the cigar out of his mouth. He remained impassive, but there was a curious disconcerting stare in his eyes.

'Hey? What's that,' he said, 'about Marcia Tait?'

'Nothing, sir.'

'You're tryin',' said H.M., pointing the cigar at him malevolently, 'you're tryin' to intrigue my interest, that's what. You got something on your mind. I mighta known it. I mighta known nobody ever calls on me out of filial piety or whatnot. Hah!'

All the baffling images of the past two days crowded in on Bennett. He saw the flat above the bleak park—the brownpaper parcel—Marcia Tait, laughing amid her furs, being photographed in the sleek torpedo of a roadster—and, finally, the red-haired man suddenly doubling up and sliding sideways from the stool at the bar. It had missed murder. But murder had been intended. He shifted uneasily.

'Not at all, sir. I was only answering your questions. After Canifest's visit, my father made a gesture of sending me here to carry a sort of thank-you-for-the-favours-of-your-noble-countryman letter to your Home Office: that's all. There's nothing to it. I had hoped to be back home in time for Christmas.'

'Christmas? Nonsense!' roared H.M., sitting up straight. He glared. 'Nephew, spend it with us. Certainly.'

'As a matter of fact, I'd already had an invitation. To a place in Surrey. And I'll admit that there are reasons why I want to accept.'

'Oh, ah,' observed H.M. sourly. 'Girl?'

'No. Curiosity—maybe. I don't know.' He shifted again. 'It's true that some very funny things have been happening. There's been an attempted murder. And a lot of strange people have been scrambled together, including Canifest and Marcia Tait. It's all friendly and social, but—well, damn it, it worries me, sir.'

'Wait,' said H.M. Wheezing and growling to himself, he hoisted his bulk out of the chair, and switched on a goose-necked reading-lamp at the desk. A pool of green-shaded light revealed disarranged papers of official stamp sprayed over with tobacco-ash and rumpled where H.M. had put his feet on the desk. Over the white-marble mantelpiece Bennett could see the thin, Mephistophelian portrait of Fouché. From a tall iron safe H.M. took a bottle, a syphon, and two glasses. Wherever he went, his lumbering progress seemed to upset things. In a near-sighted batlike waddling between desk and safe, he contrived to knock over a set of chessmen, with which he had evidently been working out a problem, and a table of lead soldiers arranged for the solution of a puzzle in military tactics. He picked nothing up. It was litter. It was also the paraphernalia of his weird, childlike, deadly brain. After measuring the drinks he said, 'Honk, honk,' with the utmost solemnity, drained his glass at a gulp, and sat back in wooden moroseness.

'Now, then,' said H.M., folding his hands. 'I'm goin' to listen to you. Mind, I got work. The folks down the way'—he inclined his head sideways in a gesture that evidently meant another building, called New Scotland Yard, a short distance down the Embankment—'*they're* still on hot bricks about that fella at Hampstead, the one who's got the heliograph on the hill. Let 'em wonder. Never mind. You're my nephew, and besides, son, you mentioned a woman I'm rather curious about. Well?'

'Marcia Tait?'

'Marcia Tait,' agreed H.M., with a somewhat lecherous wink. 'Haah. Movies. Sex plus-plus-plus. Always go to see her films.' An evil glee stole over his broad face. 'My wife don't like it. Why do thin women always get ferocious when you say a good word for the broad charms, hey? I admit she's plump; why not?—Funny thing about Marcia Tait. I knew her father, the old general; knew him well. Had a shootin' box near me before the war. Couple of weeks ago I went to see her in that film about Lucrezia Borgia, the one that ran for months at the Leicester Square. Well, and who did I meet comin' out but old Sandival and Lady same? Lady same was snortin' into her sables. She was gettin' a bit rough on The Tait. I begged a ride home in their car. I hadda point out that Lady S. had better not walk out socially with old Tait's daughter. Accordin' to rules old Tait's daughter would go in to dinner before Lady S. Ho ho. She was nasty about it...' H.M. scowled again, and paused with his hand on the whisky bottle. 'Look here, son,' he added, peering sharply across the desk; '*you're* not tangled up with Marcia Tait, are you?'

'Not,' said Bennett, 'in the way you mean, sir. I know her. She's in London.'

'Do you good if you were,' growled H.M. But his hand moved again, and the soda-syphon hissed. 'Teach you something. No spirit in young 'uns nowadays. Bah. Well, go on. What's she doing over here?'

H.M.'s small, impassive eyes were disconcerting in their stare.

'If you know the background,' Bennett went on, 'you may know that she was on the stage first—in London.'

'A flop,' said H.M. quietly. His eyes narrowed.

'Yes. I gather that the critics were pretty rough, and gently intimated that she couldn't act. So she went to Hollywood. By some sort of miracle a director named Rainger got hold of her; they trained her and groomed her and kept her dark for six months; and then they touched off their sky-rocket. In six months she became—what she is now. It was all Rainger's work, and a press agent's: fellow named Emery. But, so far as I can read it, she's got only one ambition, and that's to make London eat its own words. She's over here to take the lead in a new play.'

'Go on,' said H.M. 'Another queen, hey? She's been playin' nothing but queens. Revenge. H'm. Who's producing it?'

'That's the whole story. It's independent. She's taken great pleasure in sneering hard at a couple of producers who offered terms. She won't touch 'em, because they refused to back her a second time when she failed in the old days. Lot of wild talk. It isn't doing her much good, Emery tells me. What's more, she walked out of the studio in the middle of a contract. Emery and Rainger are raving—but they came along...'

He stared at the pool of light on the desk, remembering another weird light. That was the last night in New York, at the Cavalla Club. He was dancing with Louise. He was looking over her shoulder through a smoky gloom, with the grotesque shadows of dancers grown big and weaving against faint gleams, towards the table where Marcia Tait sat. There were scarlet hangings behind her, twisted with gilt tassels. She wore white, and had one shoulder with a swash-buckling air against a pillar. She was drunk, but composed. He saw her teeth as she laughed, brilliant against the faintly swarthy skin. On one side of her sat Emery, very drunk and gesticulating; on the other side of her the tubby Rainger, who always seemed to need a shave and drank nothing, lifting his shoulders slightly as he examined a cigar. It was hot in the smoky room, and a heavy drum pounded slowly behind the band-music. He could hear fans whir. Through the humped shadows of dancers he saw Tait lift a thin glass; Emery's gesticulations spilled it suddenly across her breast, but she only laughed at it. It was John Bohun who leaned out of the gloom, swiftly, with a handkerchief...

'The latest,' Bennett went on, looking up from the hypnotic glow, 'is that the Cinearts people have given her a month to get back on the lot. She won't—or says she won't. The answer, she says, will be this.'

He lifted his cigar and traced letters in the air as though he were writing a poster.

John Bohun presents
Marcia Tait and Jervis Willard
in
THE PRIVATE LIFE OF
CHARLES THE SECOND,
a play by
Maurice Bohun

H.M. frowned. He pushed the shell-rimmed spectacles up and down his broad nose.

'Good!' he said abstractedly. 'Good! That'd suit her style of beauty, son. You know. Big heavy-lidded eyes, swarthy skin, small neck, full lips; exactly like one of those Restoration doxies in the Stuart room at the National Portrait Gallery. Hah! Wonder nobody's thought of it before. I say, son, go round and browse through the gallery sometime. You'll get a lot of surprises. The woman they call Bloody Mary is a baby-faced blonde, whereas Mary Queen of Scots is nearly the ugliest wench in the lot. H'm.' Again he moved his glasses. 'But that's interestin' about Tait. She's got nerve. She's not only courting hostility, but she's challenging competition. Do you know who Jervis Willard is? He's the best character-actor in England. And an independent producer has snaffled off Willard to play opposite her. She must think she can—'

'She does, sir,' said Bennett.

'H'm. Now what about this Bohun-Bohun combination, keeping it in the family? And how does it affect Canifest?'

'That,' said Bennett, 'is where the story begins, and the cross-currents too. These Bohuns are brothers; and they both seem to be contradictions. I haven't met Maurice— he's the elder—and this part of it is gossip. But it seems to strike everybody who knows him, except John, as hilariously funny that he should be the author of this play. It would be strange, Marcia says, if he wrote any play: except possibly in five acts and heroic blank verse. But a light, bawdy, quick-repartee farce of the smart school...'

'"Dr. Dryasdust,"' said H.M. suddenly. He raised his head. 'Bohun! Got it. But it can't be the same, son. This Bohun I was thinkin' of—no. Senior Proctor. Oxford. "Lectures on the Political and Economic History of the Seventeenth Century." Do you mean to tell me—?'

Bennett nodded.

'It's the same man. I told you I'd been invited to a place in Surrey for the holidays. It's the Bohuns' place called White

Priory, near Epsom. And, for a certain historical reason I'll describe in a minute, the whole crowd is going down in quest of atmosphere. The doddering scholar, it seems, has suddenly begun to cut capers on paper. On the other hand, there's John Bohun. He has always played around with theatrical enterprises; never done much, never interested in much else, I understand. Well, John Bohun appeared in America as the close friend and boon travelling-companion of Lord Canifest.

'He didn't say much; he rarely does. Bohun is the taciturn, umbrella-carrying, British-stamp type. He walked around, and he looked up at the buildings, and exhibited a polite interest. That was all. Until—it appears now it was a pre-arranged plan—until Marcia Tait arrived in New York from Hollywood.'

'So?' said H.M. in a curious voice. 'Amatory angle?'

This was the thing that puzzled Bennett, among others. He remembered the echoing gloom at Grand Central, and flash-bulbs popping in ripples over the crowd when Marcia Tait posed on the steps of the train. Somebody held her dog, autograph-books flew, the crowd buckled in and out; and, standing some distance off, John Bohun cursed. He said he couldn't understand American crowds. Bennett remembered him craning and peering over the heads of smaller men: very lean, with one corded hand jabbing his umbrella at the concrete floor. His face was a shade swarthier than Marcia Tait's. He had not ceased to glare by the time he fought his way to where she stood...

'As a lovers' meeting,' said Bennett slowly, 'no. But then you can't describe an atmosphere, any more than you can describe a sultry day. And it's atmosphere that Tait carries with her. For a public face she tries to be—what's the word?—effervescent. She's not. You've hit it exactly in saying she looks like one of those Restoration women on canvas. Quiet. Speculative. *Old-time*, if you follow me. Patches and languor, and thunder in the distance. You could feel it in the air, again like a sultry day. I suppose all these fancy words simply mean Sex, but I should say there's something else too; something,' said Bennett, with more vehemence than he had intended, 'that really did make great courtesans in the old days. I can't make it quite clear...'

'Think not?' said H.M., blinking over his spectacles. 'Oh, I don't know. You're doin' pretty well. You seem to have been a good deal bowled over yourself.'

Bennett was honest. 'God knows I was—for a while. Everybody is who has the customary number of red corpuscles. But,' he hesitated, 'competition aside, I don't think I'd care for the emotional strain of staying bowled over by that woman. Do you see, sir?'

'Oh, ah,' said H.M. 'Competition was brisk, then?'

'It was ceaseless. There was even a gleam in Canifest's eye, I'm fairly sure. Thinking back on what you said...'

'So. She met Canifest?'

'She'd known him in England, it seems; he was a friend of her father. Canifest and his daughter—Louise, her name is; she was acting as his private secretary—Canifest and his daughter and Bohun were staying at the Brevoort. Very fine and sedate and dignified, you see. So (to the astonishment of everybody) the flamboyant Tait also puts up at the Brevoort. We drove straight there from Grand Central.

Canifest was photographed shaking hands with and congratulating the famous British artiste who had made her name on the screen: that sort of thing. It was as fatherly and disinterested as though she were shaking hands with Santa Claus. Where I began to wonder was when Carl Rainger, her director, arrived the next day with almost as big a public following; and the press agent with him. It was none of my affair—I was there to escort Canifest. But Bohun had arrived with the script of his brother's play: Tait made no secret of that. There was a sort of armed truce between Tait and Bohun on one side, and Rainger and Emery on the other. Whether we liked it or not, we were all mixed up together. It was explosive material. And in the middle of it was Marcia Tait, as expressionless as ever.'

Staring at the lamp on H.M.'s desk, he tried to remember just when he had first been conscious of that ominous tension, that uneasiness which scratched at the nerves in this incongruous company. Sultriness again. Like that drumbeat, muffled under the music, at the Cavalla Club. It would be, he thought, in Tait's suite on the night Rainger arrived. An old-fashioned suite in an ancient hotel, heavy with gilt and plush and glass prisms that suggested gaslight: yet with the pale glitter of Fifth Avenue outside the windows. Tait's sultry beauty was appropriate to the setting. She wore yellow, and sat back in an ornate chair under a lamp. Bohun, who always looked thinner and more high-shouldered in black and white, was manipulating the cocktail-shaker. Canifest, fatherly and heavy-mouthed, was talking interminably with his usual unction. Nearby Canifest's daughter sat on a chair which somehow seemed lower than the others;

silent, efficient, and freckled, Louise was a plain girl made plainer still by her father's wishes; and she was permitted only one cocktail. 'Our Spartan English mothers,' declared Lord Canifest, evidently scenting a moral somewhere, 'knew nothing of it. No.' It was shortly afterwards that the house phone buzzed.

John Bohun—Bennett tried to explain it to H.M.—John Bohun straightened up and looked at it sharply. He made a movement to answer it, but Marcia Tait intercepted him: her face had a faint incurious smile, and her hair under strong light was brown instead of black. She said only, 'Very well,' before she replaced the receiver, still smiling. John Bohun asked who it was, in a voice that seemed as incurious as hers. He was answered in no very long time. Somebody knocked briefly at the outer door of the suite and threw it open without waiting for an invitation. There entered a quiet little man, pudgy but not comical in stiff-jawed anger, with two days' growth of beard on his face. Paying no attention to the others, he said quietly: 'Exactly what the devil do you mean by walking out on us?' Marcia Tait asked to be allowed to present Carl Rainger.

'—and that,' said Bennett, 'was nearly three weeks ago. It was, in a way, the beginning of it. But the question is this.'

He leaned across and put his finger on H.M.'s desk.

'Who in our party would send Marcia Tait a box of poisoned chocolates?'

II

WEAK POISON

'One of your party, eh?' said H.M. meditatively. 'Been sending her poisoned chocolates. Well. Did she eat 'em?'

'I'm getting ahead of the story. The poisoned-chocolates business occurred only yesterday morning, and it's nearly a month ago that Tait arrived in New York. I never expected to come to England, you see; I never thought I should meet the party again once I had gone back to Washington; and it wasn't as though I had made particular friends with any of them. But it was that damned atmosphere. It stuck in your mind. I don't want to make the thi'ccng sound too subtle, sir—'

H.M. grunted.

'Bah. Subtlety,' he said, 'is only statin' a self-evident truth in language nobody can understand. And there's nothing subtle about trying to poison somebody. Have another drink. Then how did you come to be tied up with these people later?'

That, Bennett tried to explain, was the curious thing: the

metamorphosis of John Bohun. No sooner had the errand-boy returned to Washington, than he was despatched with Washington's platitudinous goodwill letter to Westminster in the role of dummy diplomat. A dummy diplomat had no job: all he must do was say the wise, right, and sensible thing on all occasions. He sailed on the *Berengaria*, on a bitter grey day when the skyline was smoky purple etched out with pin-pricks of light, and the wind cut raw across a choppy harbour. He had noticed a more than usual chatter, a more than usual quickened excitement aboard. They were just out of sight of the handkerchiefs at the end of the pier when he came face to face with Marcia Tait. She wore smoked glasses, which meant that she was incognito, and was swathed in unwieldy furs, smiling. On one side of her walked Bohun, and on the other side Canifest. Canifest was already looking pale with the motion. He went to his cabin at lunch, and did not return. Rainger and Emery seldom left their own cabins until the liner was a day out of Southampton.

'Which,' said Bennett, 'threw Marcia and Bohun and myself together for the crossing. And—this is what puzzled me—Bohun was a different man. It was as though he had felt uneasy and a stranger in New York. He could talk, and he seemed to develop a sense of humour. The tension was gone while only the three of us were together. I suddenly discovered that Bohun had wild romantic ideas about this play he was going to produce. So far as I can gather, both he and his brother are steeped in seventeenth-century lore. And with reason. This house of theirs, the White Priory, was owned by the Bohuns in the time of Charles the Second.

The contemporary Bohun kept "merry house"; he was a friend of the King, and, when Charles came down to Epsom for the racing, he stayed at the White Priory.'

H.M., who was filling the glasses again, scowled.

'Funny old place, Epsom. "Merry house." H'm. Ain't that where Nell Gwynne and Buckhurst lived before Charles picked her up? And this White Priory—hold on! I'm thinkin'. Look here, it seems to me I remember reading about some house there; a pavilion or the like, attached to the White Priory, that they won't let tourists see...'

'That's it. They call it the Queen's Mirror. Bohun says that the mania for importing marble into England and building imitation temples on ornamental sheets of water is traceable to the Bohuns who built the place. That's not true, by the way. The craze didn't start until a hundred years later, in eighteenth-century fashions! But Bohun violently believes it. Anyhow, it seems that ancestor George Bohun built it about 1664 for the convenience and splendour of Charles's all-alluring charmer, Lady Castlemaine. It's a marble pavilion that contains only two or three rooms, and stands in the middle of a small artificial lake; hence the name. One of the scenes of Maurice's play is laid there.

'John described it to me one afternoon when he and Marcia and I were sitting on deck. He's a secretive sort, and—I should think—nervous. He always says, "Maurice has the intelligence of the family; I haven't; I wish *I* could write a play like that," and then smiling casually while he looks at people (especially Marcia) as though he were waiting for them to deny it. But he's got a flair for description, and an artist's eye for effect. I should think he'd make a damned good director. When he got through talking, you could *see* the path going down through lines of evergreens, and the clear water with the cypresses round its edge, and the ghostly pavilion where Lady Castlemaine's silk cushions still keep their colour. Then he said, as though he were talking to himself, "By God, I'd like to play the part of Charles myself. I could—" and stopped. Marcia looked up at him in a queer way; she said, quietly, that they had got Jervis Willard, hadn't they? He whirled round and looked at her. I didn't like that expression, I didn't like the soft way she half-closed her eyes as though she were thinking of something from which he was excluded; so I asked La Tait whether she had ever seen Queen's Mirror. And Bohun smiled. He put his hand over hers and said, "Oh, yes. That was where we first met."

'I tell you, it didn't mean anything, but for a second it gave me a creepy feeling. We were alone on the deck, with the sea booming past and the deckchairs sliding: and those two faces, either of which might have come out of canvas in an old gallery, looking at me in the twilight. But the next minute, along came Tim Emery, looking a little green but determined. He tried to be boisterous, and couldn't quite manage it. But it closed Bohun's mouth. Bohun detested both Emery and Rainger, and didn't trouble to conceal it.'

'About,' observed H.M. in a thoughtful rumble, 'about Messrs Rainger and Emery... Do you mean to tell me that a highly paid director, well known in his own name, threw up a good job to chase across the ocean with this wench?'

'Oh, no. He's on leave after two years without a vacation. But he chose to spend his vacation trying to persuade

Marcia not to be a fool.' Bennett hesitated, remembering the fat expressionless face with its cropped black hair, and the shrewd eyes that missed no detail. 'Maybe,' Bennett said, 'somebody knows what that man thinks about. I don't. He's intelligent, he seems to guess your thoughts, and he's as cynical as a taxi-driver.'

'But interested in Tait?'

'Well—possibly.'

'Signs of manifest doubt. You're very innocent, son,' said H.M., extinguishing the stump of his cigar. 'H'm. And this fella Emery?'

'Emery's more willing to talk than the others. Personally, I like him. He buttonholes me continually, because the others like to sit on him and he frankly detests 'em. He's the hopping, arm-flinging sort who can't sit still; and he's worried, because his job depends on getting Tait back to the studio. That's why he's there.'

'Attitude?'

'He seems to have a wife back in California whose opinions he brings into every conversation. No. Interested in Tait as the late Mr. Frankenstein was interested: as something he'd created or helped create. Then, yesterday—'

The poisoned chocolates. As he began to speak, the heavy gong-voice of Big Ben rose and beat in vibrating notes along the Embankment. It was a reminder. Another city, with its blue dusks and deathly lights where top-hats made faces look like masks, and where Marcia Tait's welcome had been as tumultuous as in New York. The liner had docked the day before yesterday. In the crush as the boat-train drew into Waterloo Station, he had not had the opportunity for a leave-taking. But John Bohun had elbowed through the corridor for a parting handshake. 'Look here,' he said, scribbling on a card, 'here's the address.' Once in the London atmosphere, he was himself again; brisk, efficient, humorous-eyed, because he was at home. 'Marcia will go to the Savoy for one night, as a blind; she'll slip away tomorrow morning to this address. Nobody else knows it. We shall see you, of course?'

Bennett said, 'Of course.' He knew that Bohun and Marcia had had a sharp battle about that address before it was given to Rainger and Emery. 'But it will go to Lord Canifest,' said Marcia Tait, 'of *course?*' As he fought his way to a taxi, Bennett looked back to see Tait leaning out of a train window in the sooty dimness, smiling, receiving flowers, and shaking hands with some man who had his back turned. A voice somewhere said, 'That's Jervis Willard'; and flashlights flickered. Lord Canifest, very benign, was being photographed with his daughter on his arm.

Speeding along Waterloo Bridge in a yellow December afternoon, Bennett wondered whether he would see any of them again. Ship's coteries break up immediately, and are forgotten. He went to the American Embassy, where there was solemn pomp and hand-shaking; then to fulfil his mission at Whitehall, amid more of the same. It was all done in a couple of hours. They put a two-seater Morris at his disposal, and he accepted two or three invitations that were his duties. Afterwards he felt lonely as the devil.

The next morning he was still more depressed, with Marcia Tait haunting his mind. In contrast to the easy comradeship of the liner, this dun-coloured town was even more bleak. He was hesitating whether to go out to 16a, Hamilton Place, the address on the card, and prowling aimlessly round Piccadilly Circus, when the matter was decided for him. At the mouth of Shaftesbury Avenue he heard a voice bellow his name, with friendly profanity, and he was almost run down by a big yellow car. People were staring at the car. From its massive silvered radiator-cap to the stream-lined letters Cinearts Studios, Inc., painted along the side, it was conspicuous enough even for the eye of Tim Emery, who drove it. Emery yelled to him to climb aboard, and Emery was in a bad humour. Bennett glanced sideways at the sharp-featured face, with its discontented mouth and sandy eyebrows, as they shot up Piccadilly.

'God,' said Emery, 'she's batty. The woman's gone clear batty, I tell you!' He hammered his fist on the steering-wheel, and then swerved sharply to avoid a bus. 'I never saw her like it before. Soon as she gets to this town, she goes high-hat. No publicity, she says. No *publicity*, mind you.' His voice rose to a yelp. He was genuinely bewildered and worried. 'I've just been round to see our English branch. Wardour Street branch. Swell lot of help they are! Even if she did walk off the lot, I've still got to see she gets the breaks in the papers. Can you imagine, now—can you just imagine, I ask you—any woman who...'

'Tim,' said Bennett, 'it's none of my business, but you must realize by this time she's determined to put on that play.'

'But why? *Why?*'

'Well, revenge. Did you see the papers this morning?'

'Say,' observed Emery in an awed voice, 'she's sure got it in for these Limey managers, hasn't she? That won't do her any good. But why bother about what they say in this town, when she can pull down two thousand a week in a *real* place? God, that's what burns me up! As though she'd got a…h'm,' said Emery, muttering to himself. 'Woman With A Purpose. That'd make a swell lead. You could get a great publicity story out of it. If I could shoot the works on that—but I can't. I've got to stop it.'

'Short of hitting her over the head and kidnapping her,' said Bennett, 'I don't see what you can do about it.'

Emery peered sideways. The rims of his eyes were red, and his breath in the sharp air was heavily alcoholic. Bennett saw the signs of an embarrassing and theatrical, if honest, attack of sentimentality.

'Listen,' said Emery, breathing hard. He had treated the suggestion with the utmost seriousness. 'Kidnap her? Man, I wouldn't ruffle a hair of that girl's head, I wouldn't hurt her little finger so much as, for one split second in the world; and Lord help the man who tries it, that's all I've got to say. Yes. I love that woman like she was my own Margarette, and I want to see her have everything in the world…'

'Watch the road,' said Bennett sharply. 'Where are we going?'

'Out to reason with her, if she's there.' His white, fiercely earnest face turned away again. 'She went shopping this morning—in a wig, mind you. A *wig*. But I was telling you: if she wants to make a picture of this Charles-the-Second thing, all right. Why not? It's swell box-office. Radiant Pictures did one like that last year, and it got top rating from *Variety*. (That's the show you put Nell Gwynne in, isn't it? Uh-huh. I thought so.) All right. We'll fix it up with Baumann. We'll shoot a million dollars into production. A million—dollars,' said Emery, savouring the words. 'Yes, and so everything's right we'll bring over some of these Oxford guys to act as technical advisers. You think I don't want an artistic success? Well, I do. That's just what I *do* want,' he said fiercely, and the car swerved again. He meant it. Jerking his neck sharply, he went on: 'If that's what she wants, she'll get it. But not here. What kind of a guy is this Bohun, I'm asking you?—when he don't know his own mind from one minute to the next? Soft. That's Bohun. And here's their trick. To get her away from me, in case I'd make her see reason, they're taking her down to this place in the country; then we've lost her, see? But I won't bother with that end of it. She can go to the country. But there may be ways of queering their game right here in London.'

'How?'

'Oh, ways.' He wrinkled up his forehead and lowered his voice. 'Look. Keep this under your hat. Do you know who's putting up the *money* for this show? Eh?'

'Well?'

'It's Canifest,' said Emery. 'This is where we turn.'

He manoeuvred through the traffic at Hyde Park Corner, and swung into the courtyard of a white-stone block of flats overlooking the brown earth and spiky trees of the park. Emery beat the hall-porter into submission about not announcing their names; then growled and slid a note into his hand. They went up through a cathedral dimness to a landing where the door of Number 12 stood open. 'Like a funeral,' said Emery, sniffing the thick odour of flowers; but he stopped as he heard voices inside.

In a blue drawing-room, bright with wintry sun through

wide windows, were three men. One of them, who leaned back in a window-seat smoking a cigarette, was a stranger to Bennett. On a table among a litter of crushed orchids lay a brown-paper parcel unwound from its wrappings, showing gaudy ribbon and a gaudily coloured nude siren painted on the lid of a five-pound chocolate-box. John Bohun stood on one side of the table, Carl Rainger on the other. And, as Bennett watched them, he knew that there was danger here. You had only to come into the rooms of Marcia Tait, among her belongings and things that she had touched, to feel the damnable atmosphere tightening again.

'I don't know whether you are aware of it,' John Bohun's voice rose sharply, hornet-like in suggestion, and lowered again. 'It is customary to allow people to open their own parcels. Manners, we sometimes call it. Did you ever hear anything of the sort?'

'Oh, I don't know,' said Rainger stolidly. He had a cigar between his teeth, and did not lift his eyes from the box. He reached out and touched the ribbons. 'I was curious.'

'Were you really?' said Bohun, without inflection. He leaned over the table. 'Get away from that box, my friend, or I'll smash your fat face in. Is that clear?'

The man in the window-seat said: 'Look here!' Extinguishing his cigarette with a hurried motion, he got up. Rainger did back away from the table then. He was still composed, his eyes motionless.

'It seems to me, John,' the third man observed, in a sort of humorous rumble which might have cooled any animosities but these, 'that you're kicking up the devil of a row over this thing, aren't you?' He came up to the table, a big man of slow movements, and fished among the wrappings. Then he glanced over his shoulder at Rainger, speculatively. 'And yet after all, Mr.—Mr. Rainger, it's only a box of chocolates. Here's the card. *From an admirer who has no doubts.* Does Miss Tait get so few presents that you're suspicious of this one? I say, you didn't think it was a bomb, did you?'

'If that fool,' said Rainger, pointing his cigar at Bohun, 'is sane enough to let me explain...'

Bohun had taken a step forward when Emery knocked perfunctorily at the open door and hurried in. Bennett followed him. The others jerked round to look at them. Momentarily this interruption broke the tension, but it was as though the room were full of wasps, and you could hear the buzzing.

'Hello, Tim,' said Rainger. The malice crept into his voice, though he tried to keep it out. 'Good morning, Mr. Bennett. You're in time to hear something interesting.'

'By the way, Rainger,' Bohun remarked coolly, 'why don't you get out of here?'

The other raised his black eyebrows. He said: 'Why should I? I'm a guest here, too. But I happen to be interested in Marcia, and her health. That's why I'm willing to explain even to you and Mr.,' he imitated the other's manner, 'Mr. Willard. There's something wrong with those chocolates.'

John Bohun stopped and looked back at the table. So did the man called Willard, his eyes narrowing. He had a square, shrewd, humorous face, deeply lined round the mouth, with a jutting forehead and heavy greyish hair. 'Wrong?' he repeated—slowly.

'It wasn't,' Rainger went on, his eyes never moving while he spoke with sudden sharpness, 'it wasn't any unknown

London admirer who sent that. Take a look at the address. *Miss Marcia Tait, Suite* 12, *The Hertford, Hamilton Place, W. 1.* Only half a dozen people know she intended to come here. No report could have got around even now, and yet this box was mailed last night before she had even come here. One of her—we'll say her friends sent this. One of us. Why?'

After a silence Bohun said violently: 'It looks to me like a joke in damned bad taste. Anybody who knows Marcia would know she never eats sweets. And this cheap tuppenny affair, with a nude on the cover'—he stopped.

'Yes. Do you think,' said Willard, and slowly knocked his knuckles on the box, 'it might have been intended as a warning of some sort?'

'Are you trying to tell me,' Bohun snapped, 'that those chocolates are poisoned?'

Rainger was looking at him with a dull stare. 'Well, well, well,' he said, and mouthed his cigar in unpleasant mirth. 'Nobody had mentioned that. Nobody said anything about poison except you. You're either too much of a fool or you're too discerning. Very well. If you think there's nothing wrong with them, why don't you eat one?'

'All right,' said Bohun, after a pause. 'By God, I will!' and he lifted the cover off the box.

'Steady, John,' Willard said. He laughed, and the sound of that deep, common-sense mockery restored them for a moment to sane values. 'Now look here, old boy. It's no good getting the wind up over nothing at all. We're acting like a pack of fools. There's probably nothing whatever wrong with the box. If you think there is, have it sent to be analysed. If you don't, eat all you like.'

Bohun nodded. He took a dropsical-looking chocolate from the box, and there was a curious light in his eyes when he looked round the group. He smiled thinly.

'Right,' he said. '*As a matter of fact, we're all going to eat one.*'

...High up in the dingy room at the War Office, Bennett paused in his narrative as this time the gong-voice of Big Ben clanged out the quarter-hour. He jumped a little. The remembrance had been almost as real, while he stared at the hypnotic light on H.M.'s desk, as the room here. Again he became aware of H.M.'s sour moon face blinking in the gloom.

'Well, strike me blind!' boomed H.M., as hoarsely as the clock. He made sputtering noises. 'Of all the eternal scarlet fatheads I've heard about in a long time, this John Bohun is the worst. "We're all goin' to eat one," eh? Silly dummy. The idea being, I suppose, that if somebody *had* poisoned the top layer, and that somebody was in the room—which, by the way, hasn't been proved at all, at all—then that somebody would refuse to take a snack? Uh-huh. If every one of the top layer of chocolates was loaded—which would be improbable—you poison the whole crowd. If only about half the top layer was loaded—which would be very likely— all you could be sure of was that the man who had doctored the box would be devilish careful *not* to take a poisoned one. Crazy idea. Do you mean to tell me Bohun made 'em do it?'

'Well, sir, we were all pretty worked up. And everybody was looking at everybody else.'

'Gor,' said H.M., opening his eyes wide. 'Not you too?'

'I had to. There was nothing else for it. Rainger objected; he said he was a sensible man—'

'And so he was. Quite.'

'But you could see his own bogey had scared him. After pointing out several good reasons why he shouldn't, he nearly flew off the handle at the way Bohun was smiling. Emery, who was drunker than he looked, got mad and threatened to cram the whole lot down his throat if he refused. Finally he took one. So did Emery. So did Willard, who was thoroughly amused. So did I. It was the first time I ever saw Rainger shaken out of his cynical stolidity. I admit,' said Bennett, feeling a retrospective shiver, 'it was an absurd performance. But it wasn't funny to *me*. The minute I bit into that chocolate it tasted so queer that I could have sworn...'

'Uh. I bet they all did. What happened?'

'Nothing, at the moment. We stood and looked at each other: not feeling any too good. The person we all detested—I don't know why—was Rainger, who was standing there with a kind of sickly sneer on his face and smoking hard. But he got his own back. He nodded his head and said pleasantly, "I trust the experiment will prove satisfactory to all of you," and then put on his hat and coat and went out. A few minutes afterwards Marcia came in from shopping, under a fancy incognito, and we felt like a lot of kids caught in a jam cupboard. Willard burst out laughing, which restored the balance.'

'Did you tell her?'

'No. We didn't believe the yarn, *but.* You see? When we heard her in the hall, Bohun swept up the box and wrappings and hid 'em under his overcoat. Then we had lunch there. At six o'clock yesterday evening Bohun phoned me at the hotel to come round to a nursing-home in South Audley Street for a council of war. About two hours after lunch Tim

Emery had collapsed in a bar, and the doctor found strychnine poisoning.'

There was a silence.

'No,' said Bennett, answering the unspoken question.
'Not death or near death. He hadn't swallowed a sufficient
quantity. They pulled him through; but none of us felt pleasant about our little experiment. The thing was: what was
to be done? None of us wanted to call in the police, except
Emery, and that wasn't on account of himself. He kept babbling that it was the finest publicity of the age, and ought to
be in all the papers: he was talking like that this morning.
It was Rainger who shut him up. Rainger pointed out—at
least, he didn't crow over us—that, if the police were called
in there'd be an investigation and they might not get Tait
back to the States in the three weeks' grace allowed by the
studio. They're both fanatically set on that.'

'And Tait?'

'Didn't turn a hair. In fact,' replied Bennett uneasily,
remembering the faint smile on the small full lips and the
veiled dark eyes under heavy lids, 'she seemed rather pleased.
But she nearly made good old sentimental, hard-boiled
Emery weep by the way she fluttered over him. Incidentally,
Bohun seems the most flustered of the lot. There was
another council of war this morning over too many cocktails. There was an effort to make it flippant, but everybody
realized that someone—maybe someone present—had...'
He made a significant gesture.

'H'm, yes. Now wait a bit. D'jou have those chocolates
analysed?'

'Bohun did. Two of them on the top layer, including the

one Emery ate, were poisoned. Both together contained just a little less than enough strychnine to mean certain death. One was squashed a bit along one side, we noticed afterwards, as though the person hadn't known how to do his job quite well. Also, they were set so far apart that one person, except by an unholy coincidence of bad luck, wouldn't be likely to eat both. In other words, sir, it must have been what Willard suggested: a *warning* of some kind...'

H.M.'s swivel-chair creaked. One hand shaded his eyes, and his big glasses gleamed inscrutably from its shadow. He was silent a long time.

'Uh-huh. I see. What was decided at the council of war?'

'Maurice Bohun was to be in London this afternoon to take Marcia down to the White Priory, and incidentally go over the script. Willard was to go with them—by train. John is driving down late tonight in his car; he's got a business appointment in town, and won't get home until late. They wanted me to go down with the party, but I can't get away until late myself; another of those duty receptions.'

'You goin' down tonight?'

'Yes, if the party doesn't break up too late, I'll get my bags packed beforehand to be ready.—Anyway, there's the situation, sir.' For a moment Bennett struggled between a feeling that he was making a fool of himself, and the feeling that a deadlier thing lay behind this. 'I've taken up a lot of your time. I've talked interminably. Maybe for nothing—'

'Or maybe not,' said H.M. He leaned forward ponderously. 'Listen to me, now.'

Big Ben struck six-thirty.

III

DEATH AT THE MIRROR

At six-thirty on the following morning, Bennett was studying a small and complicated map by the light of the dashboard lamps, and he was shivering. On a thirteen-mile drive out of the maze of London he had already lost his way and taken a bewildering variety of wrong roads. Two hours earlier, with the champagne still in his head, it had seemed an excellent idea to drive down to the White Priory and arrive at dawn of a snowy December morning. The reception was not to blame. But, in the course of a starched evening, he had fallen in with a group of Young England who also felt restive. Long before the awning was taken down and the lights put up at Something House, they had adjourned for a small party. Later he drove flamboyantly out of Shepherd's Market on his way to his destination in Surrey; but only the first hour had been pleasant.

Now he felt drowsy, dispirited, and chilled through, with that light-headed, unreal sensation which comes of watching car-lamps flow along interminably through a white unreal world.

It would shortly be daylight. The east was grey now, and the stars had gone pale. He felt the cold weighing down his eyelids; and he got out and stamped in the road to warm himself. Ahead of him, under a thin crust of unbroken snow, the narrow road ran between bare hawthorn hedges. To the right were built up ghostly-looking woods where the sky was still black. To the left, immense in half-light and glimmering with snow, bare fields sank and rose again into the mysterious Downs. Toy steeples, toy chimneys, began to show in their folds; but there was no smoke yet. For no reason at all, he felt uneasy. The roar of the engine as he shifted into gear again beat up too loudly in this dead world.

There was nothing to be uneasy about. On the contrary. He tried to remember what H.M. had said on the previous afternoon—years ago—and found that his fuddled brain would not work. In his wallet he had two telephone numbers. One was for H.M.'s private wire at Whitehall. The other was for extension 42 of the celebrated Victoria 7000: which would at any time reach Chief Inspector Humphrey Masters, recently promoted chief of the C.I.D. for his (and H.M.'s) work on the Plague Court murders. The numbers were useless. Nothing was wrong.

Rocketing the car along a tricky road, he remembered H.M.'s heavy inscrutable face and heavy voice. He had said there was no cause for alarm. He had chuckled a little, for some obscure reason, over the attempt on Marcia Tait. Bennett did not understand, but he supposed H.M. knew...

Marcia Tait would be asleep now. Crazy idea, waking the place up by arriving at this hour. He hoped somebody was already astir. If he could only get that damned box out of his mind; even the ribbon on a shirt-front, last night, reminded him of the chocolate-box ribbons and the obese charmer simpering on the cover... Ahead of him now a white sign-post rose out of the greyness, bristling with arms. He slewed the car round in a spurting of snow, and backed again. This was the road he wanted, to the left. It was only a narrow lane, gloomy and heavily timbered on either side. The motor ground harshly as he shifted into low.

It was broad daylight when he came in sight of the White Priory. Lying some distance back from the road, it was enclosed by a stone wall patched in snow and pierced by two iron-railed gates. The nearer gate was open. Firs and evergreens stood spiky black against the white lawns, and made a twilight about the house. He saw heavy gables and a cluster of thin chimneys built up against low grey clouds behind; it was long and low, built like the head of the letter T with the short wings towards the road; and it might once have been painted with a dingy whitewash. Bow windows looked out dully. Nothing stirred there.

Bennett climbed out on numbed feet, and fumbled at the nearer gate to push it wide open. The thumping of the motor disturbed a querulous bird. From the gate, a gravel drive curved up some distance to what seemed a modern *porte-cochère* on the left-hand side. On either side of the drive, oaks and maples had grown so thickly in interlocked branches that only a little snow could get through, and glimmered in a dark tunnel. It was then—he remembered later—that the real uneasiness touched him. He drove up through it, and stopped under the *porte-cochère*. Near him, a rug over its hood, was parked a Vauxhall sedan he remembered as John Bohun's.

That was when he heard the dog howling.

In utter silence, the unexpectedness of the second made him go hot with something like fear. It was deep and hoarse, but it trembled up to end thinly. Then it had a quiver that was horribly like a human gulp. Bennett climbed down, peering round in the gloom. On his right was the covered porch, with a big side door in the heavy-timbered house, and steps ascending to a balcony half-way up. Ahead and beyond, the driveway—here snow-crusted like the lawns—divided into three branches. One ran round the back of the house, a second down over a dim slope where he could see faintly an avenue of evergreens, and a third curved out to the left towards the low roofs of what seemed to be stables. It was from this direction…

Again the dog's howl rose, with a note that was like anguish.

'Down!' came a voice from far away. 'Down, Tempest! Good dog! Down—!'

The next sound Bennett heard he thought for a moment might be the dog again. But it was human. It was a cry such as he had never heard, coming faintly from over the slope of the lawn towards the rear.

In his half-drugged state he had a feeling of almost physical sickness. But he ran to the end of the *porte-cochère* and peered out. He could see the stables now. In a cobbled courtyard before them he saw the figure of a man, in a groom's brown gaiters and corduroy coat, who was gripping the bridles of two frightened saddle-horses and soothing them as they began to clatter on the cobbles. The groom's voice, the same voice that had spoken to the dog, rose above the snorting and champing:

'Sir! *Sir!* Where are you? Is anything—?'

The other voice answered faintly, as though it said something like, 'Here!' As he tried to follow the direction of that sound, Bennett recognized something from a description. He recognized the narrow avenue of evergreens curving down to broaden into a big circular coppice of trees, to the pavilion called the Queen's Mirror. And he thought he recognized the voice of John Bohun. That was when he began to run.

His shoes were already soaked and freezing in any case, and the crust of snow was only half an inch deep. One single line of tracks led before him down the slope to the evergreens. They were fresh tracks, he could see by their new featheriness, made only a very short time before. He followed them along the path, thirty-odd feet between the evergreens, and emerged into the ragged coppice. It was impossible to see anything clearly except the dull white of the pavilion, which stood in the middle of a snow-crusted clearing measuring half an acre. In a square about it, extending out about sixty feet with the pavilion in the centre, ran a low marble coping. A higher stone pathway cut through it to the open door of the low marble house. The line of tracks went up to that front door. But no tracks came out.

A figure appeared in that doorway, with such eerie suddenness that Bennett stopped dead; his heart was knocking and his throat felt raw. The figure was a dark blur against the grey. It put one arm over its eyes and leaned the arm rockily, like a hurt child, against the doorpost. Bennett heard it sob.

As he stepped forward, his foot crackled in the snow and the figure looked up. 'Who's there?' said John Bohun's voice, going suddenly high. 'Who—?'

As though he were fiercely straightening himself, he came a little out of the shadow in the doorway. Even at that great distance in the half-light Bennett could see the narrow rounded outline of riding-breeches; but the face under the low-drawn cap was a blur, although it seemed to be shaking. Question and answer echoed thinly across the clearing. Far away Bennett could hear the dog howling again.

'I've just got here,' he said. 'I—what—?'

'Come here,' said Bohun.

Bennett ran obliquely across the clearing. He did not follow the footsteps that went up and across the stone path to the door. He saw the sixty feet of flat snow-covered space that surrounded the pavilion, and thought it was a lawn. His foot had almost touched the low coping when Bohun spoke again.

'Don't step on that!' he cried, his voice breaking. 'Don't step on that, you damned fool. It's thin ice. That's the lake. You'll go through—'

Jerking back, Bennett altered his direction. He stumbled up the path, breathing hard, and then up the three steps at the end of it which led to the door.

'She's dead,' said Bohun.

In the silence they heard roused sparrows shrilling and bickering, and one fluttered across from under the eaves. Bohun's slow-drawn breath turned to smoke in the air; his lips hardly moved. His eyes were fixed with a dull intensity on Bennett's face, and his cheeks looked sunken.

'Do you hear me?' he cried. He lifted a riding-crop and slashed it across the doorpost. 'I tell you Marcia's dead! I've just found her. What's the matter with you? Can't you say something? *Dead.* Her head—her head is all—'

He looked at sticky fingers, and his shoulders trembled.

'Don't you believe me? Go in and look. My God, the loveliest woman that ever lived, all—all—go and see. They killed her, that's what they did! Somebody killed her. She fought. She would. Dear—Marcia. It was no good. She couldn't live. Nothing—of mine—ever stays. We were to go riding this morning, before anybody was up. I came out here and...'

Bennett was trying to fight down a physical nausea.

'But,' he said, 'what's she doing here? In this place, I mean?'

The other looked at him dully. 'Oh no,' he said at last, as though his vacant mind had found an elusive fact. 'You don't know, do you? You weren't there. No, Well, she insisted on sleeping here: all the time she was with us. That was like Marcia. Oh, everything was like Marcia. But why should she want to stay here? *I* wouldn't have let her. But I wasn't here to stop it...'

'Sir!' called a low, rather hoarse voice from across the clearing. They saw the groom craning his neck and gesticulating. 'Sir. Wot *is* it? Was it you that yelled, sir? I saw you go in, and then—'

'Go back,' said Bohun. 'Go back, I tell you!' he snarled, as the other hesitated. 'I don't need you. I don't need anybody.'

He sat down slowly on the top step, and put his head in his hands.

Bennett moved past him. He knew without self-illusion that he was afraid to go in there, that he felt empty and shaken at facing the dark, but it had to be done. He cursed himself because his right hand trembled; and he seized his own wrist with the other hand, idiotically:

'Are there,' he said, 'are there any lights?'

'Lights?' repeated Bohun, after a pause. 'In?—Oh. Oh, yes. Certainly. Electric lights. Funny. I forgot to turn on lights; forgot all about it. Funny! Ho ho! I—'

The jump in his voice made Bennett hurry inside.

So far as he could tell in almost complete darkness, he was in a little ante-room which smelt of old wood and musty silks; but there was a newer perfume trailing through. It brought the face of Marcia Tait too vividly before his mind. He did not, of course, believe she was really dead. That vital loveliness—the hand you had touched, the mouth you had (if only once) kissed, and then damned her for making a fool of you—these things did not suddenly dwindle to the flat lines of a drawing, or the wax stillness of a dummy in a coffin. Impossible. She was here, she was all about, palpable even in absence; and so was the flame. But he felt a growing sense of emptiness. Groping in the wall to the left, hurriedly, he found a door open. Inside that, he groped after an electric switch, found one, and hesitated a second before he turned it on…

Nothing. Nothing, when the light went on.

He was in a museum, or a drawing-room—a real drawing-room—of the Stuart times. Nothing had changed, except that the satin had frayed, the colours faded and gone dry. There were the three high arched windows with their square panes. There was the carven fireplace with its blackened stone hood, the floor laid out in chequered squares of black-and-white marble. And it was lit by candle-flames slowly wavering and shifting in brass candelabra on the walls. So subtly had the illusion been managed that for a second Bennett doubted his own sense, and half-expected *not* to find an electric switch in the wall when he looked. There was suggestion, too, in a disarranged chair with the Stuart arms worked into its oak filigree, in the ashes of a small fire that had gone out. There was a tall door at the rear of the room. When he opened it on darkness, he hesitated still more before the switch clicked.

Only two candelabra burned here, and the shadows were thick. He saw a shadow of the tall bedstead with its red canopy, the dull gleams in many mirrors of a small square room, and then he saw her.

In one stumbling rush he blundered over to make sure. It was true. She was dead. She had been dead for many hours, for she was stone cold: that was what brought home the shock to him most vividly.

Backing away to the middle of the room, he tried to keep himself calm and sensible. It was still impossible. She lay doubled up on the floor between the fireplace and the foot of the bed. In the same wall as the bed, and just across the room from the fireplace, rose an enormous square-paned window through which the grey light fell across her body and face. It dealt kindly with the face, despite the battered forehead and half-open eyes. He had felt blood clotted on the forehead, and matting the long tumbled hair; but Marcia Tait's last expression was less one of anguish than one of fright and defiance, mingled with that assured consciousness of fleshly powers which made her face almost grotesque in death. That, Bennett thought vaguely, was the most terrible feature of all. She wore white: a heavy white lace négligée, which lay about her in a heap, and was torn down along the right shoulder.

Murder. Head beaten in with—what? Again trying to keep himself calm and sensible, Bennett fixed his brain desperately on details, and looked about him. Under the hood of the stone fireplace were the ashes of another small fire: as though with a sort of horrible tidiness, it was exactly the size of the one in the other room. Into the ashes had rolled the end of a heavy poker from an overturned set of fire-irons. The poker? Possibly.

On the hearth, and strewing the edge of the grey carpet, he saw smashed fragments of heavy gilded glass from an ancient decanter and there were dark stains near it. Port wine: it still exhaled a stale sweetish odour. Crushed fragments of one or two—yes, two—drinking-glasses lay on the hearthstone. A low tabouret of gilded Japanese lacquer had been knocked over, and an oak chair with a wicker back and scarlet cushion. All these things were on the far side of the fireplace. On the near side of the fireplace, a similar chair stood facing the one that had been overturned.

He tried to visualize what had happened. It was not difficult. Marcia Tait had had a visitor, *somebody* who sat in the chair that was still upright. The visitor attacked. When he struck, chair, tabouret, decanter, and glasses went over. Marcia Tait ran from him. He struck again, and must have beaten her head long after he had finished her.

The thick air of the room, heavy with spilled wine and stale perfume and smoke, made Bennett feel light-headed. Air! Air, to cleanse even these images away... He moved round her body, towards the big window, and noticed something else. Strewn over the carpet, all in the general direction of the fireplace, lay a number of burnt matches. He noticed them because of their coloured stems: they were the fancy green, red, and blue-painted matches you buy on the Continent. But it made no impression on him at the time, although, as he lifted his eyes, he saw on a side-ledge of the fireplace a gold jewel-box, open and containing cigarettes, with a box of ordinary safety matches. Stumbling over to the big window, he wrenched at it, and had got it up part way when he remembered that in cases of this kind you were not supposed to touch anything. Never mind. He still had one driving-glove on; and the chill air was strengthening. He breathed it deeply for a moment before closing the window again. The curtains had not been drawn, and the Venetian blind was still tied up at the top of the window. Staring out blankly, he saw the unbroken snow touched with bluish shadows. And, beyond the lake and a thin fringe of trees, he saw on higher ground the rear of the line of stables only forty odd yards away, with a little green-shuttered house which evidently belonged to servants. You would never take this for a lake, at first glance, when the snow masked it. It was a good thing John Bohun had warned him not to—

Thin ice, and unbroken snow.

Momentarily he felt a horrible and incredible idea. Wherever he had been able to see the pavilion, it flashed back on him, the snow about it had been unbroken except for the single line of John Bohun's tracks going in. But the murderer had to go in and out. Even if there were sixty feet of *solid* ice all around the pavilion, he could not have done it without leaving a track. There must be tracks around at the rear, on another entrance somewhere.

This was insane theorizing. Of course Marcia had been dead some hours. The murderer had left while it was still snowing, and the snow had obliterated previous tracks. Why bother with it? Yet he had a vague impression that the snow had stopped fairly early in the morning, from what he remembered in London. Never mind...

He was startled by a voice rather nervously calling his name from the front room. When he hurried into the other room, Bohun was standing in the eerie electric-candle-light with another gilded decanter, which he had evidently taken from one of the drawing-room cabinets, in his hand. He lifted it and drank.

'Well?' he said. He was very quiet and composed now. 'The show's over, Bennett. All over. I suppose we had better send for a doctor or something.'

'It's murder...'

'Yes,' the other agreed, nodding. 'It's murder.' His dull eyes wandered round the room. 'When I find the man who did it,' he said quietly, 'I'll kill him. I mean that.'

'But what *happened* last night?'

'I don't know. But we're going to wake up everybody in the house and hammer the truth out of them. I was detained in town—I would be. So I didn't get here until three o'clock this morning or thereabouts. Everything was dark. I didn't even know in what room they'd put Marcia. She swore she *was* going to stay in this place, but I didn't know she meant it.' He looked round again, and added slowly: 'Maurice's work, I fancy. But she'd made me promise to ride with her early. So I got a little—a little sleep,' he said, looking at Bennett out of haggard eyes, 'and got up and woke Thompson. Butler. He'd been up half the night with a toothache, anyway. He said she was here. He said she'd fixed it with Locker to bring round the horses at seven o'clock. So I came out here, and Locker hailed me as I was going in—just when that dog—Have a drink? Or shall we go up to the house and get some coffee?'

After a long pause, while he tried to make his manner inhumanly casual, Bohun broke a little. His eyes squeezed up.

'She looked—pitiful, didn't she?' he asked.

'We'll find him,' said Bennett; 'at least, I know a man who will. Sorry, old son. Were you—were you so very much—?'

'Yes,' said Bohun. 'Come on.'

The other hesitated. He felt like a fool, and yet a nervous fear worried at him. 'I was only thinking: before we go out of here and make more tracks... There weren't any tracks beside your own coming into this place...'

Bohun whirled round. 'What the hell do you mean?'

'Wait a minute! Steady! I didn't mean—' Bennett saw his unintentional implication, and saw it too late. It startled him as much as it obviously startled John Bohun. 'The wise, right, and sensible thing.' Good God, diplomacy! He went on: 'Believe me, that wasn't what I meant at all. There was only the possibility that the man might still be in the house...'

'*What?*'

'Well, is there any other way in except the front door?'

'No.'

'And are you sure the ice is thin all around the place?'

Still Bohun did not grasp the question, though in a dull way he seemed to sense that it was important. 'I suppose so. At least, old Thompson warned me about it before I came out. He said some kids had—'

Then he stopped, and his eyes widened.

'You're talking nonsense,' he said curtly. 'What the devil's the good of mucking up the issue when we've enough on our hands as it is? Tracks! You're talking like a fool detective in a play. This is real. This is true. I'm only beginning to realize it's true. You'll be saying next that *I* killed her.'

'All the same, don't you think we'd better make sure there's still nobody hidden here?'

Again, after a long pause, Bohun stalked ahead while they searched the pavilion, muttering to himself and holding the decanter tightly in the crook of his arm. The search did not take long. There were only four rooms in the pavilion, excluding a tiny cubicle with a garish gilt-leafed bath at the back of the bedroom. A narrow hall or ante-room ran the depth of the house. On one side were drawing-room and bedroom, on the other a music-room and an uncanny replica of a seventeenth-century private salon set out with rosewood card-tables. All of it was faded; but it was swept and garnished as though for ghosts. Under the dull yellow candle glow it was as though somebody had arranged a shrine.

But there was nobody there. And, as they could see by looking out of windows on each side of the house, nowhere was there any mark in the snow.

'I've had enough of this,' said Bohun, when he had looked

out of the window of the card-room and turned sharply away. 'Let's go up to the house and not act the fool any longer. It snowed again and effaced any tracks, that's all. Don't look so worried, man. Leave that to me. When I find the man who—'

His own nervousness, the jerking of his mouth, and false brittle sarcasm of his look, was evident. He wheeled round. Bennett thought that he almost cried out when a faint voice rose outside, faint and insistent on the morning air, calling John Bohun's name.

IV
KING CHARLES'S STAIR

'Hullo, there!' the voice continued, coming nearer. They went out to the front door in time to see a big figure detach itself from the avenue of evergreens some ninety feet ahead, and stroll towards them at an unruffled pace. Jervis Willard. He was flicking powdery snow from the bushes with a stick. It was broad morning; but the light was shadowed by motionless dull grey clouds, so that they saw him only as a dark shape with a pipe protruding from under the brim of a rakish black hat.

He stopped when he saw the two of them, and took the pipe out of his mouth.

'Keep back!' Bohun shouted. He felt on the inside of the door, found a key, and locked it on the outside. Bennett saw that he was regaining all his old wiry coolness; that the mask was being adjusted, and that it was the public John Bohun who walked up the path. There was even a sort of hard malice in his face as they met Willard.

'You can't go in there, old man,' he continued. 'I dare say nobody can, until the police get here.'

Willard stood motionless. For a second he hardly seemed to breathe. In the winter light there were many more wrinkles in his face: a face that would have been rugged if the hat had not concealed the jutting forehead and heavy greyish hair. The loose mouth, which was half open, closed slowly and tightly. His eyes, a curious shade of yellowish-brown, never flickered, never wavered from Bohun's face.

'Yes, Marcia's dead,' said Bohun, as though he were striking blows against this immobility. His shoulders hunched. 'Dead as Babylon, dead as Charles the—yes. Her head's smashed in. *Do you hear?* Somebody murdered her, and nobody can go in there until the police get here.'

'So that's it,' said Willard, after a pause.

He looked at the ground for some time; as though he were tied there and helpless, and yet with his arms moving under a pain he could hardly stand. The dead immobility was even worse. He fumbled at putting his pipe back into his mouth. Then he began to speak rapidly: 'I met your ostler or groom or somebody. He said something was wrong, but that you wouldn't let him come out. He said you were going riding...'

He looked up, very white.

'I hope she didn't die painfully, John. She was always afraid of that. Shall we go back to the house now? It was my fault. After that poison affair, I shouldn't have allowed her to sleep there. I didn't think she was in danger. But I shouldn't have allowed—'

'You!' Bohun observed softly. 'Who are *you* to allow?' He walked a little ahead, and then turned sharply. 'Do you know what I'm going to do? I'm going to play detective. I'll find out who did it. Then—'

'Listen, John.' Willard stumbled against a bush as they turned round to go, and caught Bohun's arm. 'There's something I want to know. What is it like, in there? I mean what does it look like? How did she come to be dead—I can't make clear what I mean—'

'I think I know. She was entertaining somebody.'

They walked on. 'The obvious question,' Willard went on heavily, 'is one I can't ask, even of a friend. But I am afraid the police will. Do you understand me, John?'

'Scandal!' inquired the other. To Bennett's surprise, Bohun did not in the least flare out. He seemed to be weighing something in his mind, and finding it puzzling; there was almost a sardonic expression on his lean face, but it vanished immediately. 'Possibly. By God, there would be scandal about Marcia Tait if she died in a nunnery. Bound to be. It's a queer thing to say, Willard, but that side of it doesn't bother me at all. She was never jealous of her reputation; neither am I.'

Jervis Willard nodded. He seemed to be talking to himself.

'Yes,' he said. 'And I think I know why. You knew she was in love with you, and you knew that if you knew nothing else in this world.' As he turned to look at Bohun, he saw Bennett as though for the first time, and straightened up. The presence of a stranger closed his mouth instantly. 'Sorry, John. You—you, must excuse us, Mr. Bennett. Neither of us is at our best this morning.'

They reached the house in silence. Bohun led them up the steps to the side entrance, where Bennett's car still stood in the drive. At the top of the steps, just drawn back from peering out through the door, they found Thompson: not a stately specimen among butlers, but efficient as a genie. He was small, bald, and wrinkled, with the tolerant eye of one who has known the family too long. His utter respectability masked even the fact that his eyes were red-rimmed and his jaw swollen.

Bohun said 'Library,' and stopped for a conference with him while Willard led the way. Bennett found himself in a maze of narrow passages, dark and smelling of old wood, with coconut matting underfoot. There were unexpected steps, and diamond-paned windows in deep embrasures. He did not remember that he was chilled through until Willard took him to a big room where one wall was built of these windows after the Tudor fashion, and the other three walls were built of books. It was austere enough, with its stone floor and its iron book-gallery circling the walls; but there were electric lights in the twisted-iron chandelier, and the tapestry of upholstered furniture before the fireplace. Books crowded even over this fireplace; but there was a roaring blaze of wood. It dazzled Bennett's eyes, it made him shudder with a removal of the chill and he remembered how tired he was. He lay back in an overstuffed chair and stared at the groined roof with the red firelight flickering on it. The warmth seeped into him; he wanted to close his eyes. By moving his head slightly he could see the motion-less grey clouds outside the windows, and the brown slopes of the Downs rutted with snow. The house was very quiet.

'You saw her?' asked Jervis Willard's voice. Bennett roused himself.

'Yes.'

Willard was standing with his back to the fire, his hands folded behind him. The fire threw a burnished grey gleam on his hair.

'That was opportune, I should think.' His voice grew a shade quicker. 'May I ask how you happened to be there?'

'Accident. I'd just driven from town. I heard Bohun cry out—or call out—something of the sort. There was a dog howling…'

'I know,' said Willard, and passed a hand heavily over his eyes. The rumbling voice grew quicker again, soft, and suggestive. 'I should think you were cooler than John. Did you notice anything? Anything that might help us?'

'Not much. She was—'

He sketched out a picture, briefly. Willard leaned his arm along the mantelpiece, staring at the fire while the other spoke. Noting the fine if now rather flabby profile, Bennett thought: matinee idol of pre-war grandeur. Had the sense to move with the times. Something stately, something favoured of Shakespeare, in that bearing. Sensible, logical, humorous Friend of the Family; if Bohun had a niece (come to think of it, he *had* mentioned a niece), she would probably call Willard uncle.

'In all probability,' he heard himself going on absently, 'she had been taking a glass of port with somebody. There was a short fight—'

'It is unwise,' said Willard, smiling and looking sideways, 'to trust to inferences so far as that. As a matter of fact, I drank her health myself.' He straightened up. He began to walk up and down, quickly. 'Joking aside. This is rather worse… You are sure about those burnt matches?'

He paused as a door closed hollowly across the room. John Bohun came up to the fire and spread out his hands. The heavy riding-crop still dangled on a thong from his wrist. He flung it off; then he loosened the wool muffler that was knotted round his throat, and opened his tweed jacket. 'Thompson,' he said to the fire, 'will be in in a moment with coffee. James, my lad, your bags have been taken upstairs and your car's in the garage. You can get a hot bath and change the white tie.' Then he turned round. 'By the way, what's this about burnt matches?'

'I was hoping,' said Willard quietly, 'we could still blame it on a burglar.'

'Well?' demanded Bohun. He seemed to hesitate.

'When you looked—at Marcia, did you notice a lot of burnt matches scattered about?'

'I was not interested,' said Bohun, 'in burnt matches. No. I didn't turn on the lights. What the hell's wrong with you, anyway? Speak up!'

Willard went over and sat down on the other side of the fireplace. 'They were coloured matches, it seems. The kind (I think?) every bedroom in this house has been supplied with, ever since Maurice got the fancy for them. Wait!' He held up his hand. 'The police will be asking these questions, John, and it's ordinary sanity to think of them. There were no such matches at the pavilion. Unfortunately, I can swear to that. Except for the actual murderer, I must have been the last person to see Marcia alive. When they lit those fires for her last night, they left no matches in the house…'

'That reminds me!' said Bohun. 'Maid! Her maid. Carlotta! Where has Carlotta been all this time?'

Willard looked at him sharply. 'Curious, John. I thought you knew that. She left Carlotta behind in London. Leave of absence, or something. Never mind. There were no coloured matches, none of any kind, at the pavilion. I gave her a box of the ordinary sort before I left.

'Now let's face it. Casual burglars don't strew the floor with coloured matches; let me give you a hint there. But I don't need to hint very broadly. There were very queer things going on in this house itself. At some time last night, something scared old Canifest's daughter, terrified her nearly out of her wits. I heard her cry out, and found her lying on the floor in the passage near the bathroom. I couldn't get a coherent word out of her, except a reference to something or somebody *walking up and down in the passage*, and the somebody or something had seized her wrist. But she spent the rest of the night with Katharine.'

Bennett heard the fire cackle. John Bohun, who had been opening a silver cigarette-box, closed it with a snap and turned round.

'Louise,' he said, 'Louise Carewe is here?'

'Why not? She's a friend of Katharine; she's been in America for several months, and hasn't seen her. Why should it surprise you?—I wish to God you wouldn't be so jumpy, my lad,' he added, rather testily. 'It's a good thing you never did become an actor. You'd have the audience embarrassed for you in five minutes.'

'Oh, I don't know,' observed the other. His long hands cupped the match to his cigarette. The flame showed a kind of swaggering, feverish, secret mirth in his eyes. 'I don't know. I might make a better actor than you think. No, it didn't surprise me. Only I was talking to Canifest himself early last night. At his office. And he didn't mention it. Well, well. Maybe she disturbed a family ghost. Have we got any other visitors?'

'Yes. Your good friend Rainger.'

Bennett sat up. 'Steady, now,' Willard went on, as Bohun took the cigarette out of his mouth. 'Take it easy, and listen to me. There's nothing you can do. He is here, and in high favour with Maurice. I don't like to mention it, but before you suggest wringing his neck let me remind you that you're the younger brother. Maurice is foggy and absent-minded enough, but he's nasty when you cross him... And don't underestimate the Enemy. Their business was to keep close to Marcia, and they've done it.'

'So. How did the swine manage?'

Wrinkles of amusement deepened round Willard's eyes. He smiled, gradually throwing off befuddlement and shock. He was groping in his pocket after a pipe. 'Easily. Rainger is a shrewd, intelligent, and cultured—yes, don't snort; cultured—man. He was here before us yesterday afternoon. When we arrived, out bustled Maurice, patting Rainger paternally on the shoulder...'

'Maurice didn't go up to London, then?'

'No. Rainger had already sent him too interesting and suggestive a telegram. It seems that he had conceived the notion, subject to the proper authorities, that a sixteen-jewel super-special motion picture might be made of Maurice's scholarly researches, with Maurice's technical advice. It's probably a hoax, but Maurice is only human.'

'I begin to understand. Fully equipped with dancing-girls

and theme-songs, and called *The King Throws A Party.'*
Bohun's voice grew high. 'I say, Willard, has my brother
gone completely off his rocker?'

'That's where you're wrong. Look here, John; admit the
man's got some good points. His direction in *La Borgia* and
Queen Catherine was devilish good. He comes as close to
historical accuracy as it's possible to come without actually
telling the truth.'

Bohun took a step forward.

'Thank you,' he said, 'for whole-hearted admiration.
Perhaps you'll admire him still more when I tell you what
the swine's cleverness has done now.' Bennett had a feeling
that the man was saying what he ought not to admit, and
would regret; that he knew it; and yet that he could not stop
himself. 'Shall I tell you how he's blocked us? If Marcia had
lived, there would have been no play, anyhow... Canifest
has refused to back us.'

Willard's hand jerked. He caught the pipe again, and rose
half-way out of his chair.

'But he said—'

'He said to me last night, not a penny. I saw him at the
Globe-Journal office. He was as lordly as the statue of himself
over in the corner. After mature consideration (hurrum),
he had decided that for reasons of policy and discretion it
would not be well to lend the name of Canifest to theatrical
enterprises. Weight of the name! He wasn't to appear at all,
blast him... I say, Willard, it shakes you up, doesn't it? Aren't
the managers so keen on your work as they used to be—or
as Marcia was? So, if you don't get this engagement...'

He stopped.

'I never pretended to be a great actor, John,' Willard said quietly. 'But I don't think I deserved that.'

After a silence Bohun passed his hand across his eyes. Then he replied, just as quietly: 'I beg your pardon, old man. So help me God, I wouldn't have said that... I think you must know by now that I'm an egotistical ass who's usually afraid to talk; and when I do talk I only mess things up. I didn't mean it. But the shock of all these things together... Not that it matters now. Rainger must have talked to Canifest, that's all. I didn't think Rainger knew. If only Marcia hadn't been such a fool—'

Again he caught himself up, from a different cause this time. By mutual consent both of them ignored what had been just said about Willard, but Willard took him up rather sharply on this.

'Knew?' he repeated. 'What are you referring to there?'

'Nothing.'

'Not even, for instance, a suggestion that our distinguished publisher had been considering making Marcia Lady Canifest?'

Bohun cackled. 'That's rot, and you must know it. D'you think she'd have him?—Where did you pick up that idea?'

Willard looked at him, and made a slight satiric bow. 'I fancy it was the penalty of my extreme age and decrepitude. I have no particular desire to play father-confessor, but young ladies seem to think I should have. Oh, it's no particular secret. Canifest's daughter told your good niece Katharine, and Katharine (with permission, I believe) told me. The girl seems to be worried. All I could do was make strange clucking noises and say nothing. By the Lord, if

Canifest marries Marcia, the fat will literally be in the fire.'
He stopped abruptly. 'She's *dead*. She's dead—and I'd for-
gotten it. I can't get used to this, John,' he said rather wildly.
'I keep imagining she'll walk in that door at any minute.'

It intensified the grey loneliness of the room. Bohun
made a move towards a decanter of brandy on a side-table;
but he paused, tightened his shoulders, and looked back
again.

'Let's hear,' he said, 'everything that happened last night.'

Willard considered a moment, vaguely. 'It's hard to give
facts. Marcia was acting. She carried it off sheerly by force
of herself, by that damned force, that hypnosis, whatever it
was, that you couldn't resist; but I have never seen her acting—in private—become quite so high-flown. She said she
was "attuning herself," and similar absurdities...'

'You think they were absurdities?'

Willard noted his look. 'Yes, I know how you two feel
about the influence of this place. She may have believed it,
but somebody should have given her better lines to speak.
I think I see the abilities of Rainger now: he's a tamer. If
he had been directing that performance, he would have
moulded those powers in the right direction.' He looked up
briefly, and then went on filling his pipe.

'Go on.'

'At dinner, I am willing to admit, she was brilliant. It was
partly the effect of your dining-hall: the polished oak and
candle-light and big windows with the moon behind them.
Also, she wore a silver gown and had her hair arranged like
that portrait of the Duchess of Cleveland over the fireplace.
It was a good illusion, even her gestures. Rainger kept a

wooden face, but Maurice was almost dodderingly worship-
ful. He had put on his thickest-lensed spectacles in honour
of the occasion. As for Katharine and Canifest's daughter,
I do not believe they were impressed. I should think little
Louise hated her. As for Katharine, she had one sharp brush
with Her Ladyship when Marcia uttered some bubbling
absurdity...'

'Little Kate—' said Bohun. 'Gad, I never thought! I don't
seem to be able to think of anything. I stayed in London,
I didn't come down here after I'd been away for months, I
haven't even *seen* little Kate—'

Willard snorted.

'Little Kate,' he said, 'be damned. Look here, John, do
you know anything about her? Do you ever think of anything except your own dreams? She's twenty-one, she runs
this house for you, she's rather a beauty, and she's never been
farther afield than London in her life. Between you and
Maurice, this whole house is run on dreams and shadows.
Of course you haven't seen her. You've never even looked
at her.'

'You were saying?' Bohun prompted politely.

Willard seemed to debate something in his mind.

'This. That you don't even know what Marcia was like,
or why anybody should want to kill her. And you may not
feel the devilishness in this house. She inspired devilishness
wherever she went. If you didn't love her, she was just as willing to have you—or anybody else—hate her.' He struck the
arm of the chair. Momentarily his queer yellow-brown eyes
were gleaming. 'Oh, yes. *I* know. She would help it along;
she would touch and prod and crack the whip. And as for us,

we poor striped brutes went through the paper hoops and climbed up on the perches, and usually she had only to fire a blank cartridge when we got unruly. I say usually...

'Now I'm going to tell you what happened after dinner, and why I wasn't surprised at murder.

'Marcia insisted on a tour of the house by moonlight; with only Maurice carrying a candle, and explaining the romance of the White Priory. Of course Maurice was delighted. The rest of us went along. Rainger was too jocose, too attentive to the Honourable Louise: Katharine was with me. And Marcia had a word for all of us. Oh, she was vivid enough. She would sometimes take the candle from Maurice to show her eyes and her smile when she dazzled Maurice; she even got a spark out of Rainger, who was stolid enough, but he snatched up the silver cape of hers when it nearly touched the floor. The girls she treated with a kind of motherly sarcasm. I suppose I was down in the dumps—I don't know why. She chaffed me about what a poor Charles the Second I would make. This, mind you, when I was suddenly beginning to realize for the first time just how the part should be played. In those dark rooms, when you had that uncanny sense that people had just stepped out of them: I *got* it, I got the feel of a role such as I've never had since I played Peter Ibbetson! I had even begun to imagine the crashing success with the audience—

'Then we came to the Charles the Second Room.'

Willard seemed to feel his audience even then. He turned to Bennett.

'This will be gibberish to you, I fear. The Charles the Second Room is the one our friend Bohun here occupies now. It is kept much as it was. The feature of the place is a staircase in the wall, between the inner and outer walls, which goes down to a door opening on what is now a modern side porch—the porch by which we came into the house. The door (it's not a secret door, of course) is at the rear end of the porch. It was built so that Charles could go out and down the lawns to the pavilion without being observed leaving by any main entrance.'

'Yes, of course,' said Bohun impatiently. 'Well?'

'Maurice,' Willard continued, 'was showing us the secret staircase. I had seen it before, of course. But Marcia dragged me out on the little stone landing when the others crowded out there. It was draughty, and there was only the light of the candle Maurice was holding up. It is a very steep, narrow, and long flight of steps. I remember thinking it looked dangerously like a precipice. Then—

'I don't know, nobody knows, whether it was a draught that blew out the candle, or whether somebody jogged Maurice's arm, or what happened. But the candle went out. I heard somebody *giggle* in the dark. Not laugh, but giggle, and that was worse. Then I felt somebody pitch against me. I caught Marcia just as she had tripped headlong down those stairs.'

'She was,' said Bohun rather hoarse, 'she was—?'

'Pushed? Yes. Hurled, rather.'

Willard got up. He lit his pipe, inhaled a deep gust of smoke, and pointed with the pipe-stem. 'What is more, she knew it. But when a light was struck again, she turned round with one of her slowest, most radiant smiles and said—oh, I can't mimic her, but I remember her exact words—"But what an accident! I should have lulled myself." And she would have, John. Yet she enjoyed it; she enjoyed the violence that would admit her power enough to kill her.'

Bohun began to pace up and down the hearth-rug. His cigarette had smouldered down to his lip, and he burnt his hand as he knocked the stump into the fire. 'You don't,' he said, 'you don't know *who*?'

'No idea. We concluded our tour after that: it was about a quarter past eleven.'

'And then?'

Willard hesitated. 'Then was when she seemed to grow worried. Oh, I don't mean nervous about what had happened; but impatient and abstracted, as though she were expecting something. A curious film had come over her eyes.' He added softly: 'You, perhaps?'

'Possibly. I wasn't feeling like—returning. Do you realize,' Bohun demanded, 'what I'd just heard from Canifest? Ruin of all our plans. I was drinking, if you want to know the truth. And driving the streets, wondering what in God's name I should say when I got home.' He beat his hands together. 'Well? What happened then?'

'I should have thought,' Willard remarked musingly, 'her attitude was...never mind. At midnight she insisted on going to bed; a little early for Marcia. I didn't want her to go there—Maurice offered to let one of the housemaids sleep there and act as maid—but she wouldn't. We went out there with her. The night had gone clouded; that was when it started to snow, and there was a sharp wind. When we came back to the house after we had,' he snapped the word out, 'installed her, Maurice dragged Rainger off to the library to discuss motion pictures. Maurice had completely forgotten about the play. Rainger gave me a very strange, almost leering good night when I said I was going to my room.' He blew a film of ash off the bowl of his pipe. 'As a matter of fact, I walked back to the pavilion.'

'Oh.'

'I was there,' Willard answered, very quietly, 'exactly ten minutes. That was as long as she allowed me to stay. She seemed surprised when I knocked at the door, surprised and annoyed, as though she had been expecting somebody else. Twice while we were talking—it was in the bedroom— she went out and looked through the front windows of the drawing-room. And she seemed to be growing more nervous and upset. We drank a glass of port and smoked a cigarette. But the more I pointed out that there was somebody in very cool earnest, who had made two attempts to kill her, the more amused she grew. She said, "You don't understand the chocolates; and, as for the other, I'm certainly not afraid of—"'

'*Who?*'

'I don't know. She only stretched her arms up above her head (you know that gesture of hers?). As though she were breathing—life, and breathing it in a kind of glutted satisfaction. She was not acting then. In ten minutes she walked to the outer door with me. She was still wearing the silver gown, and the snow was growing thicker outside. That was the last I saw of her.'

The snow. Bennett leaned across in the firelight. His muddled brain still kept returning to that question of the snow.

'Do you remember,' he said, 'exactly what time the snow began, Mr. Willard?'

'Why—yes. Yes, if it matters. It was when we took Marcia out to the pavilion, about ten minutes past twelve.'

'But I don't suppose you'd know what time it stopped?'

The actor wheeled round. He seemed about to answer irritably, when he saw Bennett's expression, and then looked with a quick speculative glance at Bohun.

'As it happens, I do. For reasons I'll explain, I spent a very wakeful night. First there was the dog barking. I was up and at the window any number of times, although—although my room isn't at the rear of the house and I couldn't see towards the pavilion. But I noticed how very heavy a fall of snow it was to last for so brief a time. It lasted just about two hours, roughly from a little past twelve to a little past two. The number of times I looked at my watch last night—' He hesitated. 'Why?'

A knocking at the door echoed hollowly across the room. Wind was rising across the Downs and rumbling in the chimney. Out of the corner of his eye Bennett saw Thompson come in.

'Excuse me, sir,' said Thompson's voice. 'Dr. Wynne has just arrived, and the inspector of police you sent for.

'There's,'—a definite *ah* of doubtful description—'there's someone else with them...'

So Marcia Tait must have been killed before two o'clock, probably some time before two o'clock, for all footprints of the murderer to have been effaced. Why, Bennett wondered, should it bother him? He almost started when he heard Thompson go on:

'The other ma—the other gentleman asked for his card to be given to Mr. Bennett. You are Mr. Bennett, sir? Thank you.'

Bennett took the slip of pasteboard, on which was scribbled, '*Friend of Sir Henry Merrivale. Should like to see you privately.*' The neat engraving read:

> **HUMPHREY MASTERS**
>
> *Chief Inspector*
>
> *Criminal Investigation Dept*
>
> *New Scotland Yard, S.W.*

V

SHADOWS IN THE GALLERY

'Tell Dr. Wynne and the inspector,' said Bohun, becoming brisk and alert once more, 'that I'll take them down to the pavilion at once. Like to come along, Willard?' He looked at Bennett, who was still staring at the card in his hand. 'You're a very popular young man, Jimmy my lad,' he added in a curious voice. 'You arrive here at break of day. At (what time is it?) at a quarter past eight people have already begun calling on you.—May I ask who it is?'

Bennett decided to be frank, though he was a little uneasy at the wheels he seemed to have set in motion. He put the card into Bohun's hand.

'I don't know the man,' he replied, 'or how he happens to be here at eight o'clock in the morning. My uncle is—'

'I know who he is,' said Bohun. His voice was quiet, but a nerve twitched beside his eyelid.

'I'm sorry. I admit it was sheer impertinence, but I mentioned the poisoned chocolates to him: in confidence. And, considering what's happened now, don't you think that maybe it was the best thing…?'

'Good Lord, of course it was,' snapped Bohun, rather too quickly. 'We shall get things done, now. He's a jolly quick worker, I should say, to be here now. Er—"privately," he says. Yes, of course. Thompson, show Chief Inspector Masters in here. Mr. Willard and I will go down to the pavilion with Dr. Wynne. No, we won't meet the chief inspector yet. Let him have his privacy.'

It was a good deal of a relief, Bennett felt, to have Bohun and Willard out of the room. The thickness of the emotional atmosphere, through which you could hardly see a man for his nerves; all the antagonisms and hates which were Marcia Tait's only legacy, seemed to clear from the library when they left it. And he was still more heartened at the homely, genial appearance of Chief Inspector Masters.

A portly man, Masters, with his bland and shrewd face, his sedate dark overcoat, his bowler hat held against his breast as though he were watching a flag procession go by. He had the eyes of a young man, a heavy jaw, and grizzled hair carefully brushed to hide the bald spot. He came into the library with just the proper air of being impressed by it.

'Ah, sir!' said Masters, by way of greeting. He took the extended hand, and returned Bennett's grin. His deep voice fell soothingly on rattled nerves. 'You must excuse such an early morning call. I promised your uncle I'd keep an eye on you.'

'On *me*?'

'Well, well,' said Masters, waving a deprecating hand. 'Manner of speaking, d'ye see. Manner of speaking, that's all. Point of fact, he 'phoned me last night, but I'm not (exactly) on duty. No. The wife of the local inspector of police is a cousin of mine, it happens. I'd been visiting. Just between ourselves'—he lowered his voice and peered round—'I'd arranged to officiate as Santa Claus at the Christmas festival of the Methodist Junior Children's League. Eh? When Mr. Bohun's message came through this morning, I took the liberty of coming along with Inspector Potter. And I wanted a word with you.'

Bennett was rather surprised to find that Thompson had wheeled in a tea-table set with a fragrant steaming coffee-urn, hot milk, and cups. He became conscious of a gnawing in his stomach.

'Sit down,' he invited, 'by all means. Coffee?'

'Ah!' said Masters appreciatively.

'Er—cigar?'

'Ah!' said Masters voluptuously. The chief inspector lowered himself with careful motions to the edge of the sofa, and accepted a cup. Bennett felt a blast of pleasant sanity coming through the miasma. 'Now, here's how it is,' Masters went on in a confidential tone. 'I won't detain you long, because I must go down to that pavilion. But first I wanted to establish relations. In a manner of speaking. Eh? Exactly. Now I won't conceal from you,' he proceeded, again as though he were imparting a confidence, 'that this case is going to create a stir. A stir. It's likely the Yard will be asked to take it up. And I want to establish relations with somebody Sir Henry said I could trust. Very useful. I'm a very suspicious man, Mr. Bennett.' Despite his beaming shake of the head, the other felt that the shrewd eyes were ticketing his appearance and missing no detail.

'You've worked with Sir Henry before, haven't you?'

'Ah!' the chief inspector murmured, and stared at his cup. 'Why, as to that, yes. I should be inclined to say that I did the working and he did the thinking.' There was the suggestion of a wink about one eye. 'You mustn't mind Sir Henry, Mr. Bennett. He grouses and grouses, until he forgets his firm belief that he's *got* to grouse; then he goes to work on the thing like a kid building a card-house. And before you know it, his case is complete and he's grousing again. Eh? I owe him quite a lot, and that's a fact. But the messes he becomes involved with are a bit too strenuous for me. I don't like these things that couldn't have happened yet did happen. Like Darworth's murder in the stone house...'[1]

It was impossible for the man to know what he was thinking about, but, as he met the small bright eye that was shifted round on him, Bennett felt his old doubts.

He said: 'I only hope you haven't got another such case. Damn it, you *can't* have! It depends on the time a woman died.'

Masters bent forward.

'Just so. Now, there was certain information given to Inspector Potter over the 'phone. It was to the effect that you had just driven down from London,' he darted a glance at Bennett's crumpled collar and tie, 'and you and Mr. John Bohun discovered the body.

Eh?'

'Yes, that's right.—Well, more or less. He got there two or three minutes before I did.'

'"More or less." Now, suppose you tell me what happened.

1 See *The Plague Court Murders.*

Tell me in your own words,' suggested Masters, rather super-
fluously, 'what happened. *With* details.' He lit his cigar
carefully, and listened with a wooden face while Bennett
spoke. Only towards the end did he seem to grow disturbed.
'Now, now!' he urged sharply. 'Now, come! Let's be certain.
Only one set of tracks going in (Mr. John Bohun's), and none
coming out?'

'Yes.'

'Were they *fresh* tracks?'

'Yes, I'll swear they were. I noticed by the feathery condition of the snow. They'd been made very shortly before
mine.'

Masters studied him. 'Fresh tracks, and you say the body
was already cold then. Hurrum. So that the tracks couldn't
have been made hours before you saw... Tut, young man!
Tut tut tut! I'm suspecting nobody, ha ha ha. Not Mr. Bohun,
of course.' His smile looked almost genuine. 'But did anybody actually *see* him go in when he said he did? Eh? Eh?'

'Yes. As a matter of fact, a groom or somebody. I've forgotten his name.'

'Oh, ah,' said Masters, nodding. He set down his cup
and got up urbanely. 'Now, I shall want to know a great deal
about the people in this house. Everything that happened;
eh?—Death of Marcia Tait!' said Masters. 'Lummy, what a
plum! First thing under my nose since—well, since. Excuse
me if I'm interested. Mrs. M. and I go often to the pictures,
Mr. Bennett.' He seemed frankly surprised at his good or
bad fortune in being so near Marcia Tait. 'And *why* I came
to you, Sir Henry tells me you know all this group. You've
travelled with 'em, know what they're like... What? No?'

'I've travelled with them. I'm not at all sure I know what they're like.'

Masters said that was better yet; he shook hands cordially, and said he must go to see how Inspector Potter was handling matters. When he had gone, Bennett considered Masters' suggestion about John Bohun, and knew that it was absurd. But it worried and depressed him. Finding a bell-cord beside the fireplace, he summoned a flurried Thompson and suggested that he would like to find his room.

After more crooked passages and one magnificent low staircase, he found himself sitting on the bed of a very large and very cold room opening off a broad gallery on the second floor of the house. The whole place had the usual disconsolate early-morning look. What was worse, as they passed along the dusky gallery he could have sworn he heard someone sobbing in one of the rooms. Thompson had obviously noticed it, though he pretended otherwise. He said that there would be breakfast in half an hour. The man's swollen jaw (hadn't Bohun said something about a toothache?) was paining him, and the news of the murder must clearly have torn the last rags of his self-possession. When he heard that faint sobbing, he began speaking loudly as though to drown it out; stabbing his finger towards a door at the end of the gallery, and repeating, '*King Charles's room, sir. King Charles's room. Now occupied by Mr. John!*' in the fashion of a hysterical guide. The gallery ran the width of the house, and King Charles's room was just opposite the one to which Bennett had been shown.

Sitting now on a bed with a shaky-looking tester bulking

overhead, Bennett scowled at a pitcher of hot water in a wash-bowl nearby. Damn their water in pitchers and their asthmatic fires and their open windows. Sybaritic American, eh? Well, why not? At least his bags had been deftly unpacked. He found his shaving-tackle, and over the wash-stand discovered a small mirror hung at a neck-breaking angle, out of which a hideous Coney Island reflection leered at him from the wavy glass. This was worse than waking up with a hangover. Where was the old sense of humour? Hunger, loss of sleep, horrors: and across the hallway was a room where *somebody* had tried to throw Marcia Tait down a flight of stone stairs—

Then he heard it. He heard the sound, the cry, whatever it was, that trembled somewhere along the gallery outside. The razor slipped out of his fingers. For a moment he felt sheer unreasoning terror.

A scuffling noise, and then silence.

He had to do something as an outlet for anger, or fear, or both. Groping after a dressing-gown, he twisted himself into it. The thing would squeeze up like a rolled umbrella when you tried to jam your hands through the armholes; you stepped on the trailing end of the waist-cord and pulled the whole thing out. He got it over his shoulders somehow, and opened the door to peer into the gallery.

Nothing; at least, nothing of visual fear or danger. He was at the end of the gallery, where there was a big latticed window looking down on the roof of the *porte-cochère*. Smoky lights showed him the faded red runner of carpet stretching away fifty feet to the head of the stairs, the line of doors in low oaken walls, the gilt frames and claw-footed chairs. He looked across at the door directly opposite. There was no reason to suppose the noise had come from King Charles's room, except that he associated it with all the stealthy moving in this house. It was Bohun's room; but Bohun could not be there. He moved across and knocked. Then the big door creaked under his hand.

In a twilight of curtains that were nearly drawn across deep embrasures, he saw its vastness. He saw a glimmer of silver vases, a tall hearse of a bed-canopy, and the reflection of his own face in a mirror. The bed was made, but Bohun's clothes were flung about on chairs and bureau-drawers hung drunkenly open. Instinctively, he was peering round for that hidden door to the staircase. This room occupied the angles of the house that looked down on the drive and the lawns towards the rear. The staircase, then, would be in the wall at his left hand; probably between those two windows. That was where—

He heard the noise again. It was behind him; it was in the gallery somewhere; behind one of those doors that locked up the White Priory secrets. He moved a little way up the gallery, and a door opened almost in his face. It opened as quietly as the girl who came out, although she was breathing hard and her hands fumbled at her throat.

She did not see him. From the room behind her he heard a curious mutter and stir, as of a sick person, before she closed the door. She bent her head forward, slid against the wall, and then straightened up.

As she took her hands away, just before they looked at each other in the gloom, he saw the bruises on her throat. And he saw Marcia Tait's face.

VI

'—WHO WALKED, BUT LEFT NO FOOTPRINT'

He stood a little to one side, looking down at her, so that the grey light should fall on her face. Curiously enough, in the first utter blankness of the shock, he did not think of ghosts or even of a hallucination whereby he saw Marcia's face everywhere. He only thought, with a dazed feeling of relief, that the whole farce of a murder was a monstrous joke after all, a hoodwinking and a premeditated nightmare; and he wanted to laugh.

Then he saw that it was not Marcia, which was even a worse shock. In the next moment he wondered that he had seen any resemblance at all in these white features crossed by the shadow of the lattice. This girl was smaller and slighter; her dark hair was caught back carelessly behind her ears; and she wore a careless grey jumper and black skirt. Yet for one instant—an outline of her cheek, a trick of gesture, a heavy-liddedness of the dark eyes—it had been there.

But he forgot that, in the knowledge that she was hurt. He heard her voice, which was not Marcia Tait's.

'Jo—' she said, and swallowed hard. She was looking up eagerly. 'John? You haven't been to see—No; what am I saying? About Louise. It's all right; really it is. It was the shock. I've quieted her. She didn't know me. She was hysterical, after last night. She tried to...' Speaking hurt her. The hands went to her throat again; she fought down nausea, and tried to smile. 'But I wish you'd get Dr. Wynne to come up and—'

A pause.

'*You're not my uncle! Who are you?*'

'Steady,' Bennett urged, and felt somehow guilty. 'It's all right. Word of honour, it's all right! I'm a friend of your uncle. My name's Bennett. Look here, you're hurt. Let me—'

'No. I'm all right. It's Louise!... Oh! Bennett! Yes, I know who you are. Louise spoke about you. You're the man who took her father round New York. What are you doing?' She moved swiftly in front of the door. 'I say, you mustn't go in there. Really you mustn't. She's got her *night-gown* on.'

'Well, what of it?' said Bennett, so startled that he pulled up short. 'Anybody who goes berserk and tries to strangle... that's what she did, wasn't it?'

Impossible to imagine this. He remembered that freckled, rather dowdy, mechanically smiling girl who was always the background for Lord Canifest; who was quietly efficient, who expertly managed his correspondence and was not permitted a second cocktail.

'Berserk?' repeated Katharine Bohun, although it hurt her to speak. She tried to laugh, weakly. 'Louise? She can't help it; she's hysterical. After what happened last night—oh, please don't be a fool! I don't feel especially well myself...'

'I know you don't,' said the other grimly, and bent forward as she tried to support herself against the wall.

'What on earth are you doing now? Let me down! Let me down, do you hear?'

He carried a rather dazed and somewhat frightened young lady, who asked him if he had gone mad, straight to his own room, and pushed open the door with his foot. Then, because it was comfortable and also because he wanted a look at her in better light, he put her down on the cushions of the window-seat in its deep embrasure. Without looking at her he rummaged in a suitcase after the bottle of brandy he found it advisable to carry in England as preparedness against the inexorable earliness of closing-hour. When he returned she was leaning back against the corner of the window with an expression in which weariness blurred out even anger or relief.

'No,' she said, rather quickly. 'I'm all right. No brandy, thanks.'

'Drink it!—Why not?'

It was, he thought, probably utter exhaustion that made her tell the truth then; she spoke involuntarily, and in spite of herself.

'Because Uncle Maurice would say I had been drinking.'

'Good old Uncle Maurice!—Here...'

She swallowed with difficulty and a good deal of pain, while he soaked a towel in water, wrung it out, and tried to adjust it round the purplish bruises on her neck.

'That's better. That's fine. Like it?'

'Of course I like it.'

'Have another? No? Then wait till I get this thing fixed

round your neck, and then I wish you'd tell me what makes friends of yours like—like the Honourable Louise Carewe,' the name sounded fantastic in his ears as he said it, when applied to that self-effacing girl whom he had always pictured as sitting on a chair lower than that of anybody else. He tested it again. 'Friends of yours like the Honourable Louise Carewe go hysterical and try to kill you. Sit still!'

'I say, you're making a most awful mess of me. Give me that towel.' She stirred, smiled faintly, and tried to assume a businesslike briskness. He studied her as she leaned back in the window-embrasure. The resemblance? If he had not been prepared for it by some accident or trick of the light, he wondered if he would have noticed it at all.

In her quiet, casual, rather nervous way she had a beauty of her own. The face was pale and devoid of make-up; she had thin brows, curving a little upwards at the outer corners, over brown-black eyes of a curiously luminous quality. Her glance was direct, in contrast to Marcia's, and of a disturbing intensity; but she had the same heavy eyelids, the same small soft mouth and small neck.

What then? Another victim of the dreams in the cloudy absorption of this house? A background for the pompous vagaries of the brothers Bohun, as quiet Louise was for Lord Canifest? You had the whole matter in the tone of John Bohun's voice when he spoke abstractedly of Little Kate. He remembered what Willard had said.

'You must forgive me,' she said, in her somewhat nervous fashion, 'if I was upset, or said—silly things, or—I'm always doing that. But I'm very fond of Louise. She had never had a chance. Her father…you know him, don't you?'

'I know his Voice.'

'Yes. Yes, that's what I meant,' she nodded. 'You understand. Louise liked you. She's a very different person, really, when she's among friends. I expect we all are...' She stared out of the window for a moment, and then turned back. 'May I ask you something? Stella said—Stella's the maid who brought my tea up this morning—Stella said they were all talking about it downstairs, and that it was true. About Marcia. Is it true? *Is it?*'

She spoke breathlessly, and he nodded without replying.

'Stella said she was hurt, killed, out at the pavilion; and her head was all—all hurt, and John found her there. Is that true too?'

'I'm afraid so.'

Again she turned away to the window, her shoulders rigid and her eyes closed. After a pause he said quietly: 'Were you fond of her, then?'

'*Fond* of her? No. I detested her. No, that's not true either. But, oh, my God, how I envied her.'

There was nothing to say. He felt nervous and uncomfortable. He got up to fumble among his belongings for a cigarette. The disturbing influence of this girl whom nobody ever noticed... She was speaking again:

'Do they know who did it?'

'No. Except they seem to think that it was somebody in this house.'

'Of course it was somebody in this house. It was the same person who was walking in the gallery last night.'

He sat down on the window-seat again; not wanting to force confidences, not wanting to throw out blatant and

futile offers of help for—what? Yet those were the sensa-
tions, baffling and complicated, that he felt more fiercely
than he could have explained them. But she must have seen
it, for she said surprisingly:

'Thanks. Thanks you-don't-know-how much.' A steady
smile. 'Most people would say I can take care of myself. I
can. But it frightened me nearly as much as it frightened…
Yes, there was somebody in the gallery last night, blunder-
ing, searching, pacing; I don't know what. It was what drove
poor Louise out of her wits, and why we shall probably need
to have the doctor for her. Whoever it was took hold of her
wrist in the dark, and then pushed her away.'

'You don't suppose she imagined—?'

'There was blood on her,' said Katharine Bohun.

'When did all this happen?'

She shook her head blankly. 'I don't remember the time.
At close on four o'clock, I should think; I looked at the
clock afterwards.—That was my room you saw me come
out of. Something woke me up; I'm not sure what. But then
I heard somebody fumbling at my door and pawing at the
knob. Like—like a big dog. I suppose I keep thinking of
dogs because Tempest barked so much early last night, and
I heard him howling again this morning.

'But this was at my door. Then I heard a sound like a fall,
and somebody running. I didn't dare move, until I heard Jervis
Willard's voice speaking out there. He'd heard some noise, and
come out in the hall and turned on the light to see what it
was. When I opened my door he was lifting Louise: in a faint.'

Bennett said rather irritably: 'Why the devil was *she* wandering around in the dark at four o'clock in the morning?'

'I'm not sure. She hasn't been very coherent since. I think she was coming to my room; she hadn't been asleep all night and she was rather hysterical already. I suppose when she got out of her own room she wasn't able to find the light-switch, and got lost and worse frightened because she couldn't find her way either back or to me. I know she has kept saying, "*Lights, lights!*"' Katharine Bohun stared straight ahead, her hands clenched in her lap. 'Were you ever awfully frightened by thinking you were lost in a maze in the dark, and you'd never got to where you wanted to go? I've been. In dreams, sometimes.'

He leaned forward suddenly and took her by the shoulders. He said:

'I'm very fond of ghost stories and the morbid kind. That's because I've never run up against anything really morbid in my own life. But *you're* not to get frightened by a lot of damned shadows and nonsense, do you hear? You've had too much of it.'

'I say, what on earth—'

'What you need is to walk out of this forsaken house with its cold hot-water pitchers and its cockeyed mirrors and its moth-eaten ghosts. You need to make straight for London or Paris, preferably Paris, and fly off on a bender that would knock the unholy watchsprings out of anything you'd ever imagined. You need to wallow in dressmakers' shops and red-plush hotels; you need to hear bands and have a dizzy love-affair and get sozzled in every bar round the Place de Clichy; you need to see the Chinese lanterns on the lake in the Bois, and dance at the Chateau de Madrid in a postage-stamp of a dress, and see the chafing-dishes steam and the colour of Burgundy while you're jammed up in a crazy little room that's served the best in the world for two hundred years. You need to see the chestnut-trees coming out in spring on the Champs Elysées, and taste onion soup down in the markets by the river when it's just getting daylight; you need—'

He had pitched diplomacy clear out of the window. He had got up and was waving one arm in the air during the fervour of the moment. Now the balloon collapsed as he realized he must be making a fool of himself. He saw again the bleak room, the windows looking out on snow. But he was surprised at the vividness and intensity of Katharine Bohun's face. She looked up at him.

'You—you blasted *Yank!*' cried Katharine Bohun, with a violence of relief which made her voice quaver. Then she began to laugh, but not in ridicule. It seemed difficult for her to stop.

'Er—yes. Exactly.'

'You're quite the craziest person I ever met.'

'On the contrary, you blasted Limey, I am regarded as—'

'And you mustn't talk like that; at least, you see—that is, of course, I mean—where anybody else can hear you.'

'Ho?'

She caught herself up, nervously. 'Never mind. Be sensible again. I've got to be. I mean—Marcia. I can't think of anything else. Marcia could do all those things you were speaking about. Marcia was herself; she was alone; she was wonderful…in her own way.' Again she clenched her hands. 'And maybe—I've been thinking of this too—maybe she was satisfied. She's lying down there dead. But she died when she had everything she wanted; when she had everything a woman ever wanted; when she was alone and splendid and not growing old. Who *wouldn't* give death for that? And if somebody smashed in her head with the loaded end of a riding-crop, then maybe it was worth it.'

Even in her rush she stopped suddenly. You could feel unspoken words shut off as at the closing of a door. And their import was as palpable as the slam of a door in the cold room.

Bennett stared at her. 'With a riding-crop?' he said.

He should never have spoken. He realized it as soon as the words were out. That closing door was one that shut him off from her.

She rose from the window-seat.

'Wasn't it? I must have got that impression from Stella,' she said, quickly and loudly. In that moment the quiet, nervous Katharine Bohun looked dangerous, and she was breathing sharply. 'I must really get back to my patient now. Thank you so much for everything. You had better go down to breakfast, hadn't you?'

Before he could move or speak, almost with the swiftness of an illusion, she was out of the room. He remained staring at the closed door, fingering an unshaven jaw. Then he went over and kicked an empty suitcase across the room. He followed it with the intention of kicking it back; but sat down on the bed instead, lit a cigarette, and blew out smoke violently.

The muddle was growing worse. His hand was shaking, and the room was full of a mocking image of Marcia Tait. If Willard's crackling picture of her character were correct, she had never laughed in life as she would laugh in death. Riding-crop! There was no riding-crop at the scene of the crime, or near it, except the one John Bohun had carried on his wrist. Which was manifestly impossible.

The police would be back from the pavilion now. He must go downstairs. Keeping his mind grimly away from Katharine Bohun, he shaved in cold water; felt better, but a little light-headed; dressed and went downstairs.

He had intended to go to the dining-room, but there were loud voices from the direction of the library. The door was open. Lights had been turned on in the ceiling of the dusky room, and a group had gathered round the modern furniture in front of the fire. At a table behind the couch, flanked by bronze lamps with yellow shades, a tall man in the uniform of an inspector of police sat with his back to the door. He was tapping a pencil against the side of his head. Beyond him stood a very nervous Thompson, and beyond them Chief Inspector Masters, blandly inspecting books on the shelves. The person who had been speaking—with strident positiveness, and a gesture like a semaphore—was a sharp-featured little man in a shabby black overcoat and a bowler hat stuck on the back of his head. He stood with his back to the fire, a pair of black-ribboned glasses coming askew on his nose, and pointed again.

He said: 'Don't think you can tell *me* my business, Potter. I regard that as a sheer, out-and-out insult, that's what I do; and when I get you at the inquest, Potter, then dum-me, I promise you now, I'll make you smart good and proper!' He leered over the glasses, malevolently. 'I'm telling you the exact medical facts. Get your police surgeon to check up on me, if you like. Get every bloody quack in Harley Street. Yah! Then you'll find out—' His sharp gaze saw Bennett at the door. He stopped.

There was a silence in the tension of the room. Masters came up to the table.

'Ah!' he said quickly. 'Come in, Mr. Bennett. Come in, if you please. I was just going to send for you. This is Dr. Wynne—here. Inspector Potter—here. Now, we've been hearing some very unusual things in the last half hour...'

Dr. Wynne snorted. Masters had lost some of his earlier genial air; there were lines round his mouth and he looked worried.

'Which need straightening out. Just so. Now, sir, I've already told these gentlemen what you told me a while ago. Perhaps you'd better repeat it, as a matter of form, to the inspector—'

Inspector Potter looked up from his notebook. He was a bald-headed giant with a small tuft of moustache, a reddish face, and an eye like a ruminating cow; and he was dogged if bewildered. He looked at Bennett rather suspiciously. 'Nameanaddress,' recited the inspector, in gruff positiveness. 'If foreigner,' more suspicion, 'suggest references. Not under oath, but advise for own good complete frankness. Now!'

'Now, then, Potter,' interposed Masters with some asperity, 'you want my help; is that it? Eh?'

'That,' said the inspector, 'that I do, sir.'

'Well, then—!' said Masters persuasively, and waved his hand. 'I'll manage for a bit, if you don't mind. Now, Mr. Bennett, I want to stress the importance of this. I want you to get it down clear. Thompson!'

Thompson came forward. His reddish-rimmed eyes showed a very definite hostility, but his voice was docile; and he looked (Bennett thought) the most respectable man in the room.

'You told Inspector Potter,' Masters went on sharply, 'that the snowfall stopped last night at just after two o'clock—no more or less—and you can swear to it?'

'Yes, sir. I'm afraid I can.'

'Afraid? What do you mean, afraid?'

'Why, sir, only that I shouldn't want to cause any trouble,' Thompson replied without inflection, 'for the police. I can swear it. I didn't close an eye all night.'

Masters turned back.

'And Dr. Wynne tells us—'

'I tell you this,' snapped the doctor, and tapped Masters on the shoulder. 'Allowing for everything, including temperature, I definitely put the time of that woman's death as between three o'clock and three-thirty a.m. That's final. You say the snow stopped at two o'clock. Well, that's your business. What *I* say is that if the snow stopped at two o'clock, then that woman didn't die until *at least* an hour afterwards.' He leered round. 'I don't envy you your job, my lads.'

Inspector Potter came to life. 'But, sir,' he shouted, 'it's not possible! Not sense! Look here; there's two sets of tracks going into that house,' he continued with heavy impressiveness, and held up two fingers. 'Mr. Bohun tells us they were made by himself and this gentleman. Very well. There's two sets coming out, made by the same people. And that's all. Each of the four sets of prints is about equally fresh, so far as we can judge...and I've done some poac—urrr—some trapping, I meantersay, in my younger days. They were made this morning, they were made about the time Mr. Bohun says! And thassalleris.' He swept his arm about, small pencil in massive fist. Then he brought the fist down on the table. 'A hundred straight feet of unmarked snow on every side of the 'ouse. Not a tree, not a shrub. *And* sixty feet of it thin ice on every side. Not possible, not sense, and may I never go to chapel again if it is!'

The inspector was breathing heavily through his nostrils. But so was Masters, who had been trying in vain to stop a conversational steam-roller. Masters did more than merely glare. His attitude towards Inspector Potter as his family-relation made him deplorably forgetful of his dignity.

'Now, then!' he declared. 'Now, then, I'll tell you what it is, Charley Potter. You keep your ruddy head shut when you're told, or I'll report to the Chief Constable of this county your means of carrying on a case. Tell a witness what to say; eh? Makes no difference if we know it's truth. Eh? *Oh*, Lord! You in the C.I.D., my lad? I *don't* think.'

Inspector Potter closed one eye in a highly sinister fashion.

'Urrr?' he inquired with dignity. 'And 'oo may be in charge of this case, I should like to know?—You that was going to play Santy Claus! Urrr! All right. Play Santy Claus. Here. Now. I was stating well-known facts. And I'll tell you more. We've got a witness, Bill Locker that I've known all my life and is honest and trustworthy and 'as spotted the Derby winner for the last three years which is more than you can do: Bill Locker saw Mr. Bohun go in. Eh? And there was nobody in there hidden, which we proved. Now, then!'

He flung down his pencil on the table like a gauntlet. 'Until you can play Santy Claus and explain all that, sir, I'll ask you respectfully—'

'Sic 'em, my lads,' said the little doctor, with an air of refreshed interest. 'I think I'll stop on a bit. Yes. Nothing adds zest to a criminal case like a free-for-all fight among the police at the outset. But is there anything else you want to know from *me*?'

With an effort Masters regained his imperturbability.

'Ah, ah,' he said. 'Forgot myself, inspector. Just so. You're in charge, for the moment, and you're quite right and within your duties.' He folded his arms. 'I should suggest, however, that before the doctor goes you make some inquiry about the weapon.'

Dr. Wynne scowled. 'Weapon? Hum. Dunno. That's your business. All I can give you is the customary Blunt Instrument. They were hard smashes. From the position of the wounds, looks as though she'd been struck down from the front, and then smashed five or six times as she lay on her side or face. Hard blows. Yes. Your police surgeon will tell you definitely at the P.M.'

'I don't suppose, sir,' observed Potter, as a startling thought seemed to occur to him for the first time, 'I don't suppose it could have been done by a *woman*, could it?'

'M. Might have been. Why not? Given a fairly heavy weapon; why not?'

'That poker with its end in the ashes?'

'I should have said something rather thicker, with an angle or two to it. But again that's your business.'

During these questions, Bennett noticed, Masters's face

had assumed a blank and tolerant sadness as of a teacher in an idiot-school, touched now by a satiric grimness. He breathed stertorously through his nose as Inspector Potter asked:

'Ah! Might it 'a' been that decanter, now; the heavy one that was smashed?'

'Hang it, man, it could have been anything! Look round for your fingerprints or your bloodstains, or whateveritis.' Dr. Wynne set his hat on jauntily and picked up a black bag. He squinted at the inspector. 'Humph. Shouldn't think it was the decanter, would you? Seems to me she'd have been soaked in port wine, and anyway the fragments of that bottle weren't near her body at all. Looks as though it only dropped off a table or something and got smashed... Lord knows, my boy, I'd like to give you a bit of help if I could. Strikes me that with a straight-out, frank, rounded impossible situation slap in front of you, you need it.'

'*Exactly*,' said a new voice from the shadows at the other side of the room, with such suddenness that they all jumped. '*But would you like me to explain how the murder was committed?*'

VII
DESIGN FOR HANGING

Inspector Potter called violently on omnipotence, and almost upset a heavy table as he surged to his feet. Even Masters was startled. They were all standing in the little circle of light thrown by the fire and the two yellow-shaded lamps. Electric bulbs burned in a sort of crown high up against the groined roof; but the big library was still dusky, almost as though the books themselves threw shadows.

Bennett looked towards the line of diamond-paned windows in the embrasure at one end, a wall of glass against which stood a single tall tapestry-armchair with its back to the room. A head rose over the chair, and a figure leisurely detached itself. It stood squat and black against windows and grey sky; they heard glass clink and smelt the smoke of a cigar. Footsteps, not quite steady ones, rasped along the stone floor. There was something leering, something goblin-like in that round little shape, ducking and mowing with the cigar; even more so when it grew close enough for them to see the short wiry black hair, the stiff smile on a stiff face, and the staring little bloodshot eyes.

Bennett realized not only that it was Carl Rainger, swathed in a flowered silk dressing-gown much too big for him; but that Carl Rainger was very drunk.

Rainger said, in a steady voice which seemed to come from deep down in his throat: 'I must ask you to excuse me. In fact, I must *tell* you to excuse me, in view of the help I am prepared to give. I was listening, gentlemen. I was frankly listening. When you came in, you surprised me there in the chair with Betsy,' he patted the neck of a bottle protruding from the pocket of the dressing-gown, 'Betsy the second, while I communed with nature. "Straight mine eye had caught new pleasures, While the landscape round it measures." Beautiful country. Ha ha ha.'

His tubby figure stumped into the circle of light. There was a rather inhuman quality about the stiff mask-like smile and the mirth that came from behind shut teeth. He nodded and winked both eyes and made a gesture of theatrical politeness with the cigar. But the reddish little eyes, despite their staring fixedness, were very sharp.

'My name is Rainger; I think it is fairly well known. Give me that chair, Mr.—Masters. The one you're standing in front of, if you don't mind. Thank you. Ah! Now! Good morning, gentlemen.'

'Good morning, sir,' Masters answered imperturbably, after a pause. Behind his back he jerked his arm sharply at the staring Potter. 'You wish to make a statement? Eh?'

Rainger considered. He was wriggling his bristly scalp backwards and forwards, as children do, while he stared at the fire.

'Yes, I suppose I do. Yes, in a way. I can explain this impossible situation that's been bothering you. Ho ho ho.'

Masters studied him. 'Naturally, sir, we're always glad to listen to suggestions. Quite. But one thing I'll suggest, if you don't mind. You're certain you're in a condition to suggest anything important?'

'Condition?'

'Well, not taken a drop over the line, as I might say? Eh?'

Rainger turned round slowly, pulling the gaudy dressing-gown about him. His face assumed an expression as though he were slyly peering round the corner of a wall; then it lit up with an almost terrifying smile.

'God love your innocence, inspector,' he said, rather tenderly. '"Taken a drop over the line"?' He burst into choking laughter until his eyes were blurred. 'Well, well, let's compose ourselves. Of course I've taken a drop over the line. Very neatly put. As a matter of fact, I'm drunker than hell, inspector, and we both know it. What *of* it? In better days, before I was persuaded to become respectable and give it up, you would never have found me in any other condition. But I lived and moved and had my being, and my brain—*this*,' he knocked his knuckles against it, 'was much the better for it. I only gave it up because I was even too clear-seeing, and they called it morbid. Hoho!

'Shall I prove it, inspector?' he demanded, pointing the cigar suddenly. 'Shall I tell you what you're thinking? You're thinking, "Maybe this is a confession. Maybe I'd better jolly this repulsive little baboon along and get him to admit something he oughtn't." Uh? That's your innocence again. I am much more talkative than usual, yes. But *I* didn't kill her. Queerly enough, I have an alibi.'

He cackled. Masters only nodded stolidly. 'Why, sir,

if you put it like that, it's quite possible I might have been thinking some such thing.'

'And as for you—' He suddenly pointed at Bennett. 'You're thinking, "There's that son of a bitch again." Aren't you, now; aren't you?' For a second the weird stare was as terrifying as his grin; then it grew muddled, bewildered, and somehow defeated. 'Why do you think that?' he asked curiously. 'Why does everybody think it? All my life I've been trying to find out. I'm Carl Rainger. I started on a railroad construction gang. Want to see my hands, even now? I can command as high a salary as any star I ever worked with, because when I get through with that picture, whoever's in it *is* a star. That's me. That's what I can do. Then why...' He fumbled at his forehead and said in a flat voice, 'Why, to hell with 'em. That's all I've got to say.' He seemed surprised. 'They're lousy rats, every one of them. I'll trust to *this*. Yes. And now—where are you, inspector? Ah!—I'll proceed to show you what you've overlooked, and offer you proof.'

'Well, sir?'

'Proof,' said Rainger, his face lighting up again, 'that a Mr. John Bohun killed Marcia Tait.'

'Good God!' said Dr. Wynne, and stopped as Masters turned to glare.

'Thank you very much, doctor,' observed the chief inspector in a quick, colourless voice. 'You've been most helpful. We needn't detain you any longer... Er, hullo? Thompson? Still here, eh? I thought I told you; well, my mistake. You'd better wait outside, now.'

'I know the man's drunk,' snapped the little doctor, 'but does he realize who he's talking about? John Bohun, ha? His host. Well, well, well. Yes, I'm going. John's having breakfast. I think I shall just inform him he's needed here.'

Masters—big and urbane, but with a vein beating at his temple—edged the doctor away, as though he were smoothing off crumbs, and spoke in a low voice. Remembering what had happened upstairs, Bennett quickly suggested a visit to Louise Carewe; and, as he sketched out what had happened, it caught Masters's ear more easily than the doctor's. Masters said, 'Oh, ah?' and to Bennett, 'Stay here!' as he sent out Thompson and edged out Dr. Wynne. When the strident voice was fading down the hall, Masters returned to Rainger, who had got a bottle of gin out of his pocket and was tilting it to his lips while a sardonic eye rolled round at the chief inspector.

'You want to accuse Mr. John Bohun,' said Masters, with another silencing gesture at Potter, 'of murder. I dare say you realize that's rather a serious matter to speak of, even when you can back it up?'

'Certainly I can back it up, my friend. Hoho. Yes. You've had statements,' replied the director, suddenly becoming cool and sharp-faced, 'from both Bohun and an actor named Willard. Now don't put on that pawnbroker-refusing-a-loan look, my friend; I heard you discussing it, and I know what they said. They gave their version of what happened last night. Now I'll give you mine. Don't you realize why there was only one set of tracks in the snow, going in?'

'Be careful, sir. Remember, they were fresh tracks.'

'Of course they were fresh tracks.' He controlled his hard breathing. 'First! Bohun was in London last night, to see His Lordship. To see the great Lord Canifest. Did he tell you that?'

'Oh, ah?' inquired Masters, his dull eye turning sideways towards Bennett. Bennett remembered that Masters had spoken to H.M., and must know a good deal of the story. 'Mr. Bohun said he had a business appointment; that was all. You mean the newspaper-owner? Just so.'

'Now you had better know why Bohun saw him, if you don't know,' said Rainger, looking at him queerly, 'already. Canifest intended to put up the money for the play Marcia was to appear in. And last night Canifest refused. Bohun and Marcia were afraid he was going to refuse. That was why Bohun got nervous and rushed over to see him last night.'

'Well?' prompted Masters, after a pause. 'Why should this—ah—Lord Canifest refuse?'

'Because somebody had been telling him things. Lord Canifest was contemplating matrimony. He had already laid his hand and heart,' said Rainger, with an appropriate gesture, 'before our lovely nymph. His Lordship, you may know, is a very upright man, and much too discreet to risk anything *but* marriage. And then somebody told his Lordship something. Bohun was afraid there would be bad news from Canifest last night, and so was Marcia.'

Masters cleared his throat. 'Just so. I daresay you mean, now, he was told something against Miss Tait's character, eh?'

'What? Oh, God love us, inspector,' said Rainger, with a sort of wild helplessness, 'your thrice-blessed innocence! No! Don't you suppose Canifest hadn't heard all the rumours of that kind? Her family was good enough for that conduct to have seemed just prankish. Haha, no. What somebody told him, I fear, was that Marcia might have been too virtuous.'

'Too virtuous?'

'That she had a husband already,' said Rainger, and cackled.

'A husband already!' the chief inspector snapped, after a pause. 'Who—?'

Rainger indulged himself in an elaborate Frenchified shrug. He shut one eye, a tubby little Mephistopheles in a bright-flowered robe, and the other staring little bloodshot eye showed through the smoke of his cigar. He smiled.

'How should I know? That part, I grant, is theory; but it's mine, and it's a good theory. Now who might that husband be? I *wonder*. Eh?'

Before Masters could voice a suggestion, he went on softly:

'Let's go on. Do you understand now what my good friend Jervis Willard told you about Marcia being upset, distraught, desperately waiting last night?—waiting for Bohun to return. Yes, I think even you understand. If Canifest refused to back this play, it would never be put on at all.'

'Now, now,' urged Masters, with goading tolerance, 'Miss Tait was a very popular actress, I should fancy. Surely any number of producers—'

'That's where you're wrong,' the other said, nodding several times. 'Not after what she had said of them separately and individually in the newspapers, and also to their faces.' The mechanical smile broadened with rather horrible effect. 'And what she didn't say, I quoted her as saying. Get it?'

'And this was the news,' Masters said slowly, 'you say Mr. Bohun was bringing back to her last night?'

'Naturally. She was a very temperamental wench, I can

tell you. What must Bohun have thought when he had to come back and explain it was all off? They might get another angel, *but*. Marcia wasn't too popular. She certainly wasn't popular in this house. It amused me last night, when Miss Katharine Bohun attempted to give her a shove that would send her down a flight of stone stairs...'

'*What the devil's this?*'

Bennett felt his heart pounding, and an empty sensation in his chest. He took a step forward, so that Rainger caught his eye.

'What's the matter?' asked Rainger harshly. 'Friend of yours? Never mind. That's what she did. Come on, flatfoot: let me get back to the subject. Willard didn't tell you about that little episode, did he? You can forget it. I want to tell you the first step in the case that'll hang John Bohun... He told you (didn't he?) that he arrived back from London about three a.m. Well, he lied. He got back here at one-thirty, when it was still snowing hard.'

'Did he, now?' inquired Masters in a curious tone. 'Well. Get this down, Potter.—How do you know? Did you see him?'

'No.'

Masters said heavily: 'Then you'll excuse me. I've listened, and I've listened for something more than vague accusations, and I'm admitting to you I've got a little tired of it. Now I'll ask you to stop this sort of talk and go up to bed where you belong.'

Rainger's arm jerked.

'Oh, you'll listen to me, damn you.' His voice wavered a moment; it became close to a screech. 'Can't you let me explain? Can't you give me fair play? Give me a minute, two minutes, only two minutes! Oh, for God's sake let me say what I've got to say—!' His desperation to have a man hanged broke his gloss and stolidity, but briefly; for he got himself in hand, and there was only cool contempt in the unshaven face. 'Now I'll explain it. At midnight last night, after we'd left Marcia in the pavilion (what Willard told you about that is true), Mr. Bohun and I—Mr. Maurice Bohun, my host—came to the library. To this room. We talked of books and other matters you wouldn't understand. We were here for something like two hours. Naturally neither of us could see John Bohun come in: the driveway is clear at the other end of the house. And we didn't hear him, for the same reason. But we heard the dog.'

'Dog?'

'A big police dog, what you call an Alsatian. They don't turn it loose at night, because it flies at anything. They keep it chained to a sort of runway wire, so that it can run twenty or thirty feet from the kennel, but no farther. It barks at anybody, known or unknown—Mr. Maurice Bohun told me. Are you listening to me *now*? We were sitting here last night, when we heard it commence barking and keep on barking.

'I asked him, I said, "Have we got burglars, or has somebody gone out?" He said, "Neither. That will be John coming home. It's half-past one." We talked about the detective stories (he likes detective stories), and the dog that *doesn't* bark because it recognizes somebody, thus presenting a clue. That's hogwash. Real dogs bark at everybody, till you get close enough to speak.'

Rainger coughed. His forehead was damp from his

intense concentration when his head must be spinning; he brushed an arm across his face, and his speech weirdly degenerated.

'That was at ha' past one. Old Bohun held out his watch and says, "See it's ha' past one." He's always fidgety, and he got even more fidgety and nervous about the noise while he was showing me books. Late as it is, he rang for that butler and told him to 'phone down to the stable and have 'em lock the dog up. He said it would drive him crazy...'

Inspector Potter struck in, heavily and eagerly: 'That part of it's true anyhow, sir. This butler said he used the telephone at one-thirty to tell them at the stable they must lock the dog up—'

Masters waved his hand. 'And is that, Mr. Rainger,' he said, 'all you've got to accuse a man of murder?'

'No. I am going to tell you what John Bohun did.

'He arrived here at one-thirty, and left his car in the driveway. He was wearing evening-clothes and light patent-leather evening shoes—'

'How do you know that?'

'I use my brain, you see,' nodded Rainger, bending forward. 'I got that from the maid who went into his room this morning to light the fire. She saw the clothes scattered. She also told me (eh?) that his bed was still made and had not been slept in last night.'

After a pause, Masters said, 'Take that down, Potter.'

'He walked straight down to the pavilion, as he and Marcia had arranged. (The fool lied to you when he said he didn't know Marcia was there, and yet he admitted she had told him she was going there. He knew Marcia never changed her mind; you'll see why he lied.) Well, the dog barked for longer than usual. Why? Because of the time it took him to walk down. If he'd only gone into the house, the dog would have shut up.'

Inspector Potter uttered an exclamation.

'You're suggesting—?' said Masters quickly.

'Oh, he was her lover,' said Rainger. 'I know that.' He leaned over suddenly and spat into the fire.

'Now see. He had bad news for her. Marcia didn't take any bad news well; and not the smash-up of everything she wanted to do. But you don't know Bohun's character if you think he told her straight out. He's too weak. He put it off, and first told her everything was all right. There was love-making; the fool thought he could get *Marcia* into the right state of mind with that. Kuaa! Afterwards, he admitted things. And she told him for the first time how she really felt towards him.'

Rainger's voice rose. 'He smashed her head in about an hour and a half after he'd got to the pavilion. Then the fool found out that the snow had stopped long ago. His footprints going out there had been effaced. There wasn't a mark on the snow now, and if he left that place, he would leave his own footprints to hang him. *Well?* What did he do? What did even a nervous fool do?'

Rainger must have seen that he had caught his audience. For a moment Bennett thought the man had grown cold sober; that he had forced himself sober by very violence of will; and, but for the twitching of the fingers and uncertain movements of the head, Bennett would have believed it.

'Use your brains,' said Rainger, with that queer diabolical grin. 'What was the only thing that would save him?'

Masters studied him. 'If I had been in his place (oh; ah! supposing this to be true!), there was an easy way.'

'Think so? What would you have done?'

'Rummy games we're playing! Eh? Well, then, I should have left that pavilion, messing up my own trail thoroughly by shuffling and kicking and scraping over the tracks so that nobody'd know whose they were. I'd have carried that messed-up trail up over the lawn to the high road, or any-where you like. The house, even... Time? Oh, ah; I'll admit it would have taken some time, and in the dark, but there'd be all the time until daylight.'

Rainger blew out a blast of sour smoke. 'Any fool,' he said, 'would have remembered the dog.'

Masters stopped.

'The dog, my flatfoot friend, that barked like hell and for such a long time—while Bohun was only hurrying down to the pavilion before—that the old man had it locked up. Think that over, will you? Mr. John remembered that dog; it almost gave him away before. What did he think it would be doing the fifteen or twenty minutes it would take him to mess up all his tracks? How was *he* to know it was locked up? What happens in a house when a dog keeps on steadily barking at four o'clock in the morning?—They'd wake up. They'd look out. And there was Bohun in the middle of the lawn, caught.'

Bennett went over and sat down on the divan. His wits were whirling, but he knew the man was right. Bennett said:

'But what could he do? He couldn't take up the time to mess the trail, and he couldn't hurry out and leave his tracks to betray him... You've got him in the pavilion with

no tracks outside; but he says he was talking to the butler
in his riding-clothes at close on seven o'clock this morning;
and I'll swear on the Bible that, when I got to the pavilion
this morning, there was only one line of tracks—going *in*.'

'Just so. Steady, sir,' said Masters. 'He did wake the butler
up in this house at a quarter to seven. The butler says so.'

Rainger savoured a triumph. He looked from one to the
other.

'Sure, sure, sure. That was his alibi. He remembered the
riding-engagement; but didn't it smell very funny to you, eh,
that he should have said he got up early in the morning, put
on his riding-clothes, and went to wake the butler up before
he was certain they would ride that morning?... He tried to
be clever. He thought he was clever. Riding-boots are useful.
They're bigger, a good deal bigger all the way round, than
little patent-leather dancing-shoes.'

Masters whistled. He made a big gesture as Rainger said:

'He waited till it was nearly daylight, and he could see not
to bang into anything. I like to think of him sweating beside
that dead woman. Then he walked out of your pavilion, and
he walked *backwards*. When he'd changed his clothes and
made his alibi, all he had to do was walk back again in his own
footprints to "discover" the body. He couldn't have done it
if he'd had on the same-sized shoes. If he tried to step *in* the
tracks—even in a very thin plaster of snow—he'd only have
blurred the prints. If the snow had been deep instead of a
little crust, he would have sloughed the tracks up. But he
stamped a fresh print with bigger shoes all over the others,
and concealed the first outline. The sole-and-heel prints
would be messed inside the track, but they always are from

the way you walk in snow. No wonder the tracks were fresh. No wonder that stable-hand saw him—from a distance— just going in at the door. He'd literally "covered" his tracks. He'd got himself the swellest alibi a man ever had. But when you got there, young man,' said Rainger, choking with the last effort of keeping his words steady, 'didn't he seem a little rattled?'

Rainger looked round for a moment more, holding their eyes.

Then he got shakily to his feet. With the effort over, he seemed to shrink like a dough figure; and it was as though a wheel went round behind his eyes. Dizzy and breathing hard, he got the bottle out of his pocket.

'I've told you how it happened,' he said. '*Now hang him.*'

He was fumblingly trying to get the bottle to his lips when he collapsed. He would have fallen if Masters had not caught him.

VIII

DR. DRYASDUST AT BREAKFAST

'Give me a hand, Potter,' said Masters briskly. Masters's stolid, heavy-jawed face was still imperturbable. 'Get him over on the settee. Better ring for the butler and have him—no! Wait a bit. Here, get hold of his feet.'

They lifted the inert lump, with its features now gone smeary and its lips drooling; a bag of dough where there had been a brain. The breath wheezed through his nose. As they put him down on the couch his dressing-gown slid back. They saw that he was wearing evening-dress trousers and a collarless stiff shirt; his feet, as small as a woman's, were thrust into red leather slippers. Masters carefully took the cigar from his fingers and threw it into the fire. He picked up the unbroken bottle from the floor; looked at it, and then at his companions.

'Very rummy chap,' he said, 'very rummy indeed. Now I wonder?—Wait a bit, Mr. Bennett. Where are you going?'

'Breakfast,' said the other, with heartfelt weariness. 'This thing has got me nearly crazy...'

'Now, now. Easy, my lad. Just wait a bit and I'll go with you. I have something to talk about. For the moment—'

Bennett regarded him curiously. For some time he had been unable to understand why the Chief Inspector of the C.I.D. should be so anxious for his company, and almost eager to make friends with him. He learned why soon enough.

'—the question arises,' continued Masters, rubbing his chin, '*is* this man right? Did it happen as he said it did? What do you think, now, Potter?'

The county inspector shifted, chewed his cud, looked at the notebook for inspiration, and finally swore.

'It sounds all right, sir,' growled Potter. 'In a way. And yet—' he stabbed out with the pencil. 'That's it. I dunno what half of it's all about. This business of backing plays and the like. But the way it was done...well, 'ow else could it have been done? That's the worst.'

Masters's pale blue, genial eyes swung over to Bennett. 'Ah! Always glad to listen to suggestions, Potter and I are. What do you think?'

Bennett said violently that it was nonsense.

'Why nonsense?'

'Well—'

'Because Mr. Bohun's your friend? Tosh tosh tosh. Leave that out of it. Does you credit, o' course. But we shall have to admit that it does explain everything. Eh?' Masters's eyes opened wide.

'I know. But do you honestly think he could have pulled off that funny business with the footprints? If the first part of it weren't so plausible, and if it didn't account for several queer things, you wouldn't give it a minute's thought. I don't believe he could have done it. Besides, that man,' Bennett heard himself talking loudly and foolishly, 'is drunk enough to say anything. Didn't you hear all the wild statements he made?'

'Oh, ah. Yes. What statement did you refer to?'

'Well, for instance, about Bohun's niece trying to kill Marcia Tait by throwing her downstairs...'

Suddenly he saw that he had fallen into a very bland, very easy trap. Masters said affably. 'Yes, indeed. I shall want to hear all about that. I talked to Mr. Willard and Mr. Bohun both, and yet neither one of them made any mention of an attempt to kill Miss Tait. Very rummy. Somebody tried to throw her downstairs, eh?'

'Look here, let's go and get some breakfast. I don't know anything about that; you'll have to ask them again. Besides—you don't want second-hand information. And I'm no stool-pigeon.'

'Stool—' Masters had been inspecting the supine and flabby figure on the couch, whose jaws moved like a bellows with its wheezing breath. Masters' big laughter boomed. 'Stool-pigeon, yes. You mean a copper's nark? Why, no. But I want any kind of information; d'ye see? *Any* kind. Eh, Potter? This niece of Mr. Bohun's is young, good-looking, I take it? And Mr. Rainger made another interesting statement: about Miss Tait being married. We shall have to check that. I say, I wonder how Mr. Rainger got so dirty? I mean in a literal sense this time. Look at him.'

He drew back the edge of the dressing-gown. There were powdery streaks of a dead blackish colour down the front of the white shirt, as though dirt had been sifted on him; the shoulders were more grimy and a thicker black; and, as Masters lifted him a little, the arm of the shirt showed in the same condition. And, as he rolled over like a dummy, they saw that there were also stains on the back of the shirt.

'Hands new-washed; shiny-washed. Look at them. H'm. Never mind, but I also wonder what he meant by saying he had an alibi? I suppose we ought to have him taken upstairs, and yet I think I shall just leave him there... Well, Potter? You said you'd done some trapping, and know about tracks in the snow? Do you think Mr. Bohun could have worked that little trick?'

Potter ruminated, uneasily. ''Ere!' he said with irrelevance but determination, and stared up. 'I'll tell you what it is. I don't *want* this case. You said you were my superior officer, and so you are. Well, I'm going to telephone the Yard, official and all, and say we need help. Bloody little I'm going to mess about with it. There.'

'That means you don't think he could have done it. Eh?'

'I dunno. That's what beats me. But,' said the inspector, rising and slapping shut his notebook. 'I'm going out to look at those tracks and see. There might be something.'

Masters said he had some instructions for him. Masters accompanied him to the door, speaking in a low voice, and Potter uttered a pleased snort. His expression was one of heavy craftiness as he went out. Then Masters beckoned to Bennett, and spoke encouragingly of breakfast.

The big raftered dining-hall was at the rear of the house, its windows looking down over the lawns towards the avenue of evergreens and the pavilion. Sprigs of holly were fastened to the chandelier and round a darkish portrait over the mantelpiece. It was a sort of shock to see their gaiety; the gaiety of the big fire and the gleaming pewter dish-covers on the sideboard. At the table, leaning back in his chair, staring dull-faced and incurious at the ceiling, sat John Bohun. A cigarette drooped from his lips, and he had a convalescent's pallor. Across from him, industriously at work on bacon and eggs, sat a very prim fastidious little man, who rose in haste as the newcomers entered.

'I beg your pardon,' the little man said, coming across in his nervous little strut. 'You are…' A hazy expression was in his eyes, and he still dabbled at his mouth with a napkin. He had a bony face dominated by his very large hooked nose and a high-domed skull with grey hair brushed flat across it. His whole expression—with the wrinkles, the fidgety mouth, and the pale grey eyes, in which the small pin-point pupils were dead black—was one of vagueness mixed with swift moods which might be of good humour or pettishness. He was very fastidiously dressed in black, with a quiet donnish primness, and his air was that of someone wandering past shelves in a library. '… you are—how extraordinarily stupid of me! I keep forgetting. *You* will be my guest, and *you* will be the inspector of police.' After a limp handshake, he hustled them towards the table. 'Did I—ah—introduce myself? I am Maurice Bohun. This is my brother John. You have already met him, have you not? Of course. Good God, what a dreadful business all this is! I only learned of it half an hour ago, you understand. But I informed John that the best way to keep up his strength in assisting justice was, in brief, to eat. You will take breakfast with us? Excellent. Thompson! More—ah—comestibles.'

As this almost invisible genie moved out from the sideboard, Maurice Bohun sat down. Bennett noticed that he limped slightly, and that a stick with a large gold knob was propped against his chair. This fussy little man to be the author of a bawdy robust comedy! Masters studied the two brothers; especially John, who had not moved from sitting back inertly with his hands in his pockets.

'I've got to warn you, sir,' announced Masters, in his voice that always seemed to dispel tense atmospheres, 'that you take me in at your own risk. I'm not officially connected with this case, although Inspector Potter's a relative of mine. So that only makes me a sort of guest at your pleasure. So if you don't mind sitting down to table with a copper, eh? Just so... Ah! Yes, the kippers, if you please.'

John Bohun lowered his head.

'I say, inspector, you may omit the urbanity.—Have you found out anything since you talked to Willard and me?'

'I'm afraid not, sir. Matter of fact, I've been talking to a gentleman named Rainger,' Masters answered, with his mouth full.

'Your esteemed friend, Maurice,' said John, turning his head. 'The one who's going to make you a technical adviser on the films...'

Maurice put down his knife and fork gently. He peered across the table and said, 'Why not?' in a voice of such clear common-sense that Bennett turned to look at him. Then Maurice smiled vaguely and went on eating.

'I'm afraid—' said Masters, and seemed to hesitate. His big grin showed behind a loaded fork. 'Mr. Rainger's a very interesting gentleman, and I admire his work, but I'm afraid he's been drinking this morning. Eh? Just so. That, and making wild accusations he may not be able to support. Can't support.'

'Accusations?' John Bohun asked sharply.

'Um. Of murder.' Masters was deprecating. 'Point of fact, he accused *you*. Lot of such rubbish.—Ah! Real cream!'

John got up from his chair.

'He's been accusing me, has he? What's the swine been saying?'

'Now, now, sir, don't let it bother you. Everything's easily proved, isn't it?... But I wanted to talk to you, sir,' he added, turning to Maurice as though he had dismissed the subject, 'about this Mr. Rainger. He said you two had been together most of last evening; and, since he'd drunk himself a bit over the mark, I was curious as to how many other—um—hallucinations he might have got.'

Maurice pushed back his plate and meticulously folded his napkin. Then he folded his hands. Against the grey light his big forehead, unwieldy for the frail body, threw into shadow those curious pale-grey eyes with the tiny black pupils. He looked muddled and mildly deprecating.

'Ah, yes,' he said. 'Er—where was I? Let me see. You—ah—wish me to satisfy you that I did not commit this murder.'

'Sir?'

'I was, of course, ah, answering the spirit of your question rather than the precise words...' He was apologetic, as though there were nothing at all odd in this, and took the whole thing for granted. 'So Mr. Rainger has been drinking? I do not approve of drinking, because the world has a tendency to use alcohol as a drug against tedium. It is not that I disapprove of a drug against tedium, but I prefer that the drug against tedium should be purely intellectual. Do you follow me, sir?... I—ah—perceive that you do not. I was referring to a study of the past.'

Masters nodded his big head, with a show of deep interest.

'Ah,' he agreed wisely. 'Reading history, sir. Quite. Very instructive. I'm fond of it myself.'

'Surely,' said Maurice Bohun, 'that is—ah—not quite what you mean, sir?' A faint crease ruffled his forehead. 'Let me see. You mean that you once read a chapter of Macaulay or Froude, and were pleased with it and yourself when you discovered it to be a little less dull than you had anticipated. You were not inclined to read further, but at least you felt that your interest in history had been permanently aroused... But I really meant something deeper than that. I referred to the process that is nowadays slurringly termed "living in the past." I frankly live in the past. It is the only mode of existence in which I find it possible to skip the dull days.'

His smooth, pleasant voice rarely lifted or altered its tone. With his elbows on the table, and the fingers of a frail hand shading his eyes, he was still mildly deprecating. But Bennett, who had been wolfishly eating, looked up. He began to feel the power of this vague-looking man's personality; the wise and subtle strength of his ruling in this house. Bennett did not like the man, because he had a nervous schoolboy sensation, under the look of those disconcerting pin-point eye pupils, of having come to class unprepared before a gently satiric master with a habit of calling on you in the last five minutes before the bell.

'Well, sir,' said Masters, still imperturbably, 'it seems to be rather a good, um, mode of existence. The young lady's death doesn't seem to have bothered you much, I should fancy.'

'No,' said Maurice Bohun, and smiled. 'There will be others like her. That has always been so. Er—we were discussing...?'

'Mr. Rainger.'

'Ah, yes. Quite so. I was forgetting: a most abominable habit of mine. So Mr. Rainger is drunk? Yes, I—I should have imagined that such an unfortunate occurrence would have affected him in precisely that fashion. I found him very interesting and amusing, with strange claims to scholarship. For various reasons of my own, I—ah—what is the term—I "jollied him along." John, would you mind not tapping your fingers on the table? Thank you.'

'Masters,' said John Bohun violently, 'I demand to know what that swine said. I've got a right to know!' He came round the table.

Maurice interposed in an almost distressed fashion: 'Oh, come, John. Come now. Surely I am not mistaken in thinking that—ah,' he frowned, 'Mr. Masters is attempting to work you into a nervous frame of mind? In that case,' explained Maurice, with a gentle bewildered expression, 'you must not expect him to tell you. Be reasonable, my boy. He has his duties.'

Bennett's dislike of Maurice Bohun was growing with every word he uttered. It might have been his intolerable assumption of rightness in everything, especially when he happened to be right; and his old-maidish way of express- ing it. Bennett began even more fiercely to sympathize with

Katharine. He noticed, too, that Masters had been feeling the discomfort. Masters, in whose big face there was a suppressed anger, folded up his own napkin and said a surprising thing.

'Do you ever get tired, sir,' said the stolid practical Masters, 'of playing God?'

For a brief time the muddled expression held Maurice's face, as though he were on the verge of protest. Then Bennett saw a look of cool Epicurean pleasure.

'Never,' Maurice answered. 'You are shrewder than I had thought, Mr. Masters... May I suggest something? Now that you have removed the button from your foil, or perhaps I should say—ah—the tinfoil from your club, would it not be better to ask me questions in your best Scotland Yard style? I shall do my best to answer.' He looked rather anxious. 'Perhaps I can even prevail on you to state your whole problem? I should much appreciate it. I have some considerable interest in the subject of criminology. It is quite possible that I might be able to help you.'

Masters seemed affable. 'Not bad, sir. Maybe not a bad idea.—Do you know the situation we're in?'

'Er—yes. My brother has been explaining.'

'Half an inch of unmarked snow all around that little house,' said Masters, 'and no footprints, no marks anywhere, except your brother's tracks; innocent, of course...'

'Of course. I really wish you wouldn't walk about in that manner, John. I think,' said Maurice, with a cool smile, 'I can take care of you.'

'I rather think you can,' returned Masters grimly. 'But can you explain how that murder was committed, then?'

Maurice touched the bridge of his nose as though for absent spectacles, and his smile was apologetic. 'Why— why, yes, inspector,' he ventured. 'It is quite possible I can.'

'Hell's *fire!*' cried Masters, suddenly letting off steam. He got up from the table, obviously contemplating what seemed to him the queerest fish that had ever slipped into his net, while Maurice made clucking noises. Masters hesitated, swallowed, and sat down again. All the tinfoil was removed from the club now. 'Very good, sir. Everybody seems to have an explanation of it except the police. Very neat and stimulating it is. I tell you frankly, I pity old Charley Potter if he'd had to fall in among this crowd without assistance... And I don't want to listen to any rubbish about anybody flying out of that house, or walking on stilts, or vaulting, or hanging to trees. There's not even a shrub within a hundred feet of it, and *no* mark whatever in the snow. And there was nobody hidden there when we looked. But it's a very queer place, Mr. Bohun... Why do you keep it all fitted out like that?'

'A whim of mine. I told you that I lived in the past. I often spend nights there myself.' For the first time there was a sort of hazy animation about Maurice. The hand shading his eyes opened and shut. 'You would not understand, I fear. I can take the same sheer utter pleasure in talking to you as I would to a deaf person. Mr. Masters, I have done a remarkable thing. I have created my own ghosts.' He laughed softly and stopped. 'May I offer you more kippers, sir? Thompson, more kippers for the inspector.'

'Were you very much interested,' struck in Masters, 'in Miss Tait?'

Maurice looked concerned. 'To your question—ah—
"Were you in love with Miss Tait," I must answer, sir, no. At
least I do not think so. I admired her as a sort of accidental
reincarnation.'

'Yet you wrote a play for her, I think?'

'So you have heard,' murmured the other, wrinkling his
forehead, 'of my modest effort. No. I wrote it for my own
amusement. I had become rather tired of being called Dr.
Dryasdust...' He placed the palms of his hands together
before him, weirdly, as though he were going to dive, and
hesitated. 'In my younger days I suffered from illusions.
These lay in a belief that the proper value of historical study
consisted in its economic and political significance. But I
am old enough now to be aware that almost the only gift no
historian has ever possessed is any knowledge whatever of
human character. I am now, I fear, an old satyr. You will be
informed (I think you have been informed?) of my senile
ecstasies over Miss Tait? Your expression indicates it. That
is only partly true. In Miss Tait I admired the charms of all
the dead courtesans with whom I should like to have had
love affairs.'

Masters drew his hand across his forehead.

'Don't mix me up, if you please!—you encouraged Miss
Tait to sleep out in that pavilion?'

'Yes.'

'Which,' Masters went on musingly, 'you had got repaired
and restored, and which was used in the old days for a king
to visit his fancy ladies on the sly...'

'Of course, of course, of course,' interposed Maurice,
hastily and rather as though he were impatient with himself

for having overlooked something. 'I should have understood. You were thinking of a secret passage underground, perhaps, to explain the absence of marks in the snow? I can assure you, there is nothing of the kind.'

Masters was watching him; and Masters pounced now. 'We might have to take it to pieces, sir. Tear off the panelling, you know, which you mightn't like...'

'You wouldn't dare do that,' said Maurice. His voice suddenly went high.

'Or take up the floors. If they're the original marble, it would be a bit hard on you, sir; but to satisfy ourselves...'

As Maurice got up from his chair, his frail wrist knocked over the walking-stick that was propped against the arm, and its heavy gold head struck the floor with a crash. That crash had its echo in Masters's voice.

'Now, sir, let's stop this fiddling and evading and being so neat and slippery. Let's talk like men and answer questions; do you hear me?' He struck the edge of the table. 'It would be no trouble at all for me to get a warrant to take that beloved little shack of yours apart piece by piece. And, so help me, I'll get mad enough to do it before very long! Now, then, will you or won't you give assistance in this thing?'

'Surely—ah—surely I had already promised to do so?'

In the long pause afterwards, that pause when Bennett knew that the chief inspector had got his man, John Bohun walked away from the window out of which he had been staring. John Bohun's face (when both he and his brother were frightened) had a curious resemblance to Maurice's, which you would never ordinarily have noticed. It was as though Masters held two men in play, like a fencer who conceals his skill under clumsiness.

'Your—your subordinate,' said John, and pointed behind him. 'He's out there on the lawn... he's examining... *What's he doing?*'

'Only making measurements of your tracks in the snow, sir. That doesn't bother you, does it? Won't you sit down, gentlemen; both of you?... There, that's better.'

It was not better. John's face had gone white.

'An attempt was made on Miss Tait's life last night before the time she was smashed over the head. Somebody tried, I think,' Masters went on, turning to Maurice, 'to throw her downstairs. Who was it?'

'I do not know.'

'Was it your niece, Miss Bohun?'

Maurice sat down quietly. He was smiling again. 'I should not think so, my friend. If the—ah—culprit was anybody, I should say it was the Honourable Louise Carewe, the daughter of my old friend Lord Canifest... However, if you will look round now, you will see my niece just behind you. You have my full permission to make enquires.'

IX
CASUAL ALIBIS

Bennett pushed back his chair and turned. She had come in quietly, and was standing not far from the table. Bennett started to draw out a chair for her, before the imperturbable Thompson could move; but she shook her head.

'Is somebody accusing me,' she said, 'of trying to kill Marcia? And that remark about Louise...' She looked curiously at Maurice, as though she had never seen him before. 'Don't you think it was rather a foul thing to say?'

She had put on what was probably the best dress in her wardrobe, as though in a sort of defiance. It was a sombre affair in grey. Momentarily her nervousness seemed almost gone, although she was twisting a handkerchief. Katharine Bohun stood with the firelight along one side of her face; and for the first time Bennett saw her clearly. She was more mature than he had thought. And in the soft, now brilliant face was a look as though she had come to a determination. Round her neck was wound, as though carelessly, a gauze scarf that concealed bruises.

'Er—did you speak, Kate?' inquired Maurice. He was not looking at her, and seemed gently surprised. 'Surely you must be aware that I am not—what shall I say?—at all in the habit of discussing my assertions with anyone?'

She was trembling; biting at her lower lip; and the eyes had a hot, hard brightness as she came forward. Yet she was beaten, and seemed to know it the moment Maurice went on: 'Tut! Er—extraordinarily stupid of me, I fear. It is, I see, another small mutiny. You were trying to say—ah—"Go to the devil," were you not?'

The insufferable pleasure of being right, like the solving of an easy problem, made Maurice regard her with gentle satisfaction and concern. Her eyes brimmed over.

'I won't make a fool of myself!' she said, breathlessly. 'I won't let you make a fool of me; again and again and—John! John, what's the matter?'

They all turned to look. John Bohun said:

'It's all right, Kate. I'm not feeling well, that's all. Touch of something.' He straightened his head from bending down, bracing himself with one hand on the table. He looked genuinely ill, and there was sweat on his forehead. The tweed coat now seemed too big for his big lean frame. 'Come here, Kate. I haven't seen you since...since I got back.' He held out his hand, trying to smile. 'How are you, old girl? You look fit. You look different, somehow. I've got a present for you, only I haven't even unpacked my bags yet.'

'But what's wrong?'

She ran over to him. He caught her under the chin and held up her head to study her the better; and despite the twitching of the nostrils, he was smiling down apparently without a thought except for her. Bennett had a curious feeling that he was seeing the real John Bohun under a number of masks.

'Nothing's wrong, fathead. Don't let 'em frighten you, d'you hear? They've got me in rather a bad situation...but, you see, no matter what I try to prove, I'm caught out in one thing or the other. I'm bound to be hanged for something.'

Masters stepped forward, and John held up his hand.

'Steady, inspector. I'm not admitting anything. I suppose there's no reason for telling or not telling; but—maybe later. I'm going up to my room to lie down now. Don't try to stop me. You said yourself you had no official authority here yet.'

There was something so intense in his manner that nobody spoke. He seemed to realize that (for the only second in his life) he was in command of a given group of people. He went rather quickly to the door, but his steps slowed down as he neared it. He turned, and jerked his head towards them. He studied them.

'Well, cheer-o,' said John Bohun. The door closed.

There was a silence. Bennett looked across at the placid, faintly amused countenance of Maurice; and he had to crush down a somewhat undiplomatic impulse to take Maurice and break him into rather small pieces. The impulse had been troubling him for some time. This wouldn't do. He looked across at Katharine, and started to light a cigarette; but his hands trembled.

'But what's *wrong* with him?' the girl cried. 'There's something...'

Bennett went over quietly, took her by the shoulders, and made her sit down. He thought that she pressed his hand.

Masters had swung round again; and, if he read Masters's expression correctly, the chief inspector had much the same feeling towards the whole wild muddled business as he had himself.

Masters said heavily: 'There are a number of questions I've got to ask about Mr. Bohun's doings here last night and this morning. But I think it will be necessary to get things in order... Excuse me; you are Miss Bohun? Just so. Now, to begin with...'

She had been pouring out coffee, her hands trembling a little among the cups; but she did not once look across the table at Maurice.

'To begin with,' she insisted, 'oh, really, let me say it! This absurd notion—about Louise's trying to... That's as silly and nonsensical as anybody would be who made it.' After a pause, during which they heard from Maurice a sound which in anybody else might have been a snicker, she hesitated as though she had said more than she dared. She looked at Bennett, flushing hotly. 'May I give you some coffee?'

Masters's look said, 'Good girl!' Aloud he said:

'I'm bound to tell you, Miss Bohun, that the same accusation was made against you. Didn't you hear me say so?'

'That? Oh, that's silly too. Because I didn't; why on earth should I?—Who made it? Not—?'

Maurice had been making faint clucking sounds of mild protest. Again he touched the bridge of his nose as though puzzled; then he reached out and gently touched Katharine's hand, as though in reassurance.

'Of course not, my dear; could such a thought have entered your poor little head? My dear, *tut!*—be careful.

You will have that coffee across my hand. And do you mind not rattling the cups so much? Thank you...' A benevolent smile. 'I must really insist on not being misquoted, Mr. Masters. I am not aware of having made any accusation whatever. Let me see? What was I saying? Oh yes. Since all those present were unlikely to have done what you suggest, it occurred to me that, in view of Miss Carewe's fairly vehement and not entirely unjustified objections to her father's possible marriage to Miss Tait, the young lady had a stronger cause for dislike than any others. I may, of course, be mistaken.'

'Suppose we hear,' said Masters quickly, 'exactly what did happen. You, Miss Bohun; would you mind giving your account?'

'Not at all. If you'll tell me who it was that said I—I shoved her.'

'It was Mr. Rainger. Eh? Does that surprise you, Miss Bohun?'

Her hand stopped in lifting the cup. Dull anger changed to a rather hysterical laughter.

'That little—ugh! Did he say that, really? Oh, I say, he would! He was the one who was going to make me a star in pictures. Yes, I understand now.'

'*What?*'

'Our little Kate,' observed Maurice vaguely, 'has sound moral ideas. Sometimes...'

She kept her gaze fixed on Masters: a shining and rather hoydenish amusement mixed with the anger. 'Sound moral ideas,' said Katharine Bohun, with a violence of loosened breath, 'be—be—d-damned! Eee! That man; that's all.

Ugh! I could no more stand having him touch me than... I don't know what. Listen, I'll tell you about it, because it's a part of the story you wanted to hear. At dinner last night was where the suggestion started that my uncle should take— you know—Marcia, and the rest of us, over the house by moonlight, with my uncle carrying a candle, but no lights turned on.

'Well, all through dinner, you see, this man Rainger kept looking at me. He didn't say anything. But first he'd look at Marcia, and then he'd look at me for a long time, and he'd hardly answer when anybody spoke to him. But when Marcia suggested going over the house by moonlight, he said it would be a splendid idea; something like that. He was sitting—' Her eyes wandered over towards Bennett, and a rather startled expression crept into them: instantly veiled as at some thought she did not wish seen. 'Here; there; I don't remember. Anyway, what was I saying? Yes. Marcia wouldn't let the men stay at table after we'd left, and on the way through the passages to the library he came behind the others and took my arm.' She began to laugh again until she had to put her handkerchief to her eyes. 'I say, it was so jolly funny, because you couldn't understand what the blighter was about for a minute; all he could do was sort of mutter out of the side of his mouth, "What about it, baby?" After a minute I knew what he meant from the way they always say that in the films; but I said, "What about what?" And he said, "Come off that; they understand it in the States," in rather a tired way. And I said, "Yes, they understand it over here, too, but you've got to make your approach in a very different way if you want to get anywhere in England."'

Maurice Bohun involuntarily said, 'Good God!' and Bennett, also involuntarily, said, 'Great!' Maurice leaned a little forward.

'This, I think,' he said, quietly, 'is a really remarkable statement from you, in equally remarkable language. I shall have to take measures towards seeing that your mode of expressing yourself, either to me or to our guests...'

'Oh, you go to the devil!' she said, whirling on him and blazing at him at last. 'I'll say what I jolly well please!'

'No,' said Maurice after a pause, and smiled gently. 'You will go to your room, I think.'

'Now I'll tell you what it is, Mr. Bohun,' interposed Masters, in a voice of very cool sanity. 'I've got no wish to interfere in, um, domestic matters. Eh? But I'm getting a bit tired of this too. This isn't a domestic matter. It's a murder case. And when it comes to ordering witnesses about... Oh, ah. Sit still, Miss Bohun. Go on, please: what were you saying?'

Maurice got to his feet. 'Then perhaps you wouldn't mind,' he said, his voice slightly shrill, 'if my niece gave me permission to go to my room?'

'I shall want to speak to you presently, sir,' said Masters urbanely. 'But if your niece sees no reason—just so. Thank you.'

Maurice gestured to Thompson, who swiftly picked up his gold-headed stick from the floor. Maurice was white, with a smiling, deadly, lightly-sweating fury; and his eyes had the dead look of a waxwork figure's.

He said: 'I confess I had never been aware that the police, those sometimes useful servants of the superior classes, were in the habit of encouraging children to talk in the fashion of—ah—sluts. I cannot, of course, allow this to pass unnoticed, on the part of either one of you. It has been my habit to enforce implicit obedience in this house, to the end that my own comfort might be maintained, and I should be foolish if I permitted the slightest imputation of that authority to pass unchallenged. Should I not?' He smiled delicately.

'You will deeply regret your failure to minister to my comfort, Kate.'

He bowed, and the complacency returned to his bearing as he left them.

Bennett reached over and beamingly shook hands with her.

'Now, now!' protested Masters, and stroked his ploughshare chin. 'None of that, if you please. I'm a police officer, and I'm here on a definite job. I—' He tried to keep impassive, but a grin broke over his face. Peering over his shoulder Masters added in a low voice, 'Lummy, you did put the old man's back up, miss! Hum. Hurrum! Just so.'

'Nice work, inspector,' said Bennett affably. 'Good old C.I.D. If you were a Maypole, we'd both dance around you.'

Masters pointed out that he was not a Maypole. The idea seemed to make him uncomfortable, and he insisted on Katharine continuing with her story.

'There isn't much, really,' she insisted, still a little fearfully and with a nervous colour in her cheeks as she seemed to reflect on what she had said. 'I mean, about that man Rainger. He said he would put me in the films, and seemed to think that was all anybody in the world could want. Then he reached down and—nothing.' She shifted in her chair. 'It was a bit dark there, but the others were close ahead of us; and the only thing I could do without being noticed was to stamp down hard on his foot. That was all the attention he paid to me, because I hurried up and took Jervis Willard's arm. He didn't say anything more; he kept talking to Louise. But I didn't think he'd be liar enough to say that I...'

She went on rapidly to describe the incident on the secret staircase in King Charles's room, and it agreed with the description Bennett had already heard from Willard.

'... because I don't think, really, that the pushing *was* intentional. Marcia said it wasn't; and she would know, wouldn't she?'

'Um. Possibly. Then there were six of you at the top of the stairs: yourself, Miss Tait, Miss Carewe, and the three men; eh? Just so. How were you standing? Who was behind her, for instance?'

'I was. But I don't know about the others; it's a little space, and everybody was pushing about. Besides, there was only that little candle.'

'Oh, ah; the candle. How did it come to go out?'

'The draught. Really it was! There's a strong draught blowing through there from the door downstairs when you open the bedroom door.'

'Yes. And afterwards?'

'Well—nothing. The sight-seeing party broke up. They all looked rather quiet and queer; but nobody said anything. That was some little time after eleven o'clock. Marcia was the only one who was as gay as ever. Louise and I were sent to bed by uncle. The rest of them went downstairs; I know they went out to the pavilion afterwards, because my bed-room window was open and I heard them.'

'And none of you,' said Masters, knocking his fist into his palm, 'none of you saw anything at all odd in this?'

'No! Why should we? Marcia *said*...and she rather—I don't know how to express it—ruled us. She was so attractive that you almost shivered when you looked at her; that dark skin and bright eyes and the way she dressed and everything. She had on a gown that my uncle would have killed me if I'd worn, but, I say, it was...! And she was being very motherly towards me.' The long eyelashes lowered a little, speculatively. 'I think she heard what that man Rainger said to me.'

'Yes?'

'Because she turned round. Then she dropped a silver brocade cloak she was wearing (lovely thing), and he jumped to pick it up. Then she looked at him in a funny way and said something.'

'Did Miss Tait—um—did she seem to mind?'

'Mind? Oh, I see. Why, I fancy she did,' Katharine replied, with candour. 'She usually did, you know. He said, "Do you mean it?"'

'Beats *me*...' said Masters, in dull incredulity and half aloud. He scowled. 'Now there's nothing else about that staircase business; nothing you can remember; nothing at all? Please think. Everything!'

She passed the back of her hand across her forehead. 'N-no. Nothing. The only other thing was that I went down to unlock the door at the foot of the stairs for my uncle John, so that he'd find it open when he got home. But that was after the—the accident happened. When he comes in late, he always uses that door; because, you see, it opens on the side porch and he doesn't have to come up through the house.'

She picked up the cup again and forced herself to drink scalding coffee.

'Everything was wrong. I was going to meet John last night, no matter how late it was, after all that time he'd been in America. And yet I didn't, after all. When I heard Tempest barking at half-past one, I thought it must be for John coming home. But it wasn't. I got up and went to his room, and down the staircase to meet him...but nobody drove in.'

Although Masters kept a bland face, his hands tightened on the edge of the table. Shadows of moving clouds passed across the dusky room. In the stillness they could hear the falling rattle of the fire.

'Just so. You're sure, now,' said Masters suddenly, and cleared his throat; 'you're positive that he didn't come in at that time? Be careful, miss. It may prove very important.'

'Of course I'm sure. I went down and looked out on the drive... *Why?* What is it? Why are you looking so queer?'

'Ah! Nothing, miss, nothing; only that somebody told us he got back at one-thirty. He couldn't have driven down to the garage, maybe, so that you missed him?'

'No, of course not. I should have seen him. Besides, his car's in the drive this morning. I thought it was odd then, because the light was on in his room; but he wasn't there... It isn't something against him, is it? I haven't told something I shouldn't, have I? Tell me!'

'On the contrary, miss. Don't be uneasy about that. But you don't know what time he did get here, do you?'

'No. I fell asleep. Besides—' she hesitated.

'Go on!'

'Well, when I was coming back from his room after I knew he hadn't come in, I was going along the gallery, and I saw that man Rainger come upstairs…'

'So?' inquired Masters, pinching at his lip. 'A very rummy chap, that gentleman, I repeat. I don't mind informing you, miss, that he told us this: He said that after they had gone out to see Miss Tait into the pavilion—which would be a little past twelve—he and Mr. Maurice Bohun returned to the library. He said they sat there talking books and the like for at least two hours. He said that they heard the dog barking, and both of them believed it to be Mr. John Bohun returning at half-past one. Two hours would mean that they presumably stopped in the library until after two o'clock. Very well. Now you tell us, miss, that you went down to your uncle's room at half-past one; and, as you were returning, how long afterwards…?'

'A few minutes. Not long. But it's true!'

'A few minutes afterwards, you saw Mr. Rainger coming upstairs. Where was he going?'

'To his room. I saw him go in. You see, I hurried straight-away for my room; because I was—well, rather undressed, and I thought he might be—'

'Exactly. Well?'

'He wasn't. He called out to me, "You can forget what I said tonight," in a nasty but rather a triumphant way; he said, "I've got better business," and he slammed the door of his room.' She brushed Rainger aside, with a violence of impatience; she pushed the heavy brown hair back behind her ears and leaned forward with her hands clenched. 'But this other thing. What are you thinking about, John?'

Masters took a deep breath. 'You needn't be surprised to hear, miss, that among Mr. Rainger's other remarks was an accusation of murder. Now, now! Steady, miss. Fine lot of witnesses. Rainger's case, a matter of snowfall, rests on Mr. Bohun's arriving back here half an hour before the snow stopped... But if we only knew what time he did get back...'

A pewter dish-cover rattled on the sideboard. Somebody coughed.

'Excuse me, sir,' said Thompson's voice. 'May I speak?'

His expression was worried but determined; he seemed less hostile towards Masters.

'I know I shouldn't be here,' he said. 'I hear things. But I've been in this house for a long time, and they let me. I can tell you positively the time Mr. John came home last night; and my wife was awake too, and she'll tell you the same thing.'

'Well?'

'He returned at a little past three o'clock, sir. At just the time he told you he did. Tempest was barking because of something else.'

X

HOW A DEAD MAN
SPOKE ON THE 'PHONE

'I wish you had asked me that before,' Thompson continued. He sucked in on his stiff swollen jaw. 'I can swear to it. My room, and my wife's, are on that side of the house, but,' he nodded, 'higher up. Under the eaves. I heard the car come in about five or ten minutes past three. I was going down to help him out with his bags, and see if he wanted anything, sir. But I—my wife said—well, that I should only get more cold in,' he touched his jaw, 'this. I thought if he wanted me he would ring. When Mr. Maurice said I could go to bed, I'd already turned on the light in Mr. John's room and left sandwiches and whisky. But then at half-past one Mr. Maurice called me out of bed again, to ask me to telephone to the stables and have them lock up Tempest...'

'He would not,' said Masters curtly, 'he would not tele-phone himself, then?'

'No, sir.' Thompson's eyelids flickered slightly. 'That is not Mr. Maurice's way. But I felt I'd done enough.'

'But if you swear the other one didn't come home at

half-past one... you swear that, eh? Well!' said Masters, and bent forward. 'Why was the dog barking, then. Eh?'

Thompson's expression grew faintly ugly. 'It's none of my business, sir. But, after all, when it comes to a matter of accusing Mr. John, that's a different thing.—Tempest barked because somebody left this house and went down towards the pavilion. That's what my wife will tell you. She saw it.'

Whenever Masters got himself into an especially muddled state of mind, Bennett noticed, he always turned around and soothingly said, 'Now, now,' to everybody else; even though nobody had spoken. The chief inspector hoisted himself up from his chair, performed this rite with a grim stare at Katharine, and towered over the butler.

'You didn't,' he said heavily, 'tell us this before.'

'I'm sorry, sir. I don't and didn't, and never will, want to make trouble for anybody. Besides, I know now it couldn't have been—'

Thompson, with nerves frayed out of his professional indulgent calm, faced Masters with a dogged and reddish eye. He changed his words so swiftly that you were conscious of almost no break or hesitation in, 'I know it couldn't have been *would you like to hear my story, sir?*'

'Couldn't have been who?'

'Mr. John.'

'Are you sure,' said Masters quietly, 'that's what you meant?'

'Yes, sir. Do you care to hear about it? When Tempest began barking, both my wife and I thought it was Mr. John returning, especially when my bell rang from the library. I hurried to dress; and—and one must be fully dressed, and answer within two minutes according to the rule, or Mr. Maurice...' For a flash, an old and very tired man looked back at them before Thompson froze again to impassiveness. 'My wife (the cook, sir) looked out of the side window, but the roof of the *porte-cochère* is there, so she couldn't see anything. But she noticed something else. Of course it was dark and snowing, but there were a few windows lighted at the back of the house (those tall windows) and she saw somebody running down towards the pavilion. That's all, sir.'

'Oh, yes. Yes, I see. Who was this person?'

'How could she tell, sir? She couldn't! She couldn't even tell—'

'Whether it was a man or a woman,' supplied Masters, with a heavy dryness. 'Just so. Now, then. Go and get your wife and tell her to come down here.'

Thompson turned abruptly. 'I swear this is for the best, Miss Kate! They'd have found it out! And I couldn't have them thinking either Mr. John or—' He clenched his hands.

'Yes, I see,' said Masters. 'Quite. Cut along.' As the door closed, Masters turned to Katharine with an air of heavy geniality. 'Now what do you want to bet, Miss Bohun, that what he was going to say wasn't, "Mr. John or you?" Eh? I think we'll find Mrs. T. believes it was a woman. He heard a good deal. He's foxy enough. He only spoke when he was sure it couldn't have been you. Because *you* were exchanging words with Mr. Rainger upstairs in the hall by the bedrooms at the same time this, um, "person" was running towards the pavilion, and he doesn't think you'd be fool enough to invent a story like that. Eh?'

She leaned back in the oak chair, her grey dress sombre

among shadows, the gauze scarf floating at her throat. Her rather full breast rose and fell. The pale face against the oak, the luminous brown eyes with brows turning up slightly at the outer corners—that, Bennett suddenly realized, was the weirdly ancient effect like one of the gilt-framed portraits in the dining-hall, which gave her the resemblance to Marcia Tait. And that was all. He realized that he was not falling in love with a ghost, but that he was falling in love with Katharine Bohun.

'How do you know,' she said suddenly, 'that I didn't invent the story? If Rainger said I tried to kill Marcia once last night, he wouldn't be likely to support what I told you, would he? We don't know *when* Mrs. Thompson saw somebody out on the lawn, if she did see somebody. The dog was barking a long time. The person might have left the house just a little after I spoke to Rainger... Oh, I know what you're thinking, and it's absurd! Won't you see it? The person you're thinking of wouldn't hurt a fl—'

'Nothing like a good friend,' said Masters sagely. 'Excuse me, miss: where did you get those bruises on your neck?'

Her hands darted up. After a pause, she said:

'Louise was hysterical. She'd had a scare...'

'Just so. That is, miss, from what I've heard of the story as it was being described to Dr. Wynne, and a few intimations from Mr. Willard, all we can be certain of was that she was lying senseless near your door with a bloodstain on her wrist... What time was it you found her?'

'I—I don't know what to say to you,' she hesitated, studying him from under heavy eyelids, and suddenly added with her own sometimes shattering frankness: 'I'd lie to you like a shot, if I knew what time Marcia had been killed. But I don't, so I'll tell the truth. It was sometime between half-past three and four o'clock... Honestly, truthfully, now, you don't really believe—?'

Masters chuckled.

'Now, now! You've got to excuse me, you know, if I don't accuse a young lady of murder before I've ever even seen her. I'd lie to you like a shot, only I've got to have a bit more evidence. It looks queer. But then,' he hammered his fist into his palm, 'as neat a case as I've ever heard at the Old Bailey was put forward against your uncle. I mean your Uncle John. Lummy, but it was neat! And it was the only thing, you'd think, that could explain an impossible situation. Next thing we know, witnesses come along and blow it sky-high. It doesn't mean he's not guilty because he didn't get back here until three o'clock; but it means he's as innocent as anybody else. Maybe more so. Certainly more so if those tracks of his can be proved honest, but it leaves us with an impossible situation again, and what sticks in my craw even worse than that is... Yes?'

He whirled round. Inspector Potter, breathing hard, hurried into the dining-room. When he saw the other occupants, he checked himself on the point of excited speech; but Masters irritably gestured him to go on.

'Shouldn't've taken so long,' Potter said heavily, 'but the police surgeon's here and the van for the body; oh, ah— and my two men for the fingerprints and photographs. I've 'phoned the chief constable to 'phone Scotland Yard, and you may step in any time you like. But the rest of it's no good. Won't work! Those footprints...'

Masters expelled his breath hard.

'They're all right?' he demanded.

'Couldn't've happened the way that gentleman said, that's all! Excuse me, miss.' Inspector Potter removed his cap and mopped his bald head with a large bandanna. '*Couldn't.* Chap with the fingerprint outfit, who's studied such things, says if he'd tried to blot out old tracks with new ones, it would have pressed the snow inside and there'd have been a ridge inside the track that you could have spotted for a mile. He said some other things, too; I don't remember, but I know what they meant. Those tracks are big: number ten boot, and clean, sharp made all round. Clean as a whistle inside, except a little blur where the snow sticks to the instep—fingerprint man says that's all right. Anyway,' said the inspector, in explosive summing-up, ''e says there's been no hanky-panky with those tracks. And there you are. Mr. Bohun's off the list. He can take it easy now. He... *My God, what is it?*'

Bennett felt his own stiff arms pushing himself up out of the chair; his skin suddenly hot with fear, and his heart beating heavily. The big dining-hall, with Masters black against the light and turning with white eyeballs to stare, had echoed to a certain noise. The noise shook ghostly tinglings from glass on the table. It seemed to travel along the line of portraits and tremble in the Christmas holly; and they knew by instinct that it meant death. That explosion was muffled by more than the old timbers of the White Priory. It was muffled as though a heavy pistol had been held against padding before it had been fired...

In the big vault of the hall Masters spoke involuntarily against the silence.

'"He can take it easy now—"' Masters repeated, as though the words were dragged out of him. 'Oh, my *God!*'

Katharine Bohun screamed. Bennett tried to seize her arm as she ran after Masters to the door; but Inspector Potter's loud-wheezing bulk got in his way. She was ahead of Masters, who was shouting something, when they plunged through the dingy passages in reply to a cry from upstairs.

The broad gallery upstairs, with its strip of red carpet, stretched away in a dusky tunnel to the light of the window at the far end. They saw a little figure there, a grey figure that hesitated before it reached out and pushed open the door of King Charles's room—jerkily, as you might prod a dead snake—with the tip of a gold-headed cane. When the door was opened, they could smell smoke. The figure looked inside.

'The fool!' said Maurice Bohun's voice, as thin and shrill as a locust. He slid back and turned his face away.

Bennett caught the girl towards him as she started to run again. Willard and Dr. Wynne had appeared in the hall, and were running towards the room with Masters after them. They stopped only in a pause of banging footsteps at the door; then they disappeared.

She could not speak: she only shook with such a horrible trembling that he thought he could not quiet her, and she turned her face away and tried to jerk free from his grip.

'Listen!' he said rather hoarsely. 'Listen! Look at me! I wouldn't lie to you. I swear I wouldn't lie. If I go down there, and look, and then come back and tell you *the truth*, will you promise to stay right where you are? Will you?'

'He's done it,' she said, and choked a little. 'He sometimes said he would. And now he's done it.'

'Will you stay here? Answer me!'

'Yes! Yes, all right. If you hurry—and come back—and you do tell the truth; *no*, not if it's in the head. Go on!'

Inspector Potter was close beside him as he made for the room at the far end. And, as he passed, he saw out of the corner of his eye Maurice Bohun sitting on the window-seat in the embrasure of the gallery: motionless, the light along one side of his parchment face and black-pointed grey eye, his shoulders slightly lifted and one hand on his cane.

Light flooded into King Charles's room as Willard rattled back the curtain-rings. It showed a big figure in brown leather boots folded double on the floor, but being straightened out like a dummy by Masters and Dr. Wynne. There was a smell of smoke and singed cloth; John Bohun's mouth was open, and there was a thump as metal struck the carpet from his limp fingers.

More curtains billowed on the second window, and Dr. Wynne's low voice struck across the clash of rings. 'Not dead yet. Got a chance. Good thing he didn't try the head; never save 'em then. They always think the heart's lower down than it is. Hah. Stop fumbling, now; leave this to me... Back, dammit!'

'You think,' said Willard, stumbling. 'You can—?'

'How the devil should I know yet? Shut up. Something to carry him in? Can't jolt him. Eh?—Dead-wagon? Why not? Best thing of all, if it's here!'

'Hop it, Potter,' said Masters. 'Get the van up here, and a stretcher. Tell 'em it's my orders. Never mind the dead 'un. Don't stand there goggling; hop it!'

There were four windows in the room: two in the

left-hand wall by the panelled door to the staircase, and two in the rear wall looking down over the lawns. Their crooked panes made lattices of shadow across a big table and chair beside which John Bohun lay; a draught swooped between their loose fittings and the door, and papers flew from the table. One of them rustled free as though with an ugly life of its own and twisted along the floor towards the door. Bennett, staring at a discarded stiff shirt hanging across a chair, mechanically set his foot on the paper.

He remembered now John Bohun's expression, and the last words he had said before he left the group in the dining-hall. They should have known it. It was in the air. But why those words, 'No matter what I try to prove, I'm caught out in something or other. I'm bound to be hanged for something.' Why the suspicious behaviour, the behaviour that would have put a halter about any man's neck; why the manifest terror with regard to Marcia, when he could be proved innocent of...? The man with a bullet in his chest suddenly moaned and twisted. Bennett glanced down. His glance met the paper under the foot, moved away, and swiftly came back. The uneasy handwriting, with the long slopes and scrawls of a drunken man, staggered along a first line.

Sorry to mess up the house. Please forgive me, but I've got to do this. You might as well know now that I killed Canifest—

At first Bennett's stunned wits refused to take in the sense of this. He could think of nothing but that it might be a slip. Then the implications behind came on him like a light that was too bright, so that for a second he could not fit together all the cloudy puzzles it explained. He bent down and with an unsteady hand picked up the sheet of notepaper.

—that I killed Canifest. I didn't mean to do it. All my life I've been trying to explain to people and myself that I didn't mean to do what I've done, and I'm sick of it; but I wouldn't have struck him if I'd known about the heart. I only followed him home to argue with him.

Pictures of John Bohun flashed through his mind, of behaviour and attitudes and mirth: his careful insistence that he had seen Canifest early in the evening, and yet his very late arrival at the White Priory...

But I swear I didn't kill Marcia, or anything to do with it, and it's only a horrible accident you came to think so. I don't know who killed her. What difference does it make now? When she's gone, there's no reason for me to stay. God bless you and keep you, Kate. Cheer-ho, old girl.

The signature, 'John Ashley Bohun', was clear and firm-written.

There was a pungent medicinal smell in the room now. Masters was focusing a flashlight down, and Bennett heard the snip of scissors and the rapid clinking from Dr. Wynne's black satchel. That draught had blown the powder-smoke away. Bennett beckoned fiercely to Masters, holding up the sheet of notepaper. The chief inspector nodded. He gestured towards Willard, who stepped over swiftly, with no more than a quick curious glance in Bennett's direction, and took the flashlight.

'Water,' said Dr. Wynne. 'Lukewarm. Get it, somebody. None here. Where the hell's that stretcher? I can't extract the bullet here. Get his head up a little; one hand'll do it. Steady...'

Masters came over, looking rather wild-eyed. Bennett thrust the sheet of paper into his hands and hurried out after water. The door of his own room was open just across the way. He went in, got the wash-bowl, and overturned a little sheaf of coloured matches. Katharine Bohun was waiting just where he had left her. She seemed more quiet now, although her hands were clenched together.

'He didn't—quite,' said Bennett, hoping he was telling the truth. 'They think they can pull him through. Warm water: where's the bathroom?'

She only nodded, and opened a door just behind her. There was an ancient top-heavy geyser-bath in the dingy oilcloth room. With steady fingers she struck a match; the gas lit up with a hollow *whoom*, and little yellow-blue flames under the tank flickered on her face as she took the bowl. 'Towels,' she said. 'You'll want those. Sorry to be such a little fool. I'll come back with you. But...'

'Stay here. They'll be bringing him out in a minute. Easier not to watch that.'

They exchanged a glance, and suddenly she said a queer irrelevant thing. She said: 'I might be a murderer, you know.'

When he went back to the other room, Masters was standing motionless, the note half crumpled up in his hand.

He took the bowl of water over, and held it steadily at Dr. Wynne's direction. 'They'll pull him through.' Did he hope that? Better for him to die. Better that the nervous, restless, tortured man now beginning to twist and gasp on the floor should go out under Dr. Wynne's fingers than live to step into a dock for the murder of Lord Canifest. He would be cleanly dead, and blessed or damned, before the law could go fumbling with its greasy rope and splashing mud on names. Bennett tried to imagine what had happened last night—'*I followed him home to argue with him*'—after Bohun had seen Canifest at the newspaper office. But all he could see was the water turning slowly red in the wash-bowl.

When at last he was instructed to put it down, he heard Masters's voice.

'That's it, then,' said the chief inspector heavily. 'That's why. But how could we be expected to know? He came up here, got that revolver out of the drawer there,' Masters pointed; 'and sat down. It took him a long time to write that note. Look at the long and short spaces between the sentences. I suppose this *is* his writing?' Masters rubbed his forehead. 'Well. Then what did he mean by this? He had it in one hand—used two hands to put the gun against his chest—and it fell out when we picked him up.'

He extended in his palm what resembled a small triangular piece of silver, cracked along one side as though it had been broken off. Masters held it out briefly, and then clenched his fist.

'May I ask,' said a thin cool voice just behind Masters, 'whether there is any hope?'

'I don't know, sir.'

'Whether it was a pity or not,' said Maurice Bohun—in just that voice of sane, unanswerable common-sense which at certain wrong times and places can be the most infuriating—'whether it was a pity or not, I fancy, depends on what he wrote in that note I observed you reading. May I ask its contents?'

'I'll ask you, sir,' said Masters heavily, but just as quietly, 'to look at this note and tell me if it's your brother's handwriting. I'd also like to ask, Is that all this thing means to you?'

'I detest stupidity,' Maurice pointed out. He gave each syllable its complete emphasis, but a little network of veins showed in his forehead. 'And I fear he was always a fool. Yes, this is his writing. Now, then...

'So he killed Canifest? Then it is to be hoped that he will not live. If he does, he will—hang.' Maurice snapped the note back to Masters just as he snapped out the last word.

As though taking up the sound, a babble of voices sounded downstairs; and the clumping of heavy footfalls. Dr. Wynne got up with an exclamation, and Bennett hurried out into the gallery. He looked round for Katharine, but she had gone: a thing he noticed with an inexplicable sense of shock and uneasiness. Downstairs, as though echoing in his mind a summons to find her, a telephone-bell was ringing shrilly. The hall was full of alien figures as the stretcher was brought along, and still the telephone-bell kept on shrilling.

'I do not know,' said Maurice's voice, 'what is delaying Thompson. He has orders, most definite orders, that a telephone is in this house for the purpose of being answered immediately, if at all.—You spoke, inspector?'

'I want to know, *if* you don't mind, where you and all the others were when you heard the shot?'

Maurice moved out into the hall to let two uniformed figures pass. Then he turned. 'Surely—ah—it cannot have occurred even to your mind, inspector,' he inquired, 'that this is another murder? It really is not. I myself was first on the scene of the unfortunate business. I had rather feared something of the sort, and I was curious to speak to my brother and understand the kinks that had grown into his mind.'

There was a shuffling inside the room.

'Easy, boys,' barked Dr Wynne's voice; 'take him easy...'

Through Bennett's brain went the words scribbled on the paper: *'God bless you and keep you, Kate. Cheer-ho, old girl.'* Behind a blue-uniformed figure showed now a brown leather boot.

'It is another murder, I think,' said Maurice, staring at the body, 'that you need to concern yourself with. Lord Canifest... Yes, Thompson? Yes? What is it?'

For a second Thompson, who had almost run along the gallery, could not keep his eyes off the figure on the stretcher. His face was wrinkled up, and he opened and shut his hands spasmodically. Then, as Maurice's gentle satiric voice flowed smoothly on in asking the same question, he pulled himself together.

'Yes, sir. It was only...yes, sir. What I wished to tell you, there is a gentleman downstairs asking for Mr. Bennett. It's Sir Henry Merrivale, Mr. Maurice, and—'

Both Bennett and Masters whipped round. Through the former went suddenly a surge and exultation that was like a shout of triumph.

'—and another thing, sir...'

'Yes?'

Thompson quieted his breathing. His voice was clear when he said:

'*Lord Canifest would like to speak with you on the telephone.*'

XI

THE HUNTING-CROP

Although he was now in a state of being able to believe almost anything, Bennett thought that this last was a trifle too much. The faces looked unreal and mask-like. And, in addition, H.M. was here. However he had contrived to get here, his presence was the one thing that lifted a burden and made you feel inexplicably that matters would be all right now. Others besides Bennett had known this feeling. Let the impossibilities go on; that didn't matter. After a space of silence Maurice Bohun moved forward, and Masters laid a heavy hand on his arm.

'Oh no,' he said. 'Better stay just where you are. I'll answer that 'phone.'

Maurice stiffened. He murmured: 'If Lord Canifest, inspector, had expressed the slightest desire to speak with you...'

'I said,' repeated Masters, without inflection, 'I'll answer that telephone.' He pushed Maurice with an easy motion which almost threw Maurice across the gallery; then Bennett found his own arm seized, and Masters was hurrying him along the hall as though in an arrest. 'What I wanted to tell you...come along, Thompson; we'll see Sir Henry...what I wanted to tell you about H.M.,' Masters continued in a low heavy voice, 'was this. You sent him a telegram.'

'I sent him a telegram?'

'Now, now; there's no time for argument. It's this way. He was off today for the Christmas holidays. If I'd tried to get in touch with him, he'd only have roared—really roared; not his usual kind that don't mean anything—and refused to have anything to do with it. But he's sentimental about a lot of things, though he'd murder you if you accused him of it; and one thing is Families. You're his nephew. If you were in trouble, he'd be here... Here's how it was. He'd 'phoned about you last night. When this case broke this morning, I knew it would be the biggest thing that ever happened to me, *and* the first under my direction after I was promoted. I've got to make a go of it, and it's not my kind of case. So first I came up here to—to see what sort of a young fellow you were.' Masters was breathing hard. He was trying to keep his dignity, not very successfully. 'You looked like the sort who'd back me up—um—well! If I stretched the truth in the interests of *justice*. That's it. Justice. So, when you went upstairs after I first saw you... Eh?' prompted Masters, with a pantomime leer.

Bennett whistled. He said: 'I begin to see—You sent him a telegram signed with my name, saying I was in trouble? What kind of trouble am I supposed to be in? Good God, you didn't tell him I was accused of murder, did you?'

'Ah! No; I couldn't say that, now, could I? Or he'd have found out as soon as he got here. I didn't specify the trouble.

At the time I couldn't think of anything. But afterwards, excuse me,' Masters peered round, 'I saw you looking at Miss Bohun... Well, *now!* Eh? So I've got somewhat of an explanation; that is, provided...'

An explanation, then, of the chief inspector's affability towards a stranger; his willingness, beyond all rules, to talk to the stranger about the case; his discretion towards Katharine, and his—

'Provided you'll say you want to help her out, that she's worried about all this, and wants help. Eh? Will you back me up?'

They had reached the top of the broad, low, heavily balustraded stairs. Thompson had gone on ahead down to the landing, where the stairs turned at right angles into the lower hall, and he was holding the receiver of a telephone. From the lower hall ascended now the heavy growl of H.M.'s voice.

'You don't know, hey?' boomed H.M. 'Well, why don't you know? Stand away, there, and gimme a look at him. Ahhh. Um. Yes...'

'And may I ask, sir,' squeaked Dr. Wynne, 'who the devil you are and what you mean by this? Do you happen to be a doctor?'

'H'm. I like the colour of that blood. No froth and no— ahh. Edges. Lemme see, now.' A pause. 'All right, son, you can take him on. Bullet missed every vital spot. I'll tell you that gratis. You look sharp and you'll bring him round without a mite of trouble. Good thing it wasn't soft-nose. Look for it high up. Humph. What kind of a house is this, hey? You walk in the door and a goddam stretcher comes downstairs...'

There was a bitter exchange of remarks, which H.M. shouted down by bellowing, 'Phooey!' Masters grasped Bennett's arm inquiringly.

'Well?' he insisted.

'Certainly I'll back you up,' said the other. 'But you've got to go down and do the pacifying. I'll follow when you've explained everything. He sounds as though he's on the warpath. Look here, Masters: is the old boy really—so—'

'Valuable at police work?' supplied Masters. 'Watch him!'

Masters hurried down to the landing to take the telephone-receiver. Bennett leaned over the banisters and tried to make out Masters's end of the conversation with Lord Canifest. A Lord Canifest, evidently, who was very much alive. But Masters had the newspaperman's trick of talking almost at a mumble into the side of the telephone, and the listener was no wiser. Hearing footsteps in the gallery behind him, Bennett pulled back and turned with a guilty start. Jervis Willard and Maurice Bohun were looking at him.

'It would seem,' Maurice observed, 'that my guests are as strange as my telephone-calls. It is an unexpected honour to receive a visit from Sir Henry Merrivale. It is an even more signal honour to receive a telephone call from a dead man... Exactly what *is* the latest news in this affair, may I inquire?' Maurice's thin features were impassive, but his voice shook.

'Good news, sir. I think you may call it pretty certain that your brother will recover.'

'Thank God for that,' said Willard. 'Why did he do it, Maurice? Why should he?'

For a second there was almost a deformity of rage in

Maurice's face, a pale and rather hideous kind of flame. 'My brother has a very curious sort of conscience. I—ah— suppose I may be permitted to see visitors in my own house? Thank you so much. I will go downstairs.'

He twisted his shoulder when he walked. His stick bumped against the balustrade on the way down.

'What happened?' Bennett asked the actor in a low voice. 'I mean about Bohun? Did he just come up here, walk to his room, and…?'

'So far as I can gather, yes.' Willard rubbed his eyes. 'I don't exactly know what did happen. The last time I saw him he said he was going to breakfast. I came upstairs, and met Kate Bohun. She asked me whether I'd sit with Miss Carewe in her room while she went down after some coffee. She went somewhere else to dress, and that's the last I saw of her until—well, you all came upstairs. Come over here a minute.'

Peering round, he drew Bennett down an angle of the gallery: a side-passage that led to a big oriel window. Willard was no longer the easy, faintly amused figure with the assured bearing. He looked old. Again his hand fumbled with his eyes as though he should have glasses.

'Tell me,' he said, 'did you summon—assistance Higher Up?'

'No! I swear I didn't. I only seem to be a kind of dummy they're using for their own purposes…'

'This Merrivale is your uncle, I understand? Do you know him well?'

'I met him yesterday for the first time in my life. Why?'

'Do you think,' asked Willard quietly, 'a man could lie

to him and get away with it?... I'll tell you why I ask. I've been sitting at Louise Carewe's bedside. She's been babbling about murdering Marcia Tait.'

Bennett whirled round. Something strange in Willard's expression caught him like a hypnosis. He tried to think of what that expression reminded him. And then a cloudy memory returned to him, of words that Willard had spoken that morning; words echoing and clanging with dull cynicism. 'We poor striped brutes went through the paper hoops and climbed up on the perches, and usually she had only to fire a blank cartridge when we got unruly.' Then he knew what it was, at last, that those queer yellow-brown eyes of Willard's reminded him of. It was of something prowling inside a cage.

'You don't mean,' Bennett heard himself saying, 'she admitted she—?'

'I don't know. It was a kind of delirium. I thought, and later found, she'd taken an overdose of some kind of sleeping drug—but I'll tell you about that in a moment. I was sitting there wondering when Dr. Wynne came in. He said you'd mentioned something about her being ill. While he was looking at her I came close to the bed, and my foot kicked something under it: a hunting-crop with a heavy silver end, loaded with lead and shaped like a dog's head...'

'That's nonsense! It wasn't *her* room; it was—'

'Kate's? Yes, I know.' Willard regarded him with a flash of curiosity. 'But Louise had the thing with her when she screamed in the gallery last night, and I picked her up in a faint. This is what I didn't tell that detective. I—quite frankly—how can I express it, anyway?' He floundered among words, and made a gesture as though to clear them away. 'Quite frankly, I don't want to run my own neck into a halter. But Louise…she's so harmless, man! That's all. I don't want to mention it. When I picked her up, she was wearing a sort of long outdoor coat over a night-gown and dressing-gown, and that hunting-crop was stuffed into the pocket.'

'And Kate knew this?' demanded Bennett. He was beginning to remember things. He remembered the girl's own slip of the tongue, instantly denied and retracted, that Marcia Tait had been killed with a hunting-crop. 'She knew it?'

'Yes. I didn't see the coat when I went into the room this morning, but Kate seemed to regard me as a kind of fellow-conspirator. Anyway, I was telling you that my foot struck the hunting-crop under the bed. I didn't dare risk Wynne's attention—so I kicked it farther under the bed. But, while Wynne was there, Louise called out something to the effect that she had tried to shove Marcia downstairs last night… Yes, I know it looks bad. Whereupon Wynne never said a word, but went about giving her some kind of emetic. Afterwards, when she seemed to be resting easier, he said he'd got something to tell me. There was rather a strange look about him. He took me out in the hall. When we came out, by the way… Willard frowned. He snapped his fingers as after an elusive memory. 'Somebody's voice was talking a bit loudly on the telephone down on the stair-landing, now that I remember it. It kept saying, *"At the pavilion, at the pavilion, I tell you."* I remember because he was making so much noise I intended to go and tell him to shut up. But Wynne said, "It's that so-and-so Rainger. I left him talking to the inspector in the library, and now I suppose he's got loose again. He's crazy drunk."'

'When was this?' demanded Bennett. 'We left him lying on the couch in the library when we went to the dining-room. I'll swear he'd passed out cold.'

'I don't know. Possibly fifteen minutes or so after Wynne had come up to look at Louise... Anyhow, Wynne said he had something important to tell me. They seem to regard me,' said Willard, wrinkling his brow and staring out of the window, 'as the guardian and father-confessor of everybody. The voice on the telephone stopped then. Wynne took me round to where we're standing now. He had just begun to talk, and was in the preparatory stage of saying nothing in an acute medical way (or so it seemed to me) when we heard the shot...

'My God, man, that was a horrible feeling! I think we both had Louise on our minds. We looked at each other, and then we both ran to Louise's room. She was all right; she was sitting up in bed as though she'd recovered herself; shaking a bit, perhaps, but very quiet and apologetic, as she always is. That fever of sorts she'd had seemed to have gone. She said, "What was that noise?" and then, "What am I doing in this room?" That was when we heard the rest of you running up the stairs.

'You know the rest.'

Willard sat down in the embrasure of the window. He seemed shaken, as though he had got through a story he was determined to tell; but he assumed unconsciously a stage gesture with one fist on his hip and his head lowered. Bennett heard his breathing.

'If,' he added after a moment, 'the police get suspicious of her—steady!'

He jerked his head round. Katharine Bohun was coming down the passage.

'I saw them,' she said, 'take John out in that—that thing they carry dead bodies in. And I heard them talking. They said, at least from what I could hear at the upstairs window, somebody had said definitely he wouldn't die. Is it true?'

Bennett took her hands, and saw the fear gradually die out of her eyes as he spoke with slow emphasis. She gave a little shudder, as of one who grows accustomed to warmth after coming in out of cold.

'It's a funny thing,' she said meditatively, 'but I'm rather glad of one thing about it. Glad he did it, in a way...'

'Glad?' said Willard.

'Because he'll never try it again. Don't you see?' she demanded: 'When he wakes up out of that stupor, he'll begin to realize things. He did it for—for her. And he'll suddenly realize that it wasn't worth it. I don't suppose I can explain what I mean, but just that act of,' she struck her hands against her breast, wincing at the thought rather than the movement, 'just that, do you see, will have done away with it for good.'

Willard stared through the window at the austerity of the snow. He spoke absently, in a low voice that slowly gathered resonance: '"—or cleanse the stuffed bosom of the perilous stuff that weighs upon the heart..."' For a moment it rose with terrible power.

His hand dropped flatly to the window-seat. He turned, smiling.

'The cure is drastic, Kate. What about Louise? Is she better?'

'She is going downstairs presently. That is what I want to ask you both about.' A pause. 'I suppose I'd better tell her what the police think?'

'Yes, in any case... Has she told you anything?'

'No!'

'But don't you think it's possible—'

She looked at Bennett. 'Let's go downstairs again, and speak to Mr. Masters. I—I'd like you to be there. You were there when Thompson told about a woman leaving this house last night; and Mrs. Thompson is probably swearing to it now. I was a fool for not thinking of it before. I can prove it wasn't Louise. Will you come along?'

She had turned without waiting for a reply. He felt a shock of fear that kept him there staring until she was out of sight; but he caught up with her at the head of the stairs. There was still a rank scent of powder-smoke in the dim gallery. It lent an even uglier suggestion to the oak and the frayed red carpet. He took hold of the newel-post and barred her way down. Then he asked quietly:

'It wasn't you, was it?'

He felt his own arm shaking with a pulse just behind the elbow. He had been staring at the bruises on her throat, only partly concealed by the scarf. She almost cried out the answer.

'Oh, suppose it had been? What difference would it make?'

'None at all, except that we've got to do some high-class lying...'

'Lie to the police?'

'If necessary, lie to Je—' He checked himself from talking louder, checked the violence that made him want to shout. She tried to pass him, pulling at his arm on the newel-post. As he bent over to tighten his hold, he felt the soft cheek brush his face: a thing from which they both moved back as though they had been stung. And, as he saw the slight opening of the small full lips, he felt his heart pounding more heavily when he went on: 'What the hell difference does it make what you did? All I'm trying to tell you, sensibly, is that we've got to invent a good story and stick to it...'

'I don't mean that I killed her. But I might have!' She shuddered. 'I envied her enough to wish somebody *would* kill her. And that's a nice thing to say, isn't it? That's almost as bad as though I'd done what I thought about. Let me go down. It makes no difference what—'

'There's something I've got to tell you first. Downstairs, Masters has got a man with him, an uncle of mine, who's got an unholy reputation of being able to see through a brick wall. Masters got him here through *me*. He used my name, and said it was because I was interested in you...'

'What are you talking about?'

'"Interested." Is that the word they use over here? All right; take it as the word. Say I'm "interested" in you. Say anything you like. Just how "interested" I can't tell you now; because there's murder here, and the whole house is poisoned, and down there's the room where somebody you'd known all your life tried to kill himself in your own home not an hour ago. I can smell that smoke from the gun too, and neither of us would dare talk about Interests here. But the house won't stay poisoned, and then maybe by God you'll know why I think you're the loveliest thing I ever saw in the world—so if somehow you've got yourself into any false position, and whatever it is you did that never mattered and never would matter, don't do any such fool thing as admitting it.'

'I know,' she said, after a long silence. 'All I'm glad of is that you said what you did,' her eyes brimmed over, 'you—you—!'

'Exactly,' he said. 'Steady, now. Let's go downstairs.'

XII

H.M. ARGUES THE CASE

A clock in the passage was striking eleven-thirty when they reached the library.

'—full reports,' Inspector Potter was intoning. 'Statement of police surgeon, post-mortem order for you to sign. Here's plaster of Paris casts of two sets of footprints, Mr. Bohun's and Mr. Bennett's: only tracks before we got there. Plan showing exact line of footprints, measured to scale. I thought that was wise; it's beginning to snow again. Here's the fingerprint reports. Photographs will be developed and sent back this afternoon. The body's still there, but it's been moved up on the bed.'

Potter was laying out articles in an orderly line on the table under the yellow-shaded lamps. It had grown darker outside, and dead tendrils of vine whipped the windows as the wind rose. There was a growling in the chimney, a draught in which one high sheet of flame cracked like thorns and flicked out spurts of fiery embers. Masters, his heavy face showing more wrinkles under the lamp, sat at the table with an open notebook. Maurice Bohun, looking interested and pleased with his bright unwinking eyes fixed on a corner of the fire-place, also sat at the table. Over at one side, in silhouette against the firelight like two Dutch dolls, stood Thompson and a grey-haired sturdy woman in black. Bennett could not see H.M. But there was a big mass of shadow in the far corner of the fireplace, where he thought he could make out a gleam of enormous glasses and a pair of white socks.

'Thanks, Potter,' said Masters. 'Here's your notebook back. I've been reading Sir Henry all the testimony we've accumulated to date. And now...any instructions, sir?'

'Uh?'

Masters moved a little to one side, so that some faint light penetrated towards the corner of the fireplace. Now Bennett could see H.M. start a little and open his eyes. The corners of his broad mouth were turned down, as though he were smelling a bad breakfast-egg, and he was ruffling the two tufts of hair on either side of his big bald head.

'Any instructions, sir?'

'I wasn't asleep, damn you,' said H.M. He put a dead pipe into his mouth and puffed at it. He added querulously: 'I was concentratin'. Now don't rush me! Don't rush me, will you? You fire a lot of undigested stuff at me and expect me to make sense of it straight off. Also, I see I got to go out to that pavilion before it snows again; and that's more work. I don't like this a little bit, Masters. It's ugly—devilish ugly. What were you askin'? Oh. Reports. No, save 'em for a min-ute until I get something straight. Stand over a little bit, son,' he gestured to Potter, 'and lemme talk to Mr. and Mrs. Thompson.'

There was something in H.M.'s presence, despite his efforts to glare, which seemed to put the Thompsons at their ease.

'Howdy, folks,' said H.M., lifting his pipe. 'I've heard what you told the chief inspector, and I'm goin' to use both of you as a check on the others in this place. If any of 'em lied, you tell the old man. Now then.' He squinted at Thompson. 'Were you on this little party that went explorin' the house by candlelight last night?'

'No, sir. My wife and I were preparing the pavilion for Miss Tait. Bed-clothing, seeing the chimneys were clear and the fires lit, water-taps working; all that sort of thing. My wife had charge of Miss Tait's clothes—'

'Such *lovely* clothes!' said Mrs. Thompson, holding up her hands and looking at the ceiling. 'She wouldn't 'ave one of the 'ousemaids do it. Only me.'

'Uh-huh. What time dj'you leave the pavilion?'

'At just a little past twelve, sir, when Mr. Maurice and the two other gentlemen brought Miss Tait out there.'

'Sure you didn't leave any matches there, hey?'

Bennett, from where he stood unnoticed with Katharine in the shadows by the doorway, could only see Thompson's back. But he thought that there was nervousness for the first time in the man's manner. Thompson glanced at Maurice, who sat impassive and pleasant-faced, a complete host.

'I'm sorry, sir. It was an oversight.'

'And after you came back to the house, what did you do?'

'That,' said Mrs. Thompson, with an air of excited remembrance, 'was when I went to bed, Mr. T.'

'That, sir, as my wife says, was when she went to bed.

I polished some silver, according to Mr. Maurice's orders, and waited for the others to return from the pavilion. They returned about a quarter past twelve, so I locked up the house then.'

'And they didn't go out afterwards?'

'Well, sir, Mr. Willard went out after Mr. Maurice and the other—person had gone to the library. But Mr. Willard stayed only about ten or fifteen minutes. He asked me if I would be up and would let him in: he said he would go out the back door of the house, which is near my pantry, and tap on the window when he returned. That's what he did, sir.'

H.M. looked down his nose, as though he were bothered by an invisible fly. He growled to himself.

'Uh-huh. It's a funny thing about that, a question nobody seems to have bothered to ask. And, burn me, it's important! Look here. Between midnight and half-past, all kinds of people were wanderin' up and down, down and back, all over the place from the house to the pavilion—and that dog Tempest never barked. But *one* person left the house at half-past one, and the dog kicked up such a row that they hadda put him inside. Now how did that happen, hey?'

Masters swore softly. He looked at his notebook, at H.M., and back to his notebook again.

'Why, sir,' said Thompson, 'that's easily explained. I know, because I spoke to Locker on the telephone to the stable. Sorry, sir; I almost forgot to tell you. Miss Tait had asked me to see that two horses were ready in the morning for her and Mr. John. It slipped my own mind until Mr. Willard came back from the pavilion; and *that* made me wonder (excuse me) why Tempest hadn't barked. So

I thought Tempest must be inside with Locker—Locker likes him, and often keeps him in the house until late. And that made me remember I hadn't 'phoned Locker about the horses. So I did, about twenty minutes past twelve, and he told me he was just taking Tempest out to the kennel...'

He was an old man, and he seemed bewildered now; but always his eye moved furtively towards Maurice. He had half turned about now, the better to look at his employer.

'I fear you forget many things,' said Maurice, still vaguely pleasant. Then Maurice literally showed his teeth. But he looked at H.M., because in his elephantine way H.M. seemed almost excited.

'Now take it easy, son,' H.M. urged blandly. 'Take all the time you want about it, but be certain. Are you tellin' me that the dog wasn't loose all last evening, up until maybe half-past twelve?'

'Yes, sir.'

'Well, strike me pink!' muttered H.M. He put the pipe back in his mouth and drew at it almost admiringly. 'Ho ho. That's the best news I've heard in this nightmare yet. I had a sort of hazy idea workin' about in the back of my mind; nothing serious, d'ye see, or any symptom of acute thought; but I thought I might as well have somebody quash it straight off. And they didn't. And I am cheerin.'' Masters hammered his fist on the table.

'I admit we overlooked it, sir!' he said. 'But what's the importance of it? I don't see it's necessarily important just because we overlooked it... The important thing is that the dog was locked up *after* one-thirty.'

'Uh-huh. We're goin' on to examine the possibilities of

that. Well, let's take it rapidly. Comrade Thompson. Now you went to bed—when?'

'After I had finished polishing the silver, sir. About one o'clock. Mr. Maurice gave me permission. I left the sandwiches for Mr. John, as I told the inspector; and I did not come downstairs again until one-thirty when Tempest barked and Mr. Maurice rang.' He swallowed suddenly, as though he had made a slip of speech, and peered again at his employer.

'More of Thompson's associations-of-ideas, I fancy,' Maurice observed. 'And this is when your good lady saw the mysterious figure leaving the house? Either my niece Katharine or the Honourable Louise Carewe?'

Thompson swiftly touched his wife's arm. But she refused to be checked. She fluttered like a black chicken, and verbal gravel flew.

She cried: 'Sir, and you too, sir, and you, I can*not*, as I keep telling you, be pinned down and hanged by that statement! Sir, I do not know if it was a lady. That was a Impression, sir, and I will not be 'anged and pinned down by a Impression. Which as for saying it were Miss Kate, I would die sooner, and that is all I 'ave to say.'

'Quite right, ma'am, quite right,' rumbled H.M., with a voice and stolid bearing which somehow suggested the elder Weller. He sniffed. 'Um, yes. You told us all that, didn't you? Well, I think that's all. You can go.'

When they had gone out, treading softly, H.M. sat for some time ruffling his hands across his head.

'Now, sir—?' prompted Masters.

'You,' said H.M., peering over towards Maurice and

extending one finger with a malevolent expression. 'Suppose you do some talkin' now, hey?'

'I am entirely at your service, Sir Henry. And I feel sure you will have no reason to complain of my frankness.'

H.M. blinked. 'Uh-huh. I was afraid of that. Son, frankness is a virtue only when you're talkin' about yourself, and then it's a nuisance. Besides, it's an impossibility. There's only one kind of person who's ever really willing to tell the truth about himself, and that's the kind they certify and shove in the bug-house. And when a person says he intends to be frank about other people, all it means is that he's goin' to give 'em a kick in the eye… Lemme see now. After you and Willard and Rainger came back from the pavilion last night, you and Rainger sat here in the library. How long did you stay here?'

'Until just after I summoned Thompson and told him to have them lock up the dog.'

'I see. Half-past one. Why did you break up then?'

Maurice was watching him warily, like a duellist, but H.M. seemed uninterested. Maurice went on: 'It was Mr. Rainger's wish. I thought it was my brother John returning then, and said so. I confess I was curious to see the effect of a meeting between Mr. Rainger and John, who did not know (I think you were told that?) of Mr. Rainger's presence. They had been having—trouble, shall I say?'

'Well, say something. You mean you thought it'ud be good fun to see whether John took a swing at Rainger's jaw? What they call a Psychological Study? And Rainger wasn't having any, and made his excuses to get away. Why'd you let him go, then?'

Maurice rubbed his palms slowly together. His forehead was ruffled.

'I should have been most unwise, sir, to take the least chance of incurring Mr. Rainger's ill-will. It was therefore politic to accept as genuine his somewhat clumsy excuses, and let him go upstairs.'

'You didn't go up to bed yourself, then?'

Maurice's smile glittered. 'You jump at conclusions, I fear. I went to bed. But my room is on the ground floor.'

'Now here's another thing that strikes me. This must be a very rummy family you got here, ain't it? You thought it was your brother returnin' at half-past one after a long stay in America; and yet you didn't even go out to say howdy-do-welcome-home to him?'

The other seemed puzzled. 'I see nothing very strange, my dear sir, in all that. I am what is known as the head of the house. If my brother had anything to say to me, I am always happy to hear it; but I really cannot put myself out or be expected to bother my head over him. My habit has always been, Sir Henry,' he lifted his eyes blandly, 'to let people come to *me*. Hence I am respected. Ah—where was I? Oh, yes. I was aware that he knew where I was. Hence...'

'That's all I wanted to hear,' said H.M., closing his eyes.

'I beg your pardon?'

'Go 'way, will you?' said H.M. irritably.

Maurice began to speak in a rapid monotone. 'I will go away with the utmost pleasure, if I receive absolute assurance from you that the Queen's Mirror will remain inviolate. I have been very patient, sir. I have endured much that is against my physical comfort and even against my peace of mind. But when your insulting subordinate suggested that such a desecration might have to be performed—tearing to pieces an almost sacred edifice in search of a non-existent secret passage—then...then...'

'Then you got the wind up,' agreed H.M. composedly. 'All right. You can hop it. I promise; there'll be no search.'

Maurice was so intent that he never saw the two figures standing by the door when he hurried out. It was the first time he had hurried; Bennett saw that there was sweat on his forehead and that he seemed to be singing to himself. Bennett's own suspicions seemed to be caught up in Masters's voice.

'Excuse me, sir,' the chief inspector growled, 'but what the devil did you want to make a promise like that for? Not search for a secret passage?'

'Because there ain't any,' said H.M. He added querulously: 'Shut up, will you? That finicky old maid is scared green that you'll lay a finger on his beautiful ghost-house. If there'd been a secret passage, he'd have told you about it in a second rather than let you sound one panel lookin' for it. Yah!'

'I'm not so sure of that, sir,' returned Masters. 'What if the secret passage led to his own room?'

'Uh-huh. I thought of that, too. Well, if it does, we still got him in a corner. But I think that secret passage idea is o-u-t.' H.M. scratched his head. For the first time something like a grin disturbed the Chinese-image austerity of his face as he rolled round to look at Masters. 'That locked-room situation has got you bothered as hell, ain't it? Your sole and particular hobgoblin. Seems as though murderers take an especial pleasure in givin' Chief Inspector Humphrey Masters the fits-and-gibbers by refusin' to keep to the rules of cricket. Only this time it's a little bit worse. If you had only the locked-room situation, you could carry on with a cheerful heart. Everybody knows several trick ways of locking a door from the outside. Bolts can be shot with a little mechanism of pins and thread. Key-stems can be turned with a pair of pliers. Hinges can be taken off the door and replaced so that you don't disturb the lock at all. But when your locked-room consists of the simple, plain, insane problem of half an inch of unmarked snow for a hundred feet round...well, never mind. There's worse than that, Masters.'

'Worse?'

'I was thinkin' about something to do with John Bohun's attempt to kill Lord Canifest, when he didn't succeed but thought he had...'

In the gloom beside him, Bennett felt the girl stiffen. She stared up at him uncomprehendingly; but he gestured her fiercely to be silent. They were eavesdroppers, but he was afraid to speak up—afraid to move now. He regretted coming down here, when something in Katharine's restless brain seemed impelling her to talk. He pressed her arm...

'But we'll skip all that for a minute,' continued H.M. drowsily, 'and look at this impossible situation. The first thing is to determine the murderer's *motive*. I don't mean his motive for murder, but for creating an impossible situation. That's very important, son, because it's the best kind of clue *to* the motive for murder. Why'd he do it? Nobody but a loony is goin' to indulge in a lot of unreasonable hocus-pocus just to have some fun with the police. And there are enough motives for Tait's murder flyin' about already without our needin' to explain the mess by simply saying that the murderer is crazy. Well, then, what reasons could there have been?'

'First, there's the motive of a fake suicide. That's fair enough. I go to your house, shoot you through the head, and shove the gun into your hand. Say it's a house like this one, with little panes in the windows. Uh-huh. I lock and bolt the door of the room on the inside. I've got with me a bag containing a piece of glass cut just right, I've got tools and putty. I remove one of the panes of glass in the window nearest the catch. Then I climb out the window, reach through, and lock it on the inside. Afterwards I replace the old pane with my new little one; I putty it round, smear it with dust so nothing shows, and walk away. And so the room's all locked up, and they'll think you shot yourself.'

Masters peered at him uncertainly.

'It strikes me, sir,' he said, 'that you know every dodge—'

'Sure I know every dodge,' H.M. grunted sourly. He stared at the fire. 'I've seen so many things, son, that I don't like to think of 'em at Christmas. I'd like to be home at my place drinkin' hot punch and trimmin' a Christmas-tree. But let's sorta poke and prod at this thing. If it's a new wrinkle in the art of homicide, I want to know all about it. First, the suicide-fake is barred. Nobody tries to stage a fake suicide by beatin' a woman's head.

'Second, there's the ghost-fake, where somebody tries to make it look like a supernatural killing. That happens seldom; it's a tricky business at best, and entails a long careful build-up of atmosphere and circumstances. And obviously that's out of the question in this murder too, since nobody's ever tried to foist any suggestion of the kind or so much as intimated that the pavilion's haunted by a murderous spook.

'Finally, there's accident. There's the murderer who creates an impossible situation in spite of himself, without wantin' to. Say you and Inspector Potter are sleepin' in connectin' rooms, and the only outside door, which is to *his* room, is barred on the inside. I want to kill you and throw suspicion on him. I come in during the night, workin' my pane-and-putty trick on the window; I stab you in the dark, and get out after replacin' the pane. Yes. What I forget or don't observe is that the door connecting your room with his is also locked on your side— and I've got an impossible situation again. Ayagh!

'Now that's the last and final refuge. But burn me,' said H.M., suddenly turning round the glare of his small eyes, 'can you see how that last and final refuge can be applied to *this* mess? Accident, hey? What kind of accident is it where a person *don't* make tracks in the snow?'

Masters scowled. 'Well, sir, I'd call that last one just about the only reasonable assumption. Like this. X, the murderer, goes out to the pavilion while it's still snowing...'

'Uh-huh. Still thinking about Canifest's daughter?'

The chief inspector had the grim and concentrated bearing of a man trying to hold his ideas steady like a pail of water on his head; and he went on doggedly:

'Wait a bit, sir! Now just wait. We were on the "accident" side of theory. Well, X goes out there before it stops snowing. Eh? Then, after X kills Miss Tait, she discovers—'

'Gal?' inquired H.M. 'Yes, you're gettin' devilish definite now.'

'Well, why not? If Miss Bohun's telling the truth about seeing Rainger upstairs in the gallery at one-thirty, when Rainger was leaving the library, that eliminates *her*. But I'm thinking of the one woman with a motive. Miss Carewe goes down there; there's a row; she kills the other woman, and afterwards discovers that the snow has stopped and she's trapped in the place!—So there's your accident, sir. She didn't intend to have an impossible situation, but there it was.'

H.M. rubbed his forehead. 'Uh-huh. And how did she get back to the house again without leaving any tracks? Also by accident?'

'You're not,' said Masters, with several adjectives, 'very helpful. This young lady, by the testimony I read you, was lying out in the gallery in a faint, with blood on her wrist, at close to four o'clock in the morning...'

H.M. nodded and scowled at his pipe.

'I know. That's another thing I wanted to ask. How was she dressed?'

Bennett saw the net begin to close. He saw it a moment before Katharine loosed her arm from his grasp and walked quickly towards the group about the fire.

'May I tell you how she was dressed?' she demanded, trying to keep her voice steady. 'She had on a night-gown and dressing-gown, with an outdoor coat over it...'

Masters got up from the table. He blocked the light in the direction of the fireplace, so that Bennett could not see H.M.

'But no *shoes*,' said Katharine. She opened and shut her hands. 'Don't you see, Mr. Masters? No shoes; only mules. She couldn't have gone out there without shoes—overshoes—something. And if she took them off afterwards they must have been wet, and they'd still be wet. Wouldn't they? Well, I went to her room this morning...'

'Steady, miss,' said Masters quietly. 'You didn't tell us this before.'

'I never *thought* of it before! But this morning I went to her room after the smelling-salts. She always carries smelling-salts; that's the—well, that's how Louise is. And I noticed all the shoes and things she'd brought down with her: I'm sure of it, because yesterday she showed me all the new things she got in the States, you see? And none of them were even damp; because I was looking for a pair of warm slippers for her... You believe me, don't you?'

The fire crackled and popped during a silence, and Bennett could see flakes of snow sifting past the grey windows.

'I believe you, miss,' said Masters quietly. 'It would be easy enough to hide away—a pair of galoshes, say. And I think it would be just as easy to find 'em again. Thanks, miss, for calling it to my attention. Potter!'

'Sir?'

'Got a couple of men here? Good! You heard it; you know what to look for. Any kind of damp shoes, *any* pair of overshoes or galoshes, in any room. No objection to looking in your room, miss?'

'Of course not. But don't disturb—'

'Hop it, Potter,' said Masters. When the inspector's heavy footfalls had died away he gestured towards a chair and stared at the girl again. 'Will you sit down, miss? I've made a good many fool omissions in this case, and I admit it, but this comes pretty close to the limit. Miss Carewe didn't go out at all last night, did she? Neither did you. Finding men's damp boots won't mean anything. But if we find anything else...'

There was a growl from behind him. 'Stand out of the light, will you?' protested H.M. 'Don't obstruct the witness, dammit. Every time a man asks a rational question around here, you go up in the air. Humph...I say, look here! You *are* a good-looking nymph, burn me if you're not!'

He lumbered to his feet as Masters moved aside, and a genuine admiration showed in his dull face. Bennett noticed now that he was wearing a vast overcoat with a moth-eaten fur collar, its pockets stuffed with Christmas packages tied in gaudy ribbon.

'Oh, and you're here, too?' he added, his expression changing as he saw Bennett. 'It seems like you started a hare, son. And now all you want me to do is catch it for you... Now, now, there's no need to be upset, Miss Bohun. Just wait till the old man gets to work. Point is, Masters there hasn't got any tact. Sit down, everybody, and be comfortable.'

'It occurs to me,' said Masters, 'that... What the devil's the matter with you, Potter?'

The chief inspector's own nerves were growing jumpy. But he had reason for it. Potter had not meant to bang the door when he came back into the room. But it echoed with a dull crash across the vault of the library, where the fire was dying now.

'Excuse me, sir,' said Potter heavily, 'but will you come here a moment?'

'Well?' demanded Masters. For a moment he seemed incapable of getting up. 'Not more—?'

'I don't know, sir! It's reporters. Dozens of 'em, and there's one I thought was a reporter; only 'e's crazy, sir, or something. *Says he killed Miss Tait, or something like that...*'

'What?'

'Yes, sir. Says he sent her a box of poisoned chocolates. His name's Emery, sir; Tim Emery.'

XIII
CIRCE'S HUSBAND

A long and satisfied grunt issued from the chimney corner.

'Aha!' said H.M., flourishing his dead pipe in triumph. 'Now we got it. I been expectin' this, Masters. Yes, I rather thought he did. Let him come in, Potter... I say, though, son: you better go out and keep the Press at bay until I can get a look at that pavilion.'

'You mean, sir,' said Masters, 'that this man—who is he? I remember hearing his name—killed Miss Tait, and...'

H.M. snorted. 'That's just what I don't mean, fathead. Oh, on the contrary, on the contrary, I'm afraid. He's one of two or three I can think of who never wanted to kill her. He sent her poisoned chocolates, yes. But she wasn't intended to eat 'em. He knew she never ate chocolates. Y'know, son, I thought it was rather funny that poisoned chocolates were sent to somebody that the whole gang knew never touched sweets. He never wanted to kill anybody. Only two of the things were loaded, and there wasn't a lethal dose in both together. And even then the poor fathead got a fit of conscience. So he mashed one with his finger when the box was offered him, so's nobody else would eat it, and swallowed the other himself. Ho ho. You'll understand why in a minute, Masters... Get him in here.'

They brought Emery in a moment later. If, when Bennett had last seen him two days ago, he had seemed restless and disconnected—with his jerking mouth, his sharp-featured narrow face and red-rimmed eyes—he now looked ill with more than the physical illness of having swallowed half a grain of strychnine. The face was waxy, and you could see the ridges of the cheek-bones; so dead a face that the sandy hair, sharply parted, looked like a wig. He wore a big camel's hair overcoat on which snow had turned to water, and he was twisting his cap round and round in his fingers. They heard his whistling, rather adenoidal breathing.

'Who—who's the boss here?' he asked, in a sort of croak.

Masters shoved out a chair for him, and H.M. bent forward.

'Easy there,' grunted the latter. 'Look here, son, what's the idea of crashing in here and shoutin' that chocolate-box business all over the place? Wanta get thrown in clink?'

'Only way the saps would let me in,' said Emery huskily. 'They thought I was a reporter. Might as well get pinched. What's the difference now anyway? Mind if I catch a drink?' He fumbled in his inside pocket.

H.M. studied him. 'Your little press-agent stunt with that chocolate box went pretty sour, didn't it?'

'Whoa there!' said Emery. His hand jerked. 'I didn't say—'

'Well, now, you might as well have. Don't be a God-forsaken fathead. She'd forbidden you to tell the papers where she was, or let you splash out with any publicity yarn. That's what you were grousin' about. So you thought you'd provide a little news she *couldn't* help, without endangerin' her life. Or anybody else's, unless it was necessary. *You* were goin' to spot that poisoned box of chocolates, only Rainger got in ahead of you. Big story in the papers, "Attempt on Marcia Tait's Life." Fine publicity, hey? Send the box to the chemist, find it was poisoned. Then John Bohun insisted on everybody there eatin' one of 'em, and you got a fit of heroic conscience... Bah.' H.M. peered at him sourly through the big spectacles. He puffed his cheeks and made bubbling noises; then he looked at Bennett. 'Are you beginnin' to understand now why I told you in my office yesterday *that there was nothin' to be afraid of,* and that Tait wasn't in any danger, hey? She wouldn't 'a' been—if we'd had only this feller Emery to deal with. But we didn't. We had somebody who meant to kill her...

'Ho, ho,' said H.M. in hollow parody, and without mirth. 'Fine work. All a sedulous press-agent got for his ingenuity was a good stiff dose of strychnine, and not even the satisfaction of breakin' the story. Because our sensible friend Rainger pointed out somethin' he overlooked: that there'd be a police investigation, and they might not get Tait back to America in time to be within her contract. Very sensible feller, Rainger.'

Masters picked up his notebook and nodded grimly.

'There's still room,' he said, 'for a police investigation. We're not very fond of that sort of journalism over here.

After all, when you send poison to somebody, that constitutes an act of attempted murder. I daresay you knew that, Mr. Emery?'

Emery's red-rimmed eyes were puzzled. He made a vague gesture as though he would whisk away a troublesome fly.

'Yes, but—oh, what the hell!' he said. 'It was a good story. It…what difference does that make anyway? There's something else now. I'll say there's something else!'

'You know somethin' about it?' inquired H.M. casually.

'Carl 'phoned me. He was cockeyed drunk. Can I—can I see her?'

He shuddered when he said that, and turned his hollowed eyes slowly towards H.M. 'He was cockeyed drunk. He said something about her being at a pavilion, didn't know what he was talking about or something, and in a marble casket. The—the poor softie was crying. Carl Rainger. I don't know about that, but we'll get her the best casket there is in London, unless we can take her across the ocean. He said they were going to arrest Bohun. They hang 'em over here, don't they? That's swell.'

The words rattled, but there was no force in his voice. He worked his fingers up and down the arms of the chair. Some thought tortured him, and, like the usual twist of his conscience, he could not rest until he had spoken it.

'I've got to come clean now. You'll know it sooner or later. If Bohun killed her, like Rainger said, it's *my* fault. Because I told Canifest… Told him yesterday afternoon; sneaked out of the hospital to do it. Carl only found out two days ago, and he said it was the best way of stopping it. Yeah. I mean, he found out Canifest was their angel, so…' he gestured.

'Easy there, son. Take your drink,' said H.M., with a drowsy wave of his hand, 'and let's get this in order. You told Canifest what?'

'That she was married already.'

Masters interposed heavily: 'It's only fair to warn you, Mr. Emery, that you must be careful what you say. Of your own volition you've admitted something that makes you liable to a criminal charge, a wilful and malicious attempt to kill her—'

'Kill her?' said Emery, in a sort of yelp. He jumped in the chair. 'My God, I'd never have hurt her! You've got a crazy lot of ideas about justice over here, but why do you have to keep harping on that? Listen, you poor sap, *she was my wife.*'

In the abrupt silence somebody whistled. Emery looked slowly round the group, and a kind of cynical despair came into his expression.

'Yeah. I know what you're thinking. Monkey-face Me. Nobody. Not fit to get invited to swell houses. All right! Now I'll tell you something. I made Marcia Tait a star.' He spoke quietly, and with a sort of fierce triumph. 'Ask anybody who put her where she was. Ask 'em, and see what they tell you. I built her up when she was nobody. There's a lot of good directors handling good actresses; but if you think that means anything you're nuts. *That* don't make 'em stars. You need Monkey-face Me for things like that.

'I'd have done anything she wanted. I always did. One of her conditions was that nobody should know about the marriage, in case it'd hurt her career. Well, I suppose she was right. Fine thing to have it known she was tied up to *me*, uh? All I could do—now you're gonna think I'm the world's worst sap; I can't help it if you do, and you'll find it out anyway; but that's the way I felt—all I could do was *invent* a wife of mine that I could talk about, and bring into the conversation when I meant Marcia. It was a sort of consolation. I called her "Margarette," because I'd always liked that name...'

The husky voice trailed off. This last admission seemed to wrench him more with an uneasy sense of shame than anything else. He looked round defiantly. His hand, still in his breast pocket, produced an enormous flat silver flask, which he automatically made a feint of holding out to everybody before he tilted it up to drink. At the end of a long pull he released his breath in a shudder.

'Oh, what the hell!' said Tim Emery with sudden weariness, and sat back.

'You mean,' Masters boomed incredulously, 'that you *allowed*... Now, come!'

'Marriage new style. Uh-huh. I begin to see,' said H.M. He blinked drowsily, the glasses sliding down on his nose; but he sat motionless as a great Buddha despite the tired cynicism of his mouth. 'Don't mind the feller who's talkin', son. That's Chief Inspector Masters, who's just about on the verge of apoplexy, and he's gettin' suspicious of you already. I know it's not easy to talk; but if you feel like goin' on— well, I've had too much experience with a crazy world to feel very much surprised at anything I hear. You'd still hit me in the eye if I called her a leech, wouldn't you?'

'So far as I'm concerned,' said Masters, 'and whatever I happen to think about that side of it, I've got only one duty. And that's to find out who killed Miss Tait. So I'll ask Mr.

Emery whether *he* knew, as her husband, that Miss Tait and Mr. Joh—'

H.M.'s grunt drowned it out. 'You know what he's goin' to say, son. You got brains enough to answer unspoken questions. And it always makes everybody feel better to pretend that not callin' a spade a spade makes it invisible. Well?'

'Oh, cut it, will you?' said Emery, without opening his eyes. His body shook. 'Yes, I knew it. Does that satisfy you? I knew it from the beginning. She told me long ago.'

'I see,' growled Masters. 'And you didn't—'

'If it made her any happier,' said Emery dully, 'it was all right with me. Now for the lova Judas, *will you let me alone?*' His voice rose. H.M., whose eyes were fixed on him, raised a hand sharply for Masters to be silent. H.M. seemed to know that Emery would go on unprompted...

'I wanted her to go on,' he added abruptly, 'and be Great. Great: that's what I mean. To tell you the honest truth, I honestly didn't care so much whether she went back to the States or put on this play over here; I'd have backed her up whatever she did. It's hard to realize that she's dead, that's all... There's only one thing that hurts like poison. I want to get out of this country. I never realized what people must think of me. It was the way that old guy, Canifest, looked at me when I told him I was married to her. As though I was a *louse*. What's the matter with me?—Listen, I'll tell you what I've done already.' Some eagerness returned to him. 'I've hired the finest Rolls Royce in London; closed car with seats opening out into a bed inside, to take her back up to London in. Listen, I've got it here now, with a special chauffeur dressed in black. We'll fill the inside of the car with flowers, and she'll go up to London in a funeral procession that'll be the biggest thing this country has seen since—since—'

The man was absolutely serious. He was catching at the last tribute he could make, in his own way.

'Well, there'll be a few formalities to go through first,' interposed H.M. Slowly and wheezingly he got to his feet. 'Inspector Masters and I are goin' down to the pavilion to look it over. You can come along after a bit, if you like. You say you told all this to Canifest yesterday afternoon. Was it your own idea?'

'Yeah, partly—wait a minute; yeah, I think so. I don't remember. It just got started when Carl and I were talking. Carl came to see me at the hospital just before he started down for here.' Emery tried to get his own ideas straight, and had recourse to the flask again. 'He said it would be the thing to do. He said he was coming down here to butter up Bohun's brother, and promise him all kinds of crazy stuff to get into the house. God, it's funny! He was gonna offer old Bohun fifty thousand a year to act as technical adviser...'

'Uh-huh. Serious proposition, was it?'

'Don't be a sap!'

H.M., whether intentionally or unintentionally, had raised his voice, and Emery had adopted the same tone without knowing it.

'Then Rainger knew you were married to Tait, hey?'

'He guessed it. Anyhow, I admitted it when he said we had to work fast.'

'Did John Bohun know it?'

'No.'

'Now careful, son: sure you got a grip on yourself? Take it easy. Didn't John Bohun know it?'

'She told me herself he didn't! She swore to me she'd never told him.'

H.M. straightened up. 'All right,' he said in a colourless voice. 'You might find your friend Rainger and see if you can sober him up. We're goin' down to the pavilion now...' He peered round, the corners of his mouth turning down. 'Where's my nephew, hey? Where's James B. Bennett? Ah! Humph. You come along. I want to know just how she was lyin' on the floor when you found her. And some other things. Come on.'

Bennett looked down at Katharine, who had not spoken or uttered a murmur since Emery's arrival. She did not even speak when she motioned him to go...

With H.M. lumbering ahead and Masters making swift scratches in his notebook, he followed them through the passages to the side-door, where Inspector Potter fought with the Press. Bennett hurriedly picked up somebody's overcoat, not his own. 'Stay behind,' growled H.M. to Masters, 'and give 'em a statement. Then come down. *Nothing to say! Nothing to say!*' He opened the door. 'Get inside, boys, and talk to the chief inspector.' He elbowed through the scramble, jealously and with sulphurous murmurs guarding an ancient rusty top-hat in the crook of his arm. Then the door slammed.

They stood for a time on the side-porch, breathing the bitter cold air. To their left the gravel driveway sloped and curved down, under the interlocking branches of the oaks, towards the highway some two hundred yards away. To their right the lawn sloped down again, and the sky was a moving flicker of snow. There was something insistent, something healing, about those silent flakes, that would efface all tracks in the world. They were a symbol and a portent, like one car in the driveway. Although the drive was now crowded with cars, the long Rolls with its drawn blinds stood black against the thickening snow: as though Death waited to take Marcia Tait away. Its presence was an absurdity, but it was not absurd. It looked all the more sombre by reason of Emery's gaudy yellow car, with Cinearts Studio sprawled in shouting letters across it and the thin bronze stork above a smoking radiator: dwarfed by the black car, Life and Death waiting side by side. Bennett found himself thinking of symbols as clumsy as life, a stork or a sable canopy, and along mysterious roads the black car always overtaking the yellow. But most of all there rose in his mind the image of Marcia Tait.

He tried to shake it off as he tramped down the lawn beside H.M. Looking at his watch, he saw that it was nearly half-past one. At this time last night, also when the snow was falling...

'Yes, that's right,' he heard H.M.'s voice. He glanced round to see the uncanny little eyes fixed on him. Dark in the mist of snow, with his unwieldy top-hat and moth-eaten fur collar, H.M. looked like a caricature of an old actor.

'It was this time last night that the whole business started to happen.—What's this I hear about you and the girl?'

'I only met her this morning.'

'Uh-huh. She looks like Marcia Tait. Is that the reason?'

'No.'

'Well, I got no objection. Only thing to make sure is that she's not a murderer, or,' H.M. scratched his chin, 'related to a murderer. Very uncomfortable in the first case, and a bit embarrassin' in the second. Can you look at it from that viewpoint? No, I don't suppose you can. You wouldn't be worth your salt if you could. Anyhow, you can set your mind at rest about one thing. *She* didn't come down here last night to interview La Tait... No, no, son. She was much too anxious to prove that Canifest's daughter didn't. She thinks Canifest's daughter did.'

'Do *you* think so?'

'You've all got your mind set on a woman, haven't you?' inquired H.M. 'That Mrs. Thompson didn't swear it was a woman. No, no. She wouldn't. Widen your horizon a bit. Imagine it wasn't... Besides, there's another reason why it sticks in the old man's throat to believe this Louise Carewe came down and bashed Tait's head in. I'll pass over the girl's remarkable ingenuity at bein' able to fly over a hundred feet of snow. I'll only ask you, What took her so long to do it?'

'How do you mean?'

'She came down here at half-past one. Accordin' to what Masters says, Tait wasn't killed until some time after three. "She came down to argue and expostulate," says you, "and when that wouldn't work, she acted." It took nearly two hours. I can't imagine anybody arguin' with Tait for two hours without being chucked out. But disregard that, and look at the big point. Tait was expecting a visitor—John Bohun. If you've got any doubts of that, root 'em out of your mind. She was expecting important news about Canifest. Well, can you picture Tait wantin' *anybody* there on the premises when her *cher amant* dropped in during the night, especially the daughter of the man she had on the string for proposed matrimony? She got rid of Willard fast enough, but we're supposed to imagine she allowed the Carewe girl to stop there for two hours when she expected Bohun any minute. And two hours can be an awful long time, son.'

'But look here, sir! Are you coming back to Rainger's idea that Bohun might have come down here at some time during the night? Because we know John didn't get back here until three o'clock.'

H.M. had stopped. They had followed fading lines of tracks down towards the entrance to the avenue of ever-greens. H.M. pushed his hat forward as he peered about. He glanced back towards the house, some hundred yards back up the slope. His eye seemed to be measuring distances.

'At the moment I won't say anything, my lad, except that Rainger's notion of hocussed tracks was even sillier than you thought. John Bohun went down there when he said he did, and no flummery there; and before he got there there were *no tracks*... No, no. That's not the part of the feller's behaviour that bothers me. The part that does bother me to blazes is his behaviour in London: that attack on Canifest, when he thought he'd killed him...'

Then Bennett remembered what had almost been lost in the twists and terrors of development. He asked what had happened, and what Canifest had said to Masters on the telephone. H.M., who seemed to be inspecting the end of the evergreen-avenue, scowled more heavily.

'I dunno, son. Except what Masters told me. It seems Masters tried to imitate Maurice's voice, and said, "Yes?"

Then Canifest said somethin' like, "I wanted to speak to you, Bohun, but I hope it won't be necessary to explain my reasons for asking that my daughter be sent home at once." Like that. Masters said he sounded weak and very shaky. Then Masters said: "Why? Because John landed one on your chin and thought you were a goner when you keeled over with a heart attack?" Of course the feller tumbled to its not being Maurice's voice, and kept gabbling, "Who is this, who is this?" Then Masters said he was a police officer, and Canifest had better come out here and give us a spot of help if he didn't want to get into an unholy mess. He piled it on, I understand. Said Canifest's daughter was accused of murder, and so on. All Masters could gather was that Bohun had followed the old boy home last night; got in a side entrance or something and tried to reopen "some business subject"; and there was a row during which John cut up rough. Naturally Canifest ain't likely to be garrulous about the subject. Masters said to come out here, heart attack or no heart attack; and hung up while Canifest was still digestin' the gruesome result of publicity if he refused to play fair with the police.'

'That seems straightforward enough…'

H.M. grunted. 'Does it? Come on out to the pavilion.' As he waddled on he was slapping irritably at the trees with his gloved hand. 'Look here, didn't they say they'd left the body out here and used the dead van to haul Bohun to the doctor's? H'm, yes. I was hopin' for that. Got a handkerchief? My glasses get all snowed up. What's botherin' *you?*'

'But, hang it all, sir, if there were no footprints whatever, and here's a woman murdered—!'

'Oh, that? You're like Masters. Funny thing, but that's the easiest part of it. Mind, I'm not sayin' I know how the trick was worked before I even have a look at the pavilion. But I got a strong hunch; oh, a very strong hunch. And if I find what I expect to find out here...'

'You'll know the murderer?'

'No!' said H.M. 'Burn me, that's just it. All I could tell you right now is the two or three people it *isn't*. And that's not accordin' to rule either. As a general rule, these sleight-of-hand tricks are a dead give-away to the murderer once you've tumbled to the means of workin' the illusion. A special sort of crime indicates a special set of circumstances, and those circumstances narrow down to fit one person like a hangman's cap when you know what they are. Well, this is the exception. Even if I'm right I may not be any closer, because...'

'Because?'

They had come out into the vast, dusky open space before the frozen lake, churned now with many lines of tracks. The pavilion was unlighted now; it looked darker against the spectral whiteness of snow. So quiet was this muffled world that they could hear the snowflakes tickling and rustling in the evergreen branches.

'When I was raggin' Masters,' said H.M., 'I thought I'd be very neat and unanswerable. I asked, Was it by accident that the murderer went to and from the crime without leavin' a footprint? And I chuckled in my fatheaded way. But that's it, son; and it's the whole difficulty. That's exactly what happened.'

Bennett stared round. He was beginning to experience

the same eerie sensation he had felt when he first came into this clearing at dawn: a feeling of being shut away into a twilight place where the present did not exist, and where Marcia Tait dead among the Stuart finery was no less alive than the beribboned ladies, with their paint and their wired ringlets, who smiled over plumed fans at the card-tables of the merry monarch…

He glanced up sharply.

A light had appeared in the pavilion.

XIV

ASHES AT THE PAVILION

Level slits of light showed yellow through the Venetian blinds in the windows of the room on the left-hand side of the door: a lonely glow in the midst of the lake. H.M., who had put the dead pipe into his mouth, rattled it against his teeth.

'It might be one of Potter's men still there,' he said. 'Or it might not. Strike a match and see if there are any fresh tracks…'

'The snow's covering them,' Bennett answered, when he had wasted several matches; 'but they look like fresh ones. Big shoes. Shall we—'

H.M. lumbered ahead, as quietly as his own squeaky shoes would permit. The causeway was again muffled in snow, but they need not have used any secrecy. The front door of the pavilion was opened just as they reached it.

'I rather imagined,' said Jervis Willard's voice, out of the gloom in the doorway, 'that I saw someone out there. I must make my deepest apologies if I came down here without permission. But the police had gone, and the door was open.'

He stood courteously, his head a little inclined, the glow from the drawing-room shining down one side of his handsome face, where none of the wrinkles showed now. The light brought out rich hues and shadows; a brocade curtain behind his stiff black clothes, a shadow-trick whereby he seemed to be wearing a black periwig.

'You are Sir Henry Merrivale,' he stated. 'I'll go now. I hope I didn't intrude. She is still—in the bedroom.'

If H.M. caught a curious undercurrent in the man's voice, he paid no attention. He only looked briefly at Willard, and stumped up the steps.

'Point of fact, you're the man I wanted to talk to,' he announced, with a sort of grudging absent-mindedness. 'Don't go. Come on in here. H'm. Yes. So this is it?' Pushing back the brocade curtain over the door to the drawing-room, he studied the room a moment before he lumbered in. 'Bah!' he added.

The electric candles were fluttering again over the black-and-white marble floor, the hammered brass vases on cabinets of Japanese lacquer, the whole stiff black and white and dull red colour of that fading room. Willard, following Bennett into the room, stood quietly with his back to the fireplace.

H.M. said: 'I saw you in "The Bells." You weren't Irving, but you were devilish good. And your Othello was the best thing you ever did. Mind tellin' me why you're playin' around in polite drawing-room comedy?'

'Thanks. Probably,' Willard answered, and looked slowly round, 'because it's this sort of drawing-room, and had *that* sort of occupant.'

'I mean, I was only wonderin' if you were another of 'em who walked into her parlour.'

'Only into the parlour.'

'Uh-huh. That's what I thought. I want to get this right about last night, because you must 'a' been the last person to see her before the murderer got here. Now, when you and Bohun and Rainger came out here with her, where did you make yourselves comfortable? In here?'

'No. In the bedroom. But we didn't make ourselves comfortable; we didn't even sit down. We left after a very few minutes.'

'And when you came back here, as they tell me you did, where were you two?'

'Also in the bedroom. I drank a glass of port with her.'

'Right,' grunted H.M. absently. 'Got a match?'

There was a faint flicker of amusement in Willard's eyes. 'Sorry. I gave away my last box to Marcia last night, and I don't carry about that coloured kind they supply at the house. Will a lighter do?'

'Just as well,' nodded H.M. The corners of his mouth turned down again. He advised gently: 'Don't ever get the notion that I'm tryin' to be clever. It's bad policy to advertise suspicion. Either on my part or yours. If I'd had any doubts, I'd have asked for a lighter to begin with. Point of fact, I wanted to look at that fireplace...'

Snapping on the lighter Willard handed him, he looked carefully at the fluffy grey wood ashes and the few stumps of charred wood. He put his hand under the broad flue, and craned his neck to peer up under it.

'Pretty strong draught. Notice that? That chimney's as

big as a house. H'm, yes. They got iron steps for the sweep. Still, I don't suppose…'

His dull eye wandered out over the hearth and the edge of the carpet.

'Other room now. I'll keep this lighter for a minute.'

Willard went ahead, reached to the left of the bedroom door, and switched on the lights. Although Bennett nerved himself to keep steady, the sight was less disturbing than he had feared. There was a businesslike look about the little room with the many mirrors and the high red-canopied bedstead. A stale reek of flashlight powder still hung in the air; white grains from the fingerprint dust clung to most surfaces where prints might have been found. Except for the fact that the body was now laid out on the bed and covered with a sheet, Potter's men had replaced the other objects just as they had been when Bennett first saw them. The fragments of the decanter lay at the edge of the carpet before the fireplace; fragments and crushed pieces of the glasses were still on the hearth; the poker had been put back with its tip in the little heap of ashes; the one chair upright, the other overturned to the right of the fireplace, the overturned tabouret and the scattered burnt matches—these things again played the dumbshow of murder.

'H'm,' said H.M.

He blundered in his near-sighted fashion over to the fireplace, where he examined the ashes carefully. In peering up the chimney with the aid of the lighter, he endangered his tall hat, and growled curses to himself. Next he picked up the poker, snorted, and put it down again. With infinite labour he got down to blink at the crushed fragments of glass, which seemed to put him in a little better humour. The match-ends, nearly burned down to the end of the stem, engaged his attention next. He moved over to examine a curtained recess containing wearing apparel, and pawed over its contents until he found a silver gown. After one glance into the primitive bathroom, he came back to the middle of the room, where he lifted one finger and pointed malevolently at his two companions in the doorway.

'Dummies!' roared H.M.

The dummies looked at each other.

'Yes, I mean you,' amplified H.M., still stabbing his finger at them. 'You and Masters and everybody else who's been out here. Ain't anybody got any brains nowadays? To mention only one item in a whole chart of clues especially provided for you, don't a single fleetin' glance at that fireplace tell you anything?'

'Well, sir,' said Bennett, 'if you mean that the murderer made his entrance and exit by crawling up and down the chimney, it seems entirely feasible. But I shouldn't think it would do him much good. The problem is how he came to and left the *pavilion.* I mean, even if he got up to the roof he'd still have to cross a hundred feet of snow. So far as the Santa-Claus business is concerned, he'd have found it less complicated by simply walking to the front door.'

H.M. swelled.

'So you're givin' the old man sauce, are you? Tryin' to sauce me, hey? That's gratitude for you, that is! All right. All right! Now just for that, young man, I *won't* tell you what I did mean. Haa. Haa, that'll fix you!—Point o' fact, I wasn't thinking about the chimney very much at all.'

'Exactly what,' said Willard, 'does "very much at all" mean, Sir Henry?'

H.M. nodded malevolently. 'I'll tell you what it means. It means what my old friend Richter said when he was conductin' the London orchestra, and the second flute played the same sour note twice over in the same place at rehearsal. And Richter he slammed his baton down on the floor, and he said, "You, secgonde vlute! I can stand your damma nonsense occasionally then and now, but sometimes, always, by God nevair!" That's what I feel about this, and I'm goin' to tell Masters so when he gets here. I didn't come here to get insulted. Now I'm goin' to ask some questions...'

He waddled over to the bed, lifted a corner of the sheet, and made a brief examination. The mere lifting of the sheet brought another atmosphere into this cold room. A little light from the big window at the side of the bed, and flickered with the shadow of snowflakes, fell across a face they had sponged off with water, and whose dark hair had been arranged behind her head...

Bennett, who had turned away, looked back to see H.M.'s small eyes fixed sharply on him from his wizard-like stoop over that still beauty.

'A quarter past three o'clock,' said H.M., 'is about the time she died... Now, when you came in here this morning, was the blind on this window up or down? Think back, and make sure.'

'It was up. I definitely remember that, because I tried to put up the window to let some air in, and remembered that you weren't supposed to touch anything in cases of this kind.'

H.M. replaced the sheet and peered out of the window.

'The windows of somebody's livin'-quarters over the stables are in a direct line with this. You noticed that, hey... All right. Now go over there and show me how she was lyin' on the floor when you first saw her. I know you'll feel like a fool, but get down and do it... Uh-huh. All right; you can get up. That would mean a good many of those burnt matches must have been scattered close to her. As though they'd been aimed at the fireplace... Now, then: when you came in, did it look as though she'd gone to bed? Was the bed disturbed?'

'I don't think so.'

'Excuse me for butting in,' said Willard, rather restlessly, 'but it seems to me that there's been a devil of a fuss about those burnt matches when they may mean nothing at all.'

'Think so, hey?' inquired H.M., stiffening. 'You got an idea somebody sat here lightin' innumerable cigarettes and then tossin' the match-ends on the floor? One match burned nearly down to a stump, or even two, I might admit as rather a lengthy light for a cigarette; but twelve or fifteen of 'em argued that somebody was strikin' 'em in the dark.'

'But put it this way,' urged Willard. 'Suppose it was innocent. Suppose that when Bohun discovered the body, coming on it all of a sudden in half-light, he bent over and struck a match to make sure...'

H.M. puffed his cheeks in and out. 'Why, aside from the fact that he said he didn't, and there seems to be no earthly reason why he should have denied it, a man don't need a dozen matches to make sure somebody's dead. Besides, I rather imagine it was light enough at that time to see without 'em...wasn't it?' He swung sharply. Bennett felt that there was an underlying purpose in the question apart from what it seemed.

'Yes,' he said, 'just. I remember noticing how the light from the window fell directly on her.'

'But, damn it,' snapped Willard, 'she wasn't killed in the dark!'

H.M., for some reason, was suddenly imbued with a fantastic jollity. He set his hat on the side of his head; he was almost affable.

'Oh, it's a funny business, son. An exceedingly rummy business. Why does the Visitor strike matches in the dark? Why are the two fires exactly the same? Why does the Visitor get mad and put two drinking-glasses down on the hearth and stamp on 'em—By the way, you didn't do that, did you?'

'*What?*'

'Uh-huh. I'd better point that out to you. Come over here and look. You see that decanter? Notice how heavy it is? Notice where it is?—not on the hearthstone, but on the carpet. I defy you to smash that decanter merely by upsettin' a low tabouret and havin' it hit the floor. The Visitor busted it, son... Now look at those smashed glasses. Did you ever see any parts of a glass *crushed* by failin' on the floor? I'll lay you a fiver you didn't. They're on the stone, where the Visitor put 'em and deliberately smashed 'em.'

'But in a struggle—'

'Ho, ho,' said H.M., settling his coat over his shoulders. 'Try the experiment some time. Put a round drinking-glass on the floor, imitate somebody staggerin' over the room in a struggle, and see if you will land a bull's-eye on one glass.

They roll, son. They're as slippery as eels. And when you discover the probabilities of your breakin' not one glass, but *two* at the same time, I think you'll find that the old man's right. Did I hear somebody say we're not any better off than we were before? Now, about these chimneys...'

They had not heard the door to the drawing-room open, or any steps there. But they felt a cold current of air, which stirred the ashes in the fireplace, and (as Bennett could see from the corner of his eyes) the sheet over Marcia Tait's body. There was something so eerie about it that for a moment nobody turned round. It was like the thin voice which spoke across the room.

'So,' said the voice, 'somebody has thought of the chimney at last? I must congratulate him.'

Maurice Bohun, his throat swathed round in a wool muffler, and a raffish-looking tweed cap pulled over one eye, stood leaning on his stick in the doorway. His glazed stare wandered over to the figure on the bed; then he removed the cap with a gently satiric gesture, and became all deprecation. Behind him towered a bewildered and savage-looking Masters, who was making signals over his shoulder.

'But even if it has already occurred to you, which is surprising,' said Maurice, with a curious snap of his jaws, 'I think I can supply more complete details than anyone. Do you mind coming into the other room? I—I cannot stand the sight of death!'

He backed away suddenly.

'Mind, sir,' Masters said over his shoulder, and appealing violently to H.M. 'I don't say I believe this. I don't say it's true. But if you'll listen to what Mr. Bohun has to say...'

'My humblest thanks, inspector.'

'...then there may be something in it. At least it explains a lot of things that've been putting the wind up us. And in a way I should think was rather tit-for-tat and sauce for the goose...'

'Don't gibber, Masters,' said H.M. austerely. 'I detest gibbering. What the devil is all this, anyhow? Can't a man have any peace without somebody rushin' in and gabblin' nonsense?'

Maurice leaned forward a little.

'You must excuse the chief inspector,' he protested. 'In his somewhat unliterary fashion, he is referring to what is known as poetic justice. I agree. Mr. Carl Rainger, from the depths of sheer spite, attempted this morning to fasten Marcia Tait's murder on my brother John. He provided for this impossible situation a clumsy explanation which would not stand scrutiny for five minutes.'

He paused, still backing away with his dead-glazed eyes fixed on the quiet figure. Then he snapped:

'If you will come into the other room, Sir Henry, I will undertake to show you exactly how this Mr. Carl Rainger himself killed Miss Tait, and attempted by a clumsy sub-terfuge to escape *my* notice. I did not wish to speak to you in the house, in case it should entail unpleasantness... You will accompany me? I thank you. I—cannot—endure— the—sight of death.'

He backed so swiftly out of the room that he stumbled and supported himself only by clinging to the frame of the door.

XV
SECOND DESIGN FOR HANGING

At half-past six that evening, Bennett was sitting in a lumpy armchair before the fire in his own room, without energy to finish dressing for dinner. His brain felt literally heavy from weariness; draughts played in the creaky room; and Katharine had not yet returned from Dr. Wynne's, although she had telephoned that John would definitely pull through. Telephone messages: 'This is Lord Canifest's secretary speaking. His Lordship will be quite unable to undertake a motor journey at this moment, owing to a heart attack experienced last night, and is confined to his room. Should there be any doubt of this in the mind of the policeman who had occasion to 'phone, it is suggested that he communicate with his Lordship's physician...' Blaah, blaah, blaah.

Bennett looked up at a murky painting hung over the mantelpiece, and down at the studless shirt in his lap. Murder, suicide, or holocaust, the business of calories and black ties must go on as usual. Maurice was in very high feather tonight; he had even issued orders that some special sherry was to be served, in place of cocktails, for the benefit of Sir Henry Merrivale. Sir Henry Merrivale had consented to spend the night at the White Priory. In other words (Bennett thought) what in the devil's name was on H.M.'s mind?

Which brought up the worst and most insistent question: was Maurice right about the murder? While Bennett and Masters and H.M. were walking back from the pavilion, with Bohun and Willard a little distance behind, H.M. had relieved his mind with a few *sotto voce* comments about Maurice, Maurice's character, and Maurice's habits, which sizzled the ear of the listener with their force and sulphurousness. But that was all. He had only grunted when Maurice expounded his theory of the murder. He had sat back with a wooden face, under the spurious candle-light in the drawing-room of the pavilion, while Maurice deftly wove a halter for Carl Rainger. Masters had been impressed. So, evidently, had Willard. Bennett was willing to admit that he himself was more than impressed. But H.M. had been neither one thing nor the other.

'You say,' he growled, 'Rainger's still dead to the world and in his room? Right-ho. Let him keep. I s'pose you're not afraid to face *him* with this story?'

Well, then? That H.M. believed this explanation Bennett doubted. But the thing was so ingenious, and so plausible, that it appealed all the more for its retributive effort. When Rainger flung out an accusation on the strength of John Bohun's tracks, he had touched a snake that could sting in return. Again Bennett heard Maurice speaking quietly, levelly, with something like a similar warning *whir* in his voice.

'I knew this morning that this man Rainger was in all

probability guilty, and I could have told you how he had done it.' Here his little head had turned snakily towards Masters. 'You may recall, inspector, that I intimated a possibility of explaining the problem that troubled you? Ah, yes. I fancy you do remember. Of course it will be obvious why I could not speak?'

Masters blurted: 'I don't know what to make of you, sir, and that's a fact. Yes, I know why. You wondered whether this man Rainger's business proposition was on the level. And if he *did* mean to offer you some fantastic job at some fantastic salary, you mean to say you were willing to cover him up in a murder?'

Maurice had only looked mildly puzzled and troubled.

'Surely it was the logical thing, was it not?'

'And you believed in this very fishy offer of Rainger's?'

'Admitting,' said Maurice with sudden harshness, 'that I was for a moment taken in! What would anyone have thought? These Americans are all notoriously fools about money. The brethren of the cinema are worse than any. Besides, if you will allow me to say so, I am not unaware of my own worth. But when I had the good fortune to overhear a conversation between you, Sir Henry, and this offensive person named Emery, then whatever doubts I had were destroyed. He had been deliberately making a fool of me—!' Maurice conquered his tone before his words made a fool of him there. He became cool again. 'I am only wondering whether Sir Henry deliberately spoke in a loud tone to this man Emery...'

H.M. blinked sleepily. A sound came from somewhere deep in his chest.

'Oh, maybe. Maybe. My sight ain't as good as it might be, but I noticed somethin' grey and ghostly floatin' around outside the door; and I thought you might as well know. Well?'

Trying to force these images to the back of his mind, Bennett got up and stalked about the room as he continued dressing. He would put *that* problem aside until he could discuss it with somebody: preferably Katharine, since the tangle involved Louise Carewe. H.M. had insisted that Louise should not be questioned until this evening, and Maurice (even afire with his theory) had been content to let it rest.

The trouble was... He had adjusted his tie, and was getting into his coat, when somebody knocked at the door.

'May I come in?' said Katharine's voice. 'I know it's the wrong time, but I had to see you. Everything's all right; I've just left John. He's still unconscious, but he's in no danger.'

She was hatless, and wore a heavy tweed coat still powdered with snow. The cold had brought brilliant colour into her cheeks.

'In fact, I've got good news all around; surprising news. I've looked in on Louise. She's up and about, and she'll come down to dinner. It's a funny thing, but I feel better than I have for years.' She came up to the fire, spreading out her hands, and tossed her hair back as she looked over her shoulder. 'By the way, what *is* the matter with Uncle Maurice?'

'Matter?'

'High spirits. That's what I don't like. When I came in, Thompson said there'd been some sort of row about that man Rainger; and that—the other one, the nice one, Emery, had been here all afternoon trying to sober him up. Only he wouldn't be sobered, and from what Thompson said, he'd been raving and singing about the house; and that's what Uncle Maurice hates. But when I came in, this Mr. Emery was coming downstairs, and Uncle Maurice came out, and—slapped him on the shoulder. I say, it's unbelievable! That is, if you knew Maurice. And he said, "Where are you going?" Emery looked ill; I mean really ill. I wanted to stop him and ask if I couldn't do something, only I didn't know him. But he said he'd got a room in a hotel at Epsom nearby where they were keeping *her* . . .'

'Steady! No Price Terrors now. Go on.'

'It was only that Uncle Maurice said, "Are you a friend of Mr. Rainger?" Emery said, "Certainly; what about it?" And Uncle Maurice said, "Then you've got to stay to dinner. You'll hear something very interesting." Emery looked at him in a queer sort of way; and there must be something on his mind, because he said, "You'd invite Me to dinner? You don't think what Canifest does?" I say, he was upset! Something about people thinking he was a—a—well, he used the word "louse." And Uncle Maurice said, "If you're a friend of Mr. Rainger, nobody will be more welcome." It simply doesn't sound like him, that's all.'

'It sounds more like him than you think.'

She dropped her hands and turned round to look at him fully.

'I know what you mean,' she said, 'but I don't understand . . .'

He told her. He told her only of the accusation, and added: 'Sit down, and let me explain it, because it concerns you. It also concerns Louise. Will you be frank with me now?'

'Yes. That is, except about one thing, and that doesn't concern—murders.'

That sharp directness of hers had come through; it would have come through, even if she had tried to prevent it. She was looking up at him, her head back as though defiantly, but he could see her shoulders quivering and the rise and fall of her breast.

'No!' she said suddenly and almost hysterically, as he took a step forward. 'That's what I meant when I said I wouldn't be frank. Not now! Not now, do you see? I'm a nasty little—little—I don't know! But I'm—I'm even postponing my feelings, until there's nothing else except them to think about or worry about; when every single thing that I think and care can all be set on one... Quick! Tell me what you were going to say about Maurice. That's only fair.'

'Maurice,' he replied, and took almost a pleasure in snapping out a name he detested, 'accused Rainger of Marcia's murder. I've told you that already. And I was going to ask if you really believed Louise had gone down to the pavilion. Because, according to Maurice, she did. Sit down. In a way it concerns you.'

'Do you really think that Rainger—? What does your man-who-can-see-through-the-brick-wall think of it?'

'That's what I don't understand. The only comment he made to me, and he was serious, was that Rainger *could have done it.* I mean, that he could be guilty; but I don't think he believes...

'Well, here's the situation. Rainger made a play for you last night, and Marcia noticed it. She didn't like it. She liked to keep her men dancing on the string, and swooped down immediately if one of them looked away; you admitted that yourself. Do you remember telling us that Marcia spoke to him, and he replied, "*Do you mean it?*" And that, Maurice says, was an invitation to the pavilion last night.'

Her eyes widened, and then narrowed again. She flushed.

'Then,' she said abruptly, 'when I saw Rainger coming upstairs at half-past one, and he said, "*You can forget what I asked you tonight; I have better business,*" what he actually meant was that he was going out to the pavilion later. Is that it?'

'Yes. And Maurice carries it farther, because he supplies a reason for everything! She wasn't inviting Rainger out there for any business of love-making; quite the contrary; although Rainger didn't know it. She was inviting him out there so that she and your Uncle John—steady, now; I don't mean anything against *him*—could corner Rainger and, if necessary, wring his neck...'

'But why?'

'Because Rainger had been the whole motivating force behind Emery's telling Lord Canifest about the marriage. She knew she could handle Emery; but not when Rainger played on Emery's nerves and uneasiness and sent him to Canifest to tell the whole thing! It's Rainger's fine Italian hand that you can see behind the whole business, whether or not you accuse him of murder. Marcia had heard rumours that the beans were spilled. That was why John had gone to see Canifest.' He hesitated, but she gestured fiercely for him to go on. 'Well, frankly, John may or may not have known about Marcia's marriage to Emery. Emery thinks he didn't; but, whether he did or not, the shock of hearing from Canifest that his great dream about the play had gone to smash was bad enough in itself. And John knew who had prompted Emery to tell. This morning, when he was talking to Willard and me, he flared out about Rainger being behind it.

'You see? Both he and Marcia had heard rumours of it. And Marcia invited Rainger down to the pavilion last night because she was expecting John back with bad news, and both she and John were going to face Rainger with it.'

'But they didn't! They couldn't have, because—'

'No. That's just it.' He wondered whether she knew about John's trouble with Canifest, and decided that the best thing was to suppress it. 'Because John was delayed in town, and, after she tried to stall Rainger off in the hope that John would return, she was forced to face him alone.

'Blast it, the thing fits together almost too accurately! Even to Louise's part in it. Louise entered unintentionally into the scheme. The mysterious woman Mrs. Thompson saw going down over the lawn at one-thirty, the person who started the dog barking, *was* Louise. She had gone down to the pavilion to make a last appeal to Marcia. If Marcia wouldn't listen to reason, she wasn't going to kill her; but that little quiet friend of yours was going to slash Marcia's face open and disfigure her with the lash of a hunting-crop...'

Katharine had gone pale. He felt a sickening sensation, a knowledge that he was right. Biting at her lips, Katharine hesitated, wavered...

'How,' she burst out, 'did Uncle Maurice know that? Nobody's said anything about that crop! I haven't told anybody. I tried to conceal—'

'Yes, I know you did. It's Maurice's quaint habit of listening at doors. He's overheard everything that's been said in this house. I shouldn't be at all surprised if he could hear us right now.'

Everywhere Bennett seemed to see that gently leering, cool, pale face with its big forehead and black-pointed eyes. So strong was the impression that he went over, opened the door, and peered out. A little reassured that the gallery was empty, he turned back.

'And he pointed out one thing we *had* overlooked: that no woman would use the loaded end of a crop as a weapon to *kill*. It had another meaning. It's clear as daylight when you think of it as a weapon like vitriol or a horsewhip: to disfigure. Very well, she went down to the pavilion at one-thirty. Rainger, on the other hand, thought the dog barking meant that John was coming home. He went to his room, and waited for some minutes so that John could go to his room and get out of the way. You see?'

'Yes, but—'

'Wait a minute. About twenty minutes to two, Rainger came downstairs (still in his evening clothes). He let himself out the back door and went down to the pavilion in high feather for a *nuit d'amour*.

'And when he got there, still during a heavy snowfall, he heard the row. It was a furious row. Louise had nerved herself up in some way, and she went for Tait with the crop. Somebody got hit, and there was a little blood; but Tait was the stronger either physically or mentally, and she got Louise out of there before Rainger showed himself to interfere. You see, Tait still didn't know Louise's father had refused to back their play, and she wanted to keep down as much trouble as possible. Louise, still with the crop in her hand, stumbled out of there, crying, with all her emotional nerve gone; and Tait only laughed. She enjoyed it.'

As he refashioned Maurice's words, Bennett understood now why the man could have written a brilliant play. He could not hope to reproduce the vividness with which Maurice's dry, precise inflexion probed into brains and reshaped the anguish of a hurt woman; again he saw Maurice bending forwards, hands clasped on his stick, gently smiling.

'What happened to Louise, according to him,' said Bennett, 'you can guess. Her worked-up nerve was gone. She came back to the house in a hysterical condition at not later than a quarter to two. She did not remove her coat, or anything except her wet shoes. She lay in the dark and brooded until she was nearly insane. Then she determined, in the night, to come to you and tell you. Can you think of a more likely motive for waking up somebody at that time of the morning? On the way to your room she lost her way in the dark—something that may have been only a shadow shattered her last shred of reason—she cried out, and when she opened her eyes, both you and Willard were bending over her. She would have told you, but she couldn't tell *Willard.* She was again the prim, nervous Miss Carewe. But she saw the blood on her, and she instantly cried out the first thing that a girl of her type would naturally think of, a "mysterious man" beloved of the spinsters, who had accosted her...'

Katharine said quietly:

'It can't be. But that doesn't matter. It doesn't have any connection with Rainger out there at the pavilion. I know

now all about the "impossible situation." Dr. Wynne carefully explained it to me. If Rainger killed her, how did he do it?'

'*It's the simplest damned trick ever worked*, if it's true. Did Dr. Wynne tell you about the conditions out there? How everything looked?'

'Yes. Carry on. I want to know!'

'All right. Rainger, when it's snowing most heavily, goes out jubilantly to his tryst. She appreciates the baboon now... Well, Tait doesn't want to pitch into him until John returns with definite news; maybe she felt Rainger might still be a valuable friend, or maybe she was a little afraid of Rainger's brains and nastiness. She was very gracious and alluring to him, while John wasn't there to take her part when she did pitch in. But—time went on, things got more strained; two o'clock, half-past two, still no John...

'The blow-up must have come about three, when Rainger was gradually getting suspicious, and Marcia suddenly realized that if the news had been good, John would have returned by that time. In other words, the plans had crashed and John was afraid to come and tell her. And it was Rainger's fault. It was the fault of the tubby little man pawing at her...'

'*Don't!*' said Katharine, and shuddered.

'I'm afraid,' said Bennett uneasily, 'you're only proving Maurice's point. Then can you imagine what she began to tell him? It's a funny thing, but when Rainger himself was telling us this morning of an imaginary interview between Marcia and John just before he said John killed her, Rainger used the words, "*She told him for the first time what she really thought of him.*"

'Lord, it comes back at him with a smash, doesn't it? Everything he said about John might have been in his mind about himself. Furious as he was (says Maurice), he kept that little kink of reason in his mind; that cunning he's always got. He realized that, if he killed Marcia by smashing her head in, the blame would probably go straight to Louise, who he knew *had* made an attack on her.

'But in any event, he didn't check himself. He killed her with one of those heavy, silvered-steel or brass vases that are all over the house, those vases with sharp edges which would make exactly the kind of wounds that were on her head. Afterwards he washed it off and put it back on one of the Japanese cabinets—so that Louise's loaded crop should be blamed.

'And there, my girl,' snapped Bennett, 'there's exactly where Maurice's theory is reasonable. There is why he says he knew Louise's story about being grabbed in the dark by a bloody-handed man was pure fabrication. Why should the fool murderer come all the way back from the pavilion *without washing his hands?* There's water down there. Even if he wasn't acquainted with the pavilion, it's the first thing he'd have looked for.'

After a pause the girl rubbed her hand dazedly across her forehead.

'And that little stain of blood,' she muttered, 'came from Louise's attempt to... But Rainger? He had to get back from the pavilion, didn't he? And the snow had stopped! And aside from *how* he could have done it, if he knew Louise would be suspected, why did he try to throw the blame on John?'

'Because, don't you see, he had to! He suddenly had to

change his plans, for the same reason we've been putting up against everybody who's been accused. The snow had stopped, and he hadn't calculated on it. It must have been a hellish shock, when he was all ready with a perfect situation at hand, to discover that the snow stopping an hour before had wrecked the entire scheme. If his footprints alone were seen leaving that pavilion, there was no chance to accuse anybody. That's why a less clever man than Rainger would never have had the strength of mind to get himself out of it. He did, brilliantly. You see...'

She protested: 'Wait a bit! Dr. Wynne told me about that accusation he made against John... But if he wanted to blame Louise, couldn't he still have done it? Somebody asked why a person trapped in the pavilion wouldn't make tracks and simply mess them up so they couldn't be recognized. And Rainger answered that it would take too much time; the dog would bark and rouse the house. But that wouldn't apply to *Rainger*. He knew Tempest had been tied up inside; he heard Uncle Maurice give the orders. Messed-up tracks would have been blamed on Louise, and he had all the time he wanted, didn't he?'

Bennett fumbled after a cigarette and lit it hastily.

He said: 'Good girl! That's exactly what Masters said to your uncle. But by the devilish arrangement of circumstances, Rainger was in an even worse position. He couldn't afford to take the time-risk either. He knew there was nothing to fear from the dog, but...'

'Yes?'

'He expected John back from town at any time!— Naturally, Marcia, when she flew out at him, would have told him she expected John. She had told him John was coming down to the pavilion, whenever he got home. Rainger knew John hadn't got back, or he would have heard the car. So, if he tries the long process of messing up his tracks, and meets John half-way up the lawn...you see?'

'I say, this is—the perverseness of things...! But what did he do? What could he do?'

Bennett drew a deep breath. 'Here we go. Now this non-arrival of John, according to Maurice, supplied Rainger with his inspiration. He knew that, *at some time during that night,* or very early in the morning, John would come down to the pavilion. He'd either go down there as soon as he got back from London, or turn up for early horseback-riding accord-ing to Tait's orders. Rainger might have to wait a long time, but the probabilities were overwhelming that John would be the first person at Tait's side in the morning. And if not John, somebody else might do as well.

'He heard John's car come in about a quarter past three. John didn't come down at the moment, but that might only mean he had gone into the house for a short time. Rainger was always in danger if he tried to venture out of the pavil-ion, not knowing what John was up to. So his inspiration grew until he worked out the whole scheme into a perfect alibi for himself... Did you see Rainger this morning?'

She looked at him queerly. 'Yes. About half-past eight. He was standing in the door of his room putting on a ghastly-looking dressing-gown. I think he was patting one of the maids—yes, it was Beryl!—he was patting her on the head and saying, "Good girl, good girl." I don't know whether he was drunk then.'

'Yes! We came back to Maurice's theory again. Beryl was the girl who told him John's bed hadn't been slept in last night. It wasn't slept in because John didn't go to bed at all. He paced the floor all night after he got in, with the light on, wondering whether he had the nerve to go and face Tait with the bad news! Do you see it? And still Rainger, as I told you, didn't dare venture out of the pavilion...because he saw the light on in John's room.

'Maurice asked the very significant question: "How did Rainger, at the very beginning of the case, before any of us knew the circumstances, *come to inquire whether or not John's bed had been slept in?* What made him think of it?" And Maurice answered, "Because Rainger saw the light on all night in that room, and he was working out his scheme to throw the blame on John."—Now, then, you saw Rainger this morning. He was still in his evening clothes, wasn't he? At least the shirt and trousers?'

'Y-yes, I think so. I don't remember...'

'He was when he spoke to us in the library. Did you notice certain very black grimy stains on his shoulders, and powdered down his shirt?'

'Yes, I did notice that, because I thought he must be even nastier than I'd thought, to let...'

Bennett got up. He put his hand slowly under the hood of the fireplace, touched lightly, and withdrew it stained in soot.

'Like this?' he asked. 'Yes. I saw the marks myself. Well, the fires were out down at the pavilion. The chimneys are enormous, and have iron steps for the chimney-sweep on the inside. Rainger took off his coat for greater freedom when he tested whether he could manage it. He found it could be done. So he waited patiently until John should come down there. He had to turn out the light a long time before daylight, in case somebody over at the stables should see an all-night light, and grow curious. But he had to keep striking matches in the dark, match after match, to look at his watch. He left the front door of the pavilion open. It would be time to act when he heard John's footsteps.

'You still don't see it? When John discovered the body, Rainger was in the chimney. He knew that he was fairly safe when the inevitable search of the house occurred. It did occur. John and I undertook it. While we were in the back part of the house...'

'But he still had to leave the pavilion!'

And now Bennett remembered the terrible subdued triumph of Maurice's face when Maurice suddenly pointed his stick at H.M. and put the last touch on his accusation.

'Have you forgotten,' said Bennett, hearing the words echo back, 'that Rainger's foot is as small as a woman's? We noticed it this morning in the library. Have you also forgotten that your uncle John wears the largest size in men's shoes?—Don't you think that *you*, for instance, could walk back to the house in his tracks, without ever touching the outside edges, while two dunderheads were searching the other side of the pavilion? Have you forgotten that, once you were across the lake, the curve of the evergreen avenue would screen you from view? With a number six shoe in a number ten, you could walk straight in your normal way; let yourself back into the house through the door John had left open to come out; and, since there might be some question about a blur in those tracks, *you could explain it later exactly in the way Rainger did,* to throw the blame on John Bohun.'

There was a long pause. Bennett's cigarette had burned crookedly down one side, and he flung it into the fire.

He added thoughtfully:

'I won't call it a conspiracy of the perverse fates, or a choice example of the innate ordinariness of human happenings. All I'll say is that in the future I'm going to be very careful when I serve on a jury. Here are two perfectly good and convincing cases, each built out of exactly the same material, each pointing to a different person, and each the only apparent way of explaining an impossible situation. But if in this nightmare of a muddle we get still a *third* way of explaining it, I'll retire to a padded cell. The case against John collapsed. If the case against Rainger likewise collapses... What do you think?'

'But that's what I was going to tell you!' she said excitedly. 'I got so wrapped up in this that I couldn't. You remember I said I had good news? It hasn't got anything to do with Rainger being guilty or not, it doesn't concern Rainger, but—'

She whirled round, in her overwrought state of nerves nearly crying out. Outside in the driveway, under the *porte cochère*, had burst a churning and back-firing of cold motors as the last protesting newspapermen were shooed down towards the high-road before the bellow of Inspector Potter. But that was not what they heard that brought them up high-strung and staring.

'It sounded like—' said Katharine, and could not go on.

XVI

THE SILVER TRIANGLE

For a part of that noise there was no name: a rather horrible gobbling sound that might have been a strangled cry, a choke, or even suppressed mirth. You could not tell whether it came from near or far away, but a sort of muffled bump followed it. Bennett felt his skin go hot, despite the chill room.

Motor-gears ground under the *porte-cochère*, but it was no part of that. He went to the door and threw it open.

'Was it——?' said Katharine. 'Don't go out!'

The gallery was dark now. He saw it with the same eerie sense of close tragedy growing again.

'Shouldn't be dark,' he said. 'There were lights on a moment ago. I had a crazy idea that somebody, you know who, might be standing outside listening to us. So I looked out… What do you mean, don't go out? This is your own home, isn't it? Nothing to be afraid of in your own home.'

No movement, no creaking, in the dense shadow: as though the gallery itself were holding its breath. A window-frame rattled in the rising wind. Somebody had turned those lights out very recently. He had that feeling which sometimes comes to those who sit in old houses with darkness beyond the door: a feeling that the darkness shut him off from human kind, and that he must not venture beyond the light of his own fire lest there should be things he would not like to see. And always, irrationally, his mind would go back to the door of King Charles's Room just across the way. He had been standing here, in this spot, almost in this attitude, when he heard this morning the sound that had brought about his first meeting with Katharine Bohun. This morning, when Louise Carewe in her delirium had tried to strangle…

It was something like *that* sound, yet with a different quality. Somebody's words came back to his mind in describing the scene last night when X had tried to push Marcia Tait down the steep dangerous staircase of King Charles's Room: 'A sound like a giggle,' when the candle went out. You had only to think of the insensate fury with which the murderer had smashed in Marcia Tait's skull to walk warily when unexpected darkness came. For there grew on him an irrational conviction that the murderer was prowling now. Who was it? *Who…?*

He stepped across the gallery, touched the door of the King's Room, and almost jumped out of a crawling skin when heavy footsteps creaked far down the gallery.

'Who's been turnin' all the lights out?' sounded H.M.'s reassuring growl. 'Man can't see the edge of his glasses in front of his face. Hey! See if you can find a switch, Masters.'

Something clicked, and a dull glow sprang up. H.M. and the chief inspector stopped as they saw him.

'Hullo!' said H.M. He lumbered down and blinked sourly on his nephew. 'What's the matter with you, hey? Burn me, you got a funny look on your face!' He craned his neck round and saw Katharine in the doorway. 'You and the little gal playin' games? Evenin', miss.'

'Did you hear anything?'

'Hear anything? You got the wind up, son. I've been hearin' queer noises all day, and most of 'em come from my own head. I'm tired and I want a large brandy and nobody under the Almighty's canopy could get me into tails tonight even if I had 'em along. But there's something I've got to do...'

'We'll see,' said Bennett. He opened the door of the room, reached quickly round to switch on the lights, and braced himself as he stepped inside.

Nothing. King Charles's Room, John Bohun's room, lay heavy and swept clean now: the clothes put away, the grey carpet significantly scrubbed at one spot near the big centre table. The heavy black velvet draperies were drawn back from the windows, and moved slightly in a strong draught.

'Thanks. No bogies? That's where I was goin',' volunteered H.M. 'I got to see something, and I want to issue a couple of orders if I see what I think I will. Masters here has been holdin' out on me. Why don't you tell me about all the evidence? You find John Bohun with a bullet in his chest and a funny-lookin' little piece of silver held tight in his hand; but nobody bothers to tell me about that piece of silver. Where'd you put it, Masters?'

Masters shifted from one foot to the other. He had his hat and overcoat on, and was presumably on his way back to Inspector Potter's for a much-belated tea.

'But we don't know it's important, sir!' he protested. 'Some keepsake, perhaps. He'd got nothing to do with the murder, and it wasn't likely he'd be holding in his hand a clue to something he didn't do—especially as he'd just written a suicide note saying he didn't do it. It had some sentimental value, probably... I put it in the drawer of the table.'

'Sentimental value, hey? Well, we'll find out. Mind comin' in, Miss Bohun? Shut the door, Jimmy my boy.'

H.M. pulled out a large oak chair and lowered himself into it. He pulled open the drawer of the table...

Now, as any poker-player at the Diogenes Club could have told him, Bennett had discovered that any attempt to read H.M.'s thoughts was a highly unprofitable occupation. His face retained the same massively dull expression. From the table drawer he fished the same small triangular bit of silver, with its curious scrollwork, which Bennett had last seen when Masters held it out for inspection that morning. H.M. did not scowl or start or give any sign. But there was a perceptible pause before he spoke, as though he had heard rather than seen something.

He weighed the silver in his hand.

'Humph. No. Looks as though it's busted off some-thing... This mean anything to you, Miss Bohun? Anything of sentimental value, that he'd be likely to want in his hand when he took the Interestin' Step? Now, now, don't worry; I know he's goin' to be all right.'

She shook her head. 'N-no. I never saw it before.'

There was a clink as H.M. dropped the bit of silver back into the drawer.

'I'll tell you what, Masters. I'm goin' up to London

tomorrow mornin'. I know a silversmith, feller I did a good turn for once, lives in a funny shop back of Lincoln's Inn Fields. He'll tell me what this thing is in a second. I'll pick it up tomorrow and take it to show him. That is—if it's necessary. May be, may not be. Depends. I was thinkin' of somethin' else.' He hauled out his watch and blinked at it. 'It is now seven o'clock. We're goin' to dine at half-past... Miss Bohun, what time was it last night when you went on your sight-seein' tour by moonlight, and you came to this room, and somebody tried to shove La Tait down those stairs over there?'

'Close to eleven o'clock, as I remember it.'

'Oh, make it earlier,' said H.M. in a plaintive tone. 'Burn me, I got to get some sleep! I'd like to stick to the poetic rules, but I got to think of my constitution. Say—well, all right. Eleven o'clock it is. It'll give Masters time to eat and take a nap before he comes back. And a little after eleven it's just possible I may be able to introduce you to the murderer... We're goin' to have another moonlight tour of this room. We're goin' to reproduce the scene of the attempted pushin' down the stairs. I've got high hopes of my little playlet.'

Masters, who had been shifting meditatively from one foot to the other, stiffened. H.M. had spoken so casually that it was a second before they realized the meaning of his words.

'Is this another joke, sir?' said the chief inspector quickly. 'Or do you really mean—?'

'Sure I mean it.'

'And the person who finally killed Miss Tait is one of that

group of five who went with her to look at the staircase last night?'

'Uh-huh. That's what I mean.'

Bennett, who was enumerating the group in his own mind with a greater sense *of* uneasiness than he had yet felt, looked round at Katharine. She made a gesture as though to protest. They all jumped a little as the last of the newspapermen's cars ground into gear with a protesting squawk, and Inspector Potter's parting bellow sounded from the drive below. H.M., who was scowlingly tapping one finger against the end of his nose, seemed to be struck with an idea. He got up and lumbered to the far window in the side wall, which overlooked the end of the *porte-cochère*. A blast of freezing air rattled papers on the table as H.M. unlocked the leaves of the window and pushed them open.

'Hey!' said H.M.

Inspector Potter appeared dimly in the driveway below.

'We're up in the show-room. Hop into the house, will you, son, and get that feller Thompson? Send him up here fast. I've just thought of somethin'. Thanks.'

The window closed with a bang. Masters said:

'But look here, sir, let's get back to the subject! I don't understand this at all. You suddenly and calmly say that you expect to show us the murderer at eleven o'clock. And that you'll do it by reproducing that attempt to shove Miss Tait down the steps...'

'That's right.'

'I'm not going to question your ideas. I'd be the first to admit, sir, that they've been pretty good ones in the past. But what sort of spectacular stunt have you got in your

mind, and what *good* will it do? You can't expect the murderer to obligingly up and shove somebody else, can you?
And it's no good trying to catch anybody out in a lie about
how he or she was standing out there; I've questioned them
all, and they were so confused with only the one candle
burning that nobody remembers where anybody else was.
Well, then! What else—?'

Masters stopped. His dubious gaze wandered over to
the big narrow door of the staircase, with its iron binding
and long iron bolt above a big disused keyhole. H.M., who
watched him out of those small shrewd uncanny eyes, was
imbued with a sort of wooden mirth.

'Ho ho. I know what you're thinkin'!' he volunteered.
'Masters, you got a mind that just naturally runs to melo-
drama. I must 'uv read a dozen stories like that, and they
were funnier than watchin' somebody sit on a silk hat. I
know, I know... We dress up somebody like Tait; say Miss
Bohun here. We put her at the bottom of the stairs. Lights
are turned out; group of people assembles on landing;
light of candle is held up; mysterious ghostly figure is seen
returned from her gibberin' grave. Ghostly figure lifts her
arm and points upstairs, intonin' in a tomb-like voice, "You
done it!" Conscience-stricken murderer instantly screams
and collapses. Burn me, Masters, but wouldn't police work
be a bed of soft rose-petals if the whole business were as
easy as that?'

He meditated, ruffling his hands across his head.

'That's a funny thing, too, Masters. In nine cases out of
ten the murderer would only look bored and tell us to take
off our false whiskers... But I can't help feelin' that this is

the tenth case; and that we really would give X one hell of a shock if we worked a fungus-grown trick like that. It's the imagination that counts: the imagination workin' on a person of this particular type. Brains don't count. Besides, X has plenty of brain right enough, but it didn't help greatly in committing the murder. I said before, and I say again, that the real beauty of it lay in the luckiest accident that ever answered a murderer's prayer...

'But we're not workin' any stale tricks like that, because it'll do no good to scare him if we can't prove anything. I got other ideas. I was just sittin' and thinkin', and all of a sudden I got an idea that'll hang X higher than Judas if it works. If, if, *if!* I dunno that it will. Burn me, Masters, it worries me...'

'I suppose, sir,' the chief inspector growled, 'it's no good asking you—?'

'No. Except for instructions. I want Potter and a couple of men here, placed where I'll tell you; and it won't do any harm to have 'em armed. Then I'm expectin' an answer to a telegram, and I've got to have that or I may look foolish. Above all, I've got to ask that feller Thompson a question that's just about the most important thing in my whole case. Assemblin' my five characters on the landing of that staircase, with *me* playin' the part of Marcia Tait to make it six, won't mean a blasted thing, and it'll all be wasted effort if I get the wrong answer.'

'From Thompson?' demanded Masters. 'A question about what?'

'About his tooth,' said H.M.

'All right!' snapped Masters grimly, after a silence. 'I know this mood, and I know you're serious no matter how you sound. We'll do what you say. But there's one thing I've got to get straight and understood, and at least you can tell me that. This story of Maurice Bohun's about Rainger committing the murder—do you believe it, or don't you? You've scouted every other suggestion, but you didn't shout him down when he spoke. *Is he right?* The thing's got me fair insane, sir; and I swear *I* don't know the truth of it…'

'I do,' said Katharine.

Her voice fell with quiet assurance into the cold room. She stood just in front of the table, her fingers touching it lightly. The light of the electric candles gleamed on the dark hair; her breast rose and fell rapidly under the old tweed coat, but it was the only sign of nervousness.

'You insist,' she said, 'on going through with this—this scheme of yours for tonight, whatever it is?'

'Well, now!' said H.M. He shifted. One hand shaded his eyes. 'I think we'd better, somehow. *You* don't mind, do you?'

'No. But before you start you can rule out one person. Maybe two.'

'That's interestin'. Why, Miss Bohun?'

'Just before you came in here, I heard all about Uncle Maurice's theory. I heard every bit of it. Oh, it's clever. It sounds like him. I don't know whether that man Rainger committed the murder. But I do know that the whole case against him, so far as I can see it, is built up on one person. Without that one person, it may not mean that the case goes to smash…'

'You mean—?'

'Louise.' She brought her fingers down sharply on the table. Then she began to speak more rapidly. 'That Louise went to the pavilion. That afterwards there really wasn't anybody walking in the gallery, who smeared blood on her wrist, and that she invented it all… Now I'll tell you. I heard it all from Dr. Wynne, and he'll swear to it. This morning, after he'd examined Louise, he took Jervis Willard out in the gallery and was going to tell him something. That was when they heard the shot…' Her eyes darted to the scrubbed space on the grey carpet; and she could not continue. 'That was when they heard it. And Dr. Wynne was so busy taking care of John that he didn't mention it again then.

'But it's this. Sometime late last night, he says Louise must have taken a terrific overdose of some sleeping-drug like veronal. You may be able to guess why. Well, she took so much that it had exactly the opposite effect: that is, it kept her mind awake and wild, but it partly paralysed her body. She might have had the idea of going down to that pavilion; she might get hallucinations and even try to go. That may have been where she was going when she collapsed outside my room. But Dr. Wynne is willing to swear after his examination that she took the drug not later than one o'clock, and that for the next four or five hours it would have been absolutely impossible to have walked more than twenty or thirty feet from her own room. It simply couldn't have been done. The farthest she could get was where she did get. She bumped into this person in the dark because she was stumbling all over the gallery; and there was a person, and she didn't imagine it, and, finally, it proves you can't possibly accuse her of murder.'

Masters, who had got out his notebook, lowered it to the table and swore. He stared at H.M.

'Is that possible, sir?'

'Uh-huh. Quite possible. Depends on the dose, and depends on the person even more. Bit reckless to speculate without knowin' a patient's nerve status, but let Wynne have his way. He may be right, he may be wrong. I rather imagine he's wrong, but suit yourself.' A sluggish grin crept over H.M.'s face. 'Well, Masters?'

'You mean, sir, that you believe in Mr. Bohun's explanation?'

H.M. shifted uncomfortably.

'Look here, Masters, I don't want to mix you up any more than's necessary for a very definite purpose. This business is black enough, and tangled enough, as it is. All I can tell you is that I'm not wavin' my hands over the crystal and makin' mysterious noises out of pure cussedness. But there's somethin' you can see for yourself. Miss Bohun's right about one thing. If you accept the hypothesis that Rainger is guilty, then you can't take only the parts of it that appeal to you: you've got to accept all of it or none of it. And the keystone arch of that theory is the girl who says somebody smeared her wrist with blood. If you believe that prowler-in-the-gallery was a myth, all right. But, if you believe he was a real person, then you've got to discard the theory of Rainger's guilt. Because why? Because it would be too staggerin' and monstrous a coincidence to imagine *two* people with blood-stained hands wanderin' about these grounds. And, at the time that girl says she bumped into her man in this house, by the very basis of Maurice Bohun's theory *Rainger must have been at the pavilion.* He never left the pavilion until he walked back in John's tracks. Right you are, then. Either the prowler-in-the-gallery is a myth, or else he ain't. But if he ain't a myth, then you've shaken the theory and done somethin' towards establishin' Rainger's innocence.'

Masters took a few lumbering paces, as though he were measuring spots in the carpet. Then he turned in angry uneasiness.

'Just so. Just so, sir. And that's what jars me about your orders. You've refused to let me question Miss Carewe, or question her yourself—'

'Ho ho! You're jolly well right I have, son.'

'And you don't seem to want to question Rainger either. Eh? Barring, I mean, your going into a conference with Emery and telling him to get Rainger sober as soon as possible...'

H.M. opened one eye. 'I don't think you quite understood what I said, Masters. My instructions to Emery were to keep Rainger as sodden drunk as possible. Uh-huh. To sit by his bedside with a wary eye out, and shove a drink under his nose the moment he showed signs of stirrin'. Emery thinks I'm off my onion. Like you. But I promised to introduce him to the murderer of his wife, and he's obeying orders. Like you.'

A slow, weird expression began to dawn across Masters's face, and H.M. nodded with malevolent glee.

'At last! I knew sooner or later you'd see it. Uh-huh. And you're exactly right. That's it. I don't *want* to question either the Carewe girl or Rainger, especially Rainger. I tell you frankly, son, that if once Rainger gets the opportunity of replyin' to the accusation against him, then I'm *licked*... All I need is a couple of hours free, but I need 'em badly. And this is by way of prelude to requestin' you, Miss Bohun, whatever else you do in the next three hours, for God's sake don't mention Dr. Wynne's report about your friend. Got it?'

His voice was very low, lower than the wind that had begun to rumble in the chimney, but it seemed to echo in the cold room. He was bending forward with his dusty bald head under the light; but it was as though he grew to enormous size against massive grey-and-black furnishings. Snowflakes ticked and flew against the windows. The nightmare sensation had come back to Bennett. With that shift in the wind, he thought he could distinguish in its blast an echo of something he had heard that morning.

'Do you,' said Katharine suddenly, 'do you hear a dog howling?'

They all heard it; but nobody spoke until Katharine turned round and nodded briefly. 'You'll have to excuse me,' she said in a colourless voice. 'It's late. I must dress.'

XVII

CONCERNING MURDER
ON A LAMP-SHADE

'Rummy, sir,' said Masters, with genial uneasiness, 'the ideas you get, eh?' He clucked his tongue and tried to smile. 'I've been interviewing servants, you know. They all said that Alsatian was howling this morning just before—I'm very fond of dogs. Now what?'

H.M. pinched the side of his jaw. His dull eye wandered round the room; and his stolid bulk conveyed somehow an impression of restlessness.

'Hey? Oh! Now! Well, I'll tell you what. You and the young 'un go down and look in on Rainger. Make sure he's sleepin' the sleep of the just. Dammit, where do you suppose Potter's got to with that butler? I want to talk with him, and then I want a look round this room. Ah!' He nodded almost affably when there was a knock at the door. Inspector Potter towered behind a rather frightened Thompson.

'*Enfin!*' growled H.M. 'You're the man I want to see. Tut, now, I ain't goin' to hurt you! You may stay, Potter. Cut along, you other chaps. Come back here when you've finished.

Rrrum! Now, then. I want to know just how bad that jaw of yours was last night, Thompson. Toothache's the devil, ain't it? I know. I was wonderin' if it let you get any sleep at all last night? If, for instance, you might have dozed off a bit towards the end of the night, about four or five o'clock...'

That was all Masters and Bennett heard, for Masters closed the door. Then the stolid chief inspector lifted a big fist and shook it with violent pantomime in the dimly lighted gallery. Bennett said:

'What's on his mind? Have you got the cloudiest notion what's on his mind?'

'Yes,' said Masters, and let his hand fall. 'Yes. But, I tell you straight, I don't like to think what it means. Or—no. 'Tisn't exactly that I don't like to think of it, if he's got his eye on the man I think he has. But I don't see how he's going to prove it. There's gentlemen that are apt to be a bit too canny even for him. Above all, I don't see what he hopes to gain by reconstructing that attempt on the lady's life last night. Blast it, that seems unimportant! It's not as though the thing succeeded, you know.'

'Yes. That's it. Can you hear that dog howling now?'

'All dogs howl,' said Masters curtly. 'It seems we've got a job of work. Let's go to the chap's room and take his pulse. Great work for the C.I.D. Eh? If he's not satisfactorily in a stupor, we shall probably catch it from Sir Henry. This way.'

Rainger's room was near the head of the staircase, just at the turn of the gallery in the comparatively modern part of the house. A light shone out over the transom, and the door was partly open. Almost instinctively Masters jerked back as he heard voices. One was a woman's, and it choked

something between sobs. The other was Emery's, shrill
with a sort of wild patience.

'Now listen!' Emery urged. 'I've been trying to tell you
for five minutes—stop bawling, will you? You've got me so
jittery I can't sit still. Quit it! If you've got anything to tell
me, go on and tell it. I'm listening. Here, for God's sake, have
some of this—have a drink of gin, huh? Now, listen, Miss
Umm—what'd you say your name was?'

'Beryl, sir. Beryl Symonds.'

'All right! Now take it easy. What were you trying to say?'
The choking voice controlled itself. 'I tried, sir, honestly I
tried to tell the gentleman this afternoon, really I did, but
he was so *awful* blued that all he did was make a g-grab for
me. And I was going to tell him I couldn't tell the master,
because, of course, the master w-wouldn't understand and I
should simply get the *s-sack!*'

'Look,' said Emery. 'Are you trying to tell me Carl made a
pass at you? Is that it?'

'They said you were a friend of his, sir, and you won't
make me tell! You mustn't. He told me this morning when
I brought him his tea, "You was right"; that's what 'e said;
"you was right!" I mean, for turning the key last night. And
I told him what they was saying about the murder being
done, and he turned a funny colour first—he was already
getting blued, you see—and he come running after me,
truly he did, pulling on a bathrobe and saying, "Good girl,
good girl; well, if I come into this, you know where *I* was last
night, don't you?" And I said, Yes. But—'

Masters knocked at the door and pushed it open with
almost the same gesture.

Something that was probably sheer terror prevented the girl from screaming out. She jerked back and said, 'OhmyGod, it's the police!' It was Emery, white-faced and dishevelled, who leaped up from his chair, spilling a lurid-covered magazine out of his lap; and he choked back a nervous yelp just in time.

He had been sitting beside a tumbled bed, empty, and near him on the table burned a lamp with a newspaper tied round its shade. There were several bottles, two of them empty, on the table; it was sticky with lemon-peel, soda-water, and sugar; and even the filled ash-trays were damp. Stale smoke hung against the dull lamplight, and the air was nauseously bad.

'Quite right,' said Masters. 'It's the police. And *I'm* the one who wants to hear your story, miss.'

'Look,' said Emery. He sat down again. He took the stump of a cigarette from a corner of the ash-tray, and his hand shook when he put it to his lips. 'What kind of crazy business is going on in this place? Somebody knocks at the door, and you open it and there's nobody there. And the lights are out. And somebody ducks around a corner of the hall...'

'What's this?'

'I'm not kidding you! Ask *her*. It was a little while ago; I don't know when. It can't be Carl being funny, because he never gets that kind of a drunk. Never has, since I've known him. I'm telling you, it scared the pants off me for a second. Like somebody was calling my attention to something. I don't know. Crazy, like.'

Masters's glance darted to the bed. 'Where,' he said, 'is Mr. Rainger?'

'Oh, *he's* all right. He went out to—' Emery glanced at the girl, checked himself, and said: 'He went to the bath. They feel better when you let 'em alone. But I'm telling you, Cap, that man can't hold much more liquor, or you're gonna have a case of acute alcoholism on your hands. He—'

'Yes,' said Masters. 'The young lady.'

Beryl Symonds had backed away. She was a small brunette, with a pretty if rather heavy face, a somewhat dumpy figure, and earnest brown eyes swollen with weeping. She wore a maid's cap and apron, which she seemed trying to arrange.

She burst out suddenly: 'I seen all his pictures! He directs 'em. His name's in as big letters as 'ers. And I couldn't see the harm in talking, but I don't want the sack. Please I don't want the sack!'

'I talked to you,' said Masters, with slow deadliness, 'this afternoon. You said you knew nothing about what had happened last night. That'll tell against you, you know. Were you ever up before a magistrate?'

By degrees they got the story. Bennett, always with the twisted, despairing, and rather ludicrous figure of Rainger in his mind, wondered why he had not anticipated it. Psychologically, it was almost inevitable with Rainger. He might even have anticipated the twisted and ludicrous sequel. Beryl Symonds had been told to light the fire and prepare Rainger's room when he arrived the afternoon before. He had seen her then; but he had done nothing but give her a certain jocose pinch ('which some gentlemen does, and some gentlemen doesn't'), and mutter arch incomprehensibilities as she left the room. She had been All of a Flutter, really. And flattered. She had not seen him until late last night, at eleven o'clock, when she was going up to bed. The master and his guests had been coming back from looking at King Charles's Room. Rainger was some little distance behind the rest, seeming 'upset, and mad, and very funny.' All of a sudden he stopped and looked at her, waiting till the others were out of sight...

Inevitable? Well, the idea had been that she was to come down to his room at two o'clock when the rest were asleep and he should tell her all about Hollywood. He said that he had a bottle of gin. He said to hell with everything. And she was so much All of a Flutter with the romantic adventure, 'just like the films he makes, and think of *me* in them,' that she had said maybe. She went upstairs with the flutter grow-ing; she whispered it to Stella, who had the same room with her, and Stella had a fit and said, 'Holy Mother, don't be a daft silly; suppose the master sees you?'

'Never mind that,' said Masters. 'Did you come down at two o'clock?'

But both he and Bennett were beginning to realize the meaning of Rainger's last satiric snarl at Kate Bohun when he went upstairs at half-past one. Beryl cried out, and kept repeating over and over, that all she had meant was to come down and *look* at him. She seemed to derive strength from this notion of coming down for a last look, and reconnoitring, and making up her mind when she saw him then.

'But when I did go down, I knew I oughtn't to stay the minute I got inside the door. Because Mr. Rainger was a-drinking already, and walking about, and muttering things to himself. Then he turned round and saw me. He started to laugh. For a minute when I saw his face I was so clear awful frightened I couldn't move; that's when I knew it was wrong to come down...'

'Yes, yes; never mind that. What did you do?'

''E started over after me, sir. And then I saw the key was in the outside of the door, so I got out and pulled the door shut and turned the key in the lock.'

Masters looked at Bennett, and slowly rubbed his hand across his forehead.

'But you opened it again, I dare say?' he demanded.

'*No, sir!* I even held on to the knob outside, and I'd got such a scare I didn't move. And then he called, not very loud, so I could hear him through the transom; 'e said, "What's the idea of this?" That's what 'e said. And then started to get mad and said, "Better open that door, if you don't want me to smash it and rouse the 'ouse, and then where'll you be?" And I couldn't think of anything to say, except I said, "You'd better not," I said, "because if you do you'll look an awful silly ass, sir, won't you?"'

Beryl swallowed hard. She stared from one to the other of them.

'It was all I could think of to say!' she cried defensively. 'And, anyway, it usually stops the gentlemen.'

'Quite,' said Masters, with non-committal heaviness. 'Well?'

'Then I didn't know what to do, sir, because I *was* afraid to unlock it, and I didn't want to stay there in the gallery for fear the master might come along like 'e does. So I backed away and stood at the end of the gallery. And he didn't say anything, or make any more noise at all, till 'e tried to climb out through the transom.'

'Through the transom,' repeated Masters. 'What was he wearing then?'

'Wearing? I won't stand,' cried Beryl, 'for them hints! I won't! I'd rather get the s-sack. 'E was dressed! 'E was in shirt-sleeves. But I knew he couldn't get out by the transom, because it opens the other way; and all he did was get himself mucky on the shoulders a-trying to squeeze through. So he stopped. And I heard 'im say, "You're still there, I'll bet. Never mind. I'm a-going to get drunk." And he laughed a little. And I was so frightened at the way he said that...sir, I ran on upstairs, and that's the truth so help me, and I didn't let 'im out till morning.'

Masters lowered his head.

'Sunk,' he said. 'Second explanation shot to blazes. *And* Sir Henry knew it would be, somehow. So that's what the chap meant by saying he had an alibi!' He turned fiercely to Beryl. 'Well? What about this morning?'

'Why, I opened the door. And in the meantime there was this awful talk about murder. So I thought, "Aaoow! If 'e tries to say anything to me, and 'e's mad, I'll stop him by telling him first off Miss Tait's gone, poor lady—"' For a moment Beryl's tears nearly overflowed again. 'And it w-worked. So help me, I thought it'd kill 'im. And right away he grabbed my arm and said, "Bohun did it, didn't he? Where's Bohun now?" And I said, "The Master?" And 'e said—you know, a word I won't say—"No! the other one." And I said I didn't know what could 'ave 'appened to Mr. John, because his bed wasn't slept in, but his things was scattered about; and I told him what I'd 'eard downstairs. Then he wanted me to tell them, in case there was trouble for 'im, about being locked in the room. And I said I would, just to get away from him then. But now Stella's saying the master says 'e *did* do it, and I was trying to tell this gentleman...'

'Get out,' said Masters.

'Sir?'

'Go on, miss. Hop it! That's all. Now, now, don't come grabbing my arm, miss; I'll see what can be done about you. I'm a copper, blast it! That's all I can say, but I'll do what I can.'

When she had been urged out of the door, Masters turned back again and shook his fist.

Masters said bitterly: 'Very fine and revealing. I'm beginning to see through Rainger to the core. I understand now what's been on his mind; I understand every word he said to us this morning; and I also see why he wasn't anxious to explain what his alibi was. But it don't *help* us! Eh?'

'He's taking,' said Bennett, 'a devil of a long time to come back here.'

He was startled at his own words. Staring at the empty and tumbled bed, at the mess of bottles on the table, he found himself half hypnotized by the glow of the lamp with the newspaper round its shade. The light gleamed through smeary print, and a part of a headline was traced out on it. He could make out only one word, shaky on the crumpled paper, but it grew more clear in black letters as he looked...

'A long time,' he repeated, 'to come back. Oughtn't we—?'

'Nonsense!' said Masters. 'There's somebody coming now.'

It was not Rainger. It was H.M., alone. He stood massive in the doorway; still inscrutable, but humped and dangerous. He came in, closed the door after looking round outside, and stood against it.

Masters wearily took out his notebook. 'We've got more evidence, sir. I don't know whether you suspected it or not, but Rainger's got an alibi. There's a girl... I'll read it to you. Rainger hasn't come back yet, but it clears him absolutely.'

'You don't need it, son,' replied H.M. slowly. 'He's never comin' back.'

The terrible deadness and force of those words struck into the room as sharply as a cry. Outside the wind had fallen nearly to silence; the whole house was very still. Bennett glanced at H.M., who stood with his arms outspread against the tall door, and then back again to the dull-glowing newspaper round the lamp. The word that stood out was *murder.*

After a silence H.M. lumbered up to the table. He glanced at Masters and then Bennett and then Emery.

'We four,' he said, 'are goin' to have a council-of-war about tonight. My scheme still holds, y'see; and the insane part of all this is that the scheme's better than ever, if we've got the nerve and the callousness to put it through. D'you believe in the devil, Masters? Do you believe in the devil as a human entity, that listens at keyholes and taps at doors and moves people's lives like a set of dominoes?... Steady, now. Rainger's dead. He was strangled and thrown down those stairs in King Charles's Room. Poor swine! He was too drunk to defend himself, but not too drunk to think. Thinking killed him. What's that you got in the bottle? Gin? I hate gin, but I'll take one neat. He wasn't very pretty in life, and he's even less pretty when he's dead. I can rather sympathize with him now.'

'But,' Emery shrilled, 'he went out to—'

'Uh-huh. That's what you thought. Ever know that chap when he was too far gone to keep some part of his brain still clickin'? He went out, and surprised Somebody down in that room at the end of the gallery. Somebody strangled him and chucked him downstairs... I'm a pompous ass, ain't I?' inquired H.M., opening and shutting his hands. He peered at Bennett. 'I kept jeerin' at your bogies and noises. And, all the while I was sittin' in that room, that poor frustrated swine of a Rainger was lying at the foot of the steps with his face blue and finger-marks on his throat. But how was I to know it? I only suspected one thing. I didn't suspect murder. We only saw it when Potter and I looked at the stairs.—Easy, Masters! Where are you goin'?'

The chief inspector's voice shook a little. 'Where would I be going, sir?' he demanded. 'This puts the lid on it! I'm going to find out where everybody in this house...'

'No, you're not, son. Not if I can prevent you. Nobody else in this house is to know he's dead.'

'That's what I said. Potter's guardin' him, and Potter won't let anybody in. What can we do for him now, except piously take off our hats? He's dead. We're goin' to leave him exactly where he is, Masters, for maybe a few hours. It may be a brutal trick; it may be insultin' the clay to turn it into a dummy for a show; but the show's goin' to go on according to programme. When our little group goes to that staircase in the dark, and the candle's held up, they'll see him down there just as he fell. All right. I'll have that drink now.'

He took bottle and glass from Emery's unsteady hands, and then looked at Emery, who had sat down on the bed.

'I got some instructions for *you*, son. I want you to listen carefully, and for God's sake don't deviate from what I tell you. You're the only one who can carry it off to convince 'em, because you're Rainger's friend. You're not to go down to dinner. You're to stay here, with that door locked on the inside. If anybody comes to the door, *no matter who it is or on whatever pretext*, you're not to open it. You're to tell 'em through the door that Rainger is waking up from his stupor, but that he's a pretty unsightly object and you won't show him until he's presentable. Got that?'

'Yes, but—'

'All right. As soon after dinner as we can manage, the whole crowd of us will come up here for a little experiment in King Charles's Room. Never mind exactly what it is. If anybody tries to rout Rainger out to make him take part in it, use the same excuse as before. Jim Bennett here will take Rainger's place in the experiment, and I'm going to be Marcia Tait. I don't dare have Masters directly on the scene; and he's goin' to be, for a certain very good reason, at the foot of the staircase. When we've gone into King Charles's Room, so that they still think you're back here, sneak out of this room; go down there; stand in the doorway, and watch. They probably won't notice you. They'll be on the landing, and there'll be no lights, but a candle. *Whatever you see or hear that you don't expect*, don't say anything until I give you the word. Is that clear?'

Masters struck his fist on the table.

'But look here, sir! Can't you give us some intimation as

to what you do expect? I'll fall in with this lunacy, if you like. But you're not mad enough to imagine that the murderer will give himself away when he sees Rainger's body down there, are you? The murderer knows it's there.'

H.M. regarded him curiously. With a shark-like gulp, and without apparent effort, he swallowed three fingers of neat gin. Then he stared at the glass.

'You still don't see it, do you? Well, never mind. I got some instructions for you, too. Better come down with me and take a look at Rainger. I'm afraid the devil hasn't left much of a signature; but we'll grub round a bit and see. Hey!' He shook Emery's shoulder. 'Pull yourself together, son. Yes, and *you*, too. Fine nephew I got, lookin' pale around the gills! When you go down to dinner, act natural! Understand?'

'I'm all right,' said Bennett. 'But I was just wondering how much dinner you expect a person to eat. Is that included, with your little scheme in front of us? Look here, sir, it's not on the level! It's a damned dirty trick! Pull all the games you like on us, but what about those women? What are they going to feel like when they look down? Louise has had about enough shocks as it is; and you know she's not guilty. You know Kate isn't guilty either. Then what's the use in dangling a dead man in front of them, like a kid with a rubber spider on a wire?'

H.M. set down the glass. He lumbered to the door, and turned only when he beckoned to Masters.

'It's a conjurin' trick,' he said, 'that I can't explain now. But I've got to do it. And my rubber spider's goin' to bite somebody, son, unless I'm very much mistaken. All I've got to tell you is that you'll let me down badly, and you'll do something that won't be pleasant for you to remember when you see the consequences, if you give a hint to anybody as to what's goin' on. Understand? *Anybody.* Come on, Masters.'

He opened the door. Mellow and deep through the house, but with something in its note at once of terror and finality, quivered the stroke of the dinner-gong.

XVIII
GAMBITS REPLAYED

'I think,' said Maurice Bohun, slowly brushing one hand across the palm of the other, as though he were wiping a slate, 'I think we are almost ready to proceed with the curious experiment Sir Henry has suggested?' He looked up from contemplating his hands. 'I may say that it will not, of course, lead us to anything that concerns the actual murderer of Miss Tait. Although at Sir Henry's express wish I have refrained from telling all of you the fact—that is, until such time as a certain gentleman shall be in a condition to defend himself— nevertheless we ourselves have little doubt. *But...*'

How Bennett got through that dinner he could never afterwards remember. Against his own inclination and even against his own will, something had compelled him to go to the King's Room before he went downstairs. He could not be content, with his mind full of troubled horrors as to what the thing might look like, until he had looked at it and curbed his imagination. Afterwards he wished he had not. It was a price. Inspector Potter stood guard at the door to the gallery: there were no lights on in the room, and only a sickly moonlight had begun to penetrate through the windows. But the door to the secret staircase was open in a strong draught, and flashlights moved at the bottom where H.M. talked in low tones to Masters. He moved over to this door. He had not realized how high and steep and dangerous this staircase was: how the uneven stone steps, between narrow walls that smelled like a cellar, seemed to plunge down into a pit. Masters's light flashed up into his face so suddenly that he almost lost his balance. Then the beam turned down again on the other face, the face that was twisted back over one of the treads, and did not blink its eyes before the light.

Dinner, to which Bennett presently sat down with five others—H.M., Maurice, Willard, Katharine, and Louise— was turned by Maurice into a hideous formality. Afterwards Bennett liked to forget it. Everybody except the host was conscious of a new strain, as though they felt without being told that death had come to the house again. When he went down to the library, he saw Louise for the first time since landing in England. She sat near the fire, wearing dark blue, with her mouse-coloured hair flat and parted in the middle. In whatever cloudy mental picture he had already formed, he had always remembered her as short and thickset, her freckles predominating and her age as vaguely twenty-eight. He was surprised how thin she seemed now, her eyes dark-rimmed, but surprisingly fine. Emotional strain had made a ghost of her, and yet a far from dowdy ghost. Her age might have been forty.

He mumbled a platitude or two. There was nothing to say, and he would not make the mistake of trying to say it. She smiled mechanically when she extended her hand; then clasped it about a handkerchief and stared into the fire, seeming to forget the rest of them. Maurice—burnished out in prim elegance—was very gracious, and extolled the sherry he offered them 'to replace the detestable fashion of cocktails.' His thin laugh rang under the roof. Jervis Willard was quiet and courteous, but he had begun to pace about the library with that caged stride of his, and you saw that he needed a shave. When H.M. lumbered in, blinking and mumbling amiably at everybody, Bennett thought that they all started a little. He could not tell whether the subject of the night's experiment had yet been mentioned. Katharine came down last of all. She was in plain black, without jewellery or ornament, but her shoulders gleamed against the dark panelling.

For Bennett, her presence suddenly intensified the terror that was on this group. She was reality, she was the warmth and beauty he knew; any of the others might have been goblins behind a mask, and one of them *was*. That was the evil uncertainty which made grotesque this business of walking in to dinner, and (worse) of eating it. Of course they stumbled on the subject, which might have been accident, as soon as they went into the dim and draughty dining-hall.

'I have ordered,' said Maurice, nodding in the candlelight, 'an extra chair for the table…'

The scraping of footfalls seemed to change and waver.

'An extra place?' said Katharine.

'For Mr. Rainger, of course,' her uncle pointed out softly, 'in case he should feel well enough to come down. You did not misunderstand, Kate?' He nodded to Thompson, and he was smiling as he turned in mild surprise. 'Mr. Emery tells me that he is not in a condition to sit down with us tonight...

'You spoke, Sir Henry?' he added quickly.

'Did I?' grunted H.M. 'Well, there, now! I must 'a' been thinkin' of something else. I was only thinkin', wonderful constitution that feller Rainger must have.'

Chairs scraped. 'Most extraordinary,' Maurice agreed. 'He would struggle to the end. Even to a rope's end, I should fancy.' His ghoulish high spirits seemed to whip him on. Somewhere at the table a spoon rattled against a plate. 'Come, Kate! You really must eat. I can recommend this soup. If you insist on coming undressed to the table, you must have something to keep you warm. Or perhaps that element has already been supplied? Our young friend from America seems—ah—to evince a similar lack of appetite, from which I seem to deduce material conclusions, may I say? Yes. But it is not flattering to a host. Surely—ah, my boy, you do not think you are dining with the Borgia?'

'No, sir,' said Bennett. He felt a small and undiplomatic hammer beginning to beat in his temple. He looked up. 'With the Borgia, you at least knew what to expect.'

'But surely,' said Maurice in a remonstrating tone, 'surely American—ah—"push" and inventiveness would have found a quick way in matters culinary as well as amatory? Would you really have been afraid of poison; or would you not have found a way of giving the poison to the Borgia himself?'

'No, sir,' said Bennett. 'Only castor oil.'

'Do have some of your own soup, Uncle Maurice,' urged

Katharine. She suddenly leaned back and began to laugh hysterically. It had a thin sound in the big room; and it was as though the draught that passed over the candle-flames symbolized a new presence there. Jervis Willard's heavy and sardonic gaze moved round the table.

'I say, Maurice,' he observed, 'I don't want to interrupt all this pleasant theorizing about soup and poison. But let's be sensible for a while, shall we? In the first place, all this can't be very pleasant hearing for—' He stopped. He seemed again heavy and bewildered, as he had been that afternoon; and now it was as though he were cursing himself for saying something he had not intended.

'I don't mind,' said Louise, in a thin but clear voice. She looked up from studying the table. 'I wasn't trying to poison myself, you know. Only to sleep. It's a curious thing, but I don't mind anything now. All I want is to get a train back to town, and see that father's all right, and isn't—upset.'

They had not told her about the trouble with John Bohun even yet: so much was clear from her tone. But Bennett, glancing swiftly at Maurice, thought he could follow at least a part of the thought that twisted behind those flickering dead-grey eyes. Maurice weighed surgical knives, wondering which to apply. He chose the second knife.

'A train back to town?' he repeated. 'I feel sure we all applaud your solicitude, and so would my brother John if he were here. But I fear the police would not be so obliging. Perhaps nobody has heard? Ah! Well, we are to act our parts as of last night; we are to re-enact the attempted murder of poor Marcia on the staircase in King Charles's Room. Sir Henry thinks it should be helpful. For the moment I will say no more. I should be deeply regretful if I were to spoil anyone's dinner.'

A start went round the table; more, it seemed, of surprise than any other feeling. Thompson moved in deftly, and, as though everybody became aware of his presence, there was a silence for a long time. The moving of the dishes seemed unnaturally loud. Although Bennett did not look up, he found himself watching *hands.* Hands against the dark polished oak of the table, moving, idle, shifting against the silver. Maurice's slender hands, with shadows hollowed along the backs, brushed together with a washing motion. Louise's pink-tinted nails making a faint scraping noise on the oak. Willard's big spatulate fingers, the forefinger tapping slowly on the line of spoons. Katharine's hands, as white as the laced linen circles for the dishes, clenched and motionless. Then Bennett glanced at Rainger's empty chair, and remembered a scene at the bottom of the stairs where somebody's hands had been busy...

'What's this nonsense?' demanded Willard.

'I trust,' said Maurice, 'nobody has any objection? It would look exceedingly odd to Sir Henry, you know.'

Katharine said in a clear voice: 'I think it's rather horrible. But if we must go on with it, we must. Still, I shouldn't think *you* would take much interest in reconstructing the scene of any attempt, Uncle Maurice, if Mr. Rainger couldn't be there.'

'I have my reasons,' Maurice answered, nodding meditatively. 'It is most interesting, even if Mr. Rainger's place must be taken by somebody else. I venture to assert that our young friend from America will have considerably more success in the part than Mr. Rainger. Let us say no more about it.'

The dinner dragged on. It was, he supposed, a good dinner; but to Bennett the very steam was nauseous, and the bursts of conversation were worse. Maurice lingered over every course, descanting. A clock struck eight-thirty. When Katharine and Louise tried to withdraw from the table as Thompson set out the decanters, Maurice's thin voice forbade them. H.M., who had not spoken throughout, sat back wooden and motionless. The sharp noise of Maurice cracking nuts sounded thin in the big room. Now the firelight had begun to die down, and the moon was high beyond one wall of windows...

Crack. A faint thump as the nut-cracker was put down. Bennett suddenly pushed his cold coffee away...

'I think,' said Maurice, 'that we are almost ready to proceed with the curious experiment Sir Henry has suggested. I may say that it will not, of course, lead us to anything that concerns the actual murderer of Miss Tait. Although at Sir Henry's express wish I have refrained from telling all of you the facts, nevertheless we ourselves have little doubt. *But* this reconstruction should be most interesting to some of us, particularly'—*crack!* the little steel jaws snapped again—'my dear young friend Louise. Ha ha ha. Besides, I am always willing to lecture on the beauties of the White Priory, as I did last night. Sir Henry, do you wish me to take all of you on a full round of the house, as last night?'

'No,' said H.M. They seemed a trifle startled to remember that he was there. 'Nothin' so elaborate as that. We'll start from here, and go up to the room. Humph. I got no objection to your lecturin', if you like. Besides, I shouldn't be much good in Tait's part, should I? Hey? No. We'll simply imagine she's here. It'll be easier, in the dark. Imagine she's walkin' between you and me. We'll go on ahead, and the others can follow in the order they did last night.'

Maurice rose. 'Quite so. Louise with my friend Jervis. Little Kate with Mr. Bennett in the role of our other absent guest. I should earnestly recommend that each person act as he or she did last night. As for myself, I have so often fancied I walked and talked with dead ladies in this house that it will scarcely be a strain on my imagination to see the latest of them walking beside me... Thompson, you may blow out all the candles except one.'

As each candle puffed out, it was like the driving of a nail into a door that shut them back into the past: even though it were only the equally irrevocable past of last night. The moonlight probed down through the wall of windows, touching silhouettes and the sides of faces turned the colour of skim milk. Feet shuffled. The little yellow flame from the candle in Maurice's hand flickered as he raised it aloft. It touched a portrait, a darkened and paint-cracked portrait of a woman in a yellow gown, the semblance of whose inscrutable eyes they recognized an instant before the light lowered again.

'This way,' said Maurice.

Again the footsteps rasped on stone. The pin-point flame moved ahead. Bennett felt Katharine's arm trembling against his own. It was just when they moved out into the maze of passages that Maurice's thin voice began to speak smoothly and pleasantly.

'It is an interesting thing concerning this fleshly charmer,' he said, smirking down at an empty space under the candle-flame, 'that, apart from the one affair with a monarch which may be only likened in analogy to a tolerant Providence protecting her, her life was chiefly distinguished by the love of four men. One was a famous actor. One was a playwright. One was a dashing captain whose first name was John. One, of course, was her complacent husband.

'I refer—ah—to Barbara Villiers Palmer, first Lady Castlemaine and later Duchess of Cleveland. The actor was Charles Hart, the grand-nephew of Shakespeare and Drury Lane's great tragedian; who, they said, could teach any king how to comport himself. The playwright was William Wycherley, a witty dog, ha ha, who complimented her Grace on "understanding nothing better than obliging all the world after the best and most proper fashion." The dashing captain was John Churchill, later to become famous (for his love of money) as the Duke of Marlborough. The husband was little Roger Palmer, who never mattered at all…

'There were others, of course. There was a grubby rope-dancer of low beginnings, named Jacob Hall, who sometimes directed the Punch-and-Judy shows at St Bartholomew's Fair. Late in her career, there was an old white-haired rake called Beau Fielding, who wished to marry her, and did marry her. Beau Fielding, by the way, had a grown daughter. It has occurred to me to wonder that if the course of capricious time were turned and altered…'

Dimly ahead Bennett could see the silhouettes of Louise and Willard. From her strained tensity he could guess that Louise was staring ahead as though she tried to make out something in the gloom. She shook as though she were cold, and Willard gently touched her arm. Bennett could have sworn that a board creaked in the staircase before either Maurice or H.M. set foot on it. He looked round. He and Katharine had lagged far behind the others. He could see her eyes distinctly in the gloom as she looked up.

'This,' she said, 'is where...'

'Yes. And I'm Rainger.'

His hands touched her shoulders and tightened. It was an insane business, but the crazy fates were decreeing it as inevitably as they drew that group to King Charles's Room. It may have lasted a second or two minutes, a hot blankness while he felt her body trembling; then he felt her lips move round and heard above the enormous pounding of his heart some whisper like, '—join Willard, you with Louise.' She tore away before he could blurt out, 'When you get to that room, *don't look downstairs*'; and he thought he must have said them aloud. But he could be sure of nothing in the shaken darkness of that moment, except that his wits were bewildered and that he had forgotten for a moment where the real Rainger was.

Love and death, love and death, and Katharine's lips. The candle-flame moved on ahead up the stairs, touching tall gilt-framed portraits; and another picture of the damned woman leaped out of gloom. Barbara Villiers or Marcia Tait, the portrait was smiling... He glanced down, and was surprised to find that it was Louise who walked beside him now. She did not look at him; her hands were gripped together, a knuckle-joint cracked and Maurice's voice flowed on thinly ahead:

'—along this gallery. You will notice the chairs as being of royal property; the king's arms, a crown supported by two lions rampant and enwoven with the letters C.R., have been worked into the top of the chair-back...'

Bennett stammered something to Louise without knowing what it was, but he was startled to see the fierce fixity of her look ahead. The light approached the door of the King's Room...

'And here—' said Maurice. He stopped. 'This door,' he snapped, 'this door is locked!'

'Uh, yes. Yes, so it is,' said H.M. 'Well, never mind. I got the key. Wait till I open it, now.'

A lock clicked. Bennett thought, '*Here we go!*' with the feeling of a man who leaps from an unknown height with his eyes bandaged.

'Over to the staircase door,' boomed H.M.'s voice, rising suddenly along the gallery, 'in exactly the same positions you had last night. Don't anybody hesitate. Keep on goin'; that's it.'

The candle moved into the room. They could see dimly that the staircase door was ajar, and feel the draught. Bennett caught up in a press of more people than he had imagined were there, and he heard somebody breathing hard. Maurice went out on the landing first, shielding the candle with his hand. Katharine followed him. Bennett, not knowing where Rainger had been or what to do, followed her with the vague hope of shutting off her view downwards. Probably the glow of the candle could not penetrate so far; he hoped so. Willard went in next, and H.M. had to urge Louise by the elbow. Darting a glance over his shoulder, Bennett could as yet make out nothing in the dark at the foot of the stairs. He had a wild, irrational fancy of being jammed into a crowded subway train without lights, a train that was roaring through a tunnel as dark as itself; and the fancy was strengthened by H.M.'s big and deadly figure at the door.

'Now then,' said H.M., 'I'm goin' to close this door on you for a second. I'll come in with you as though I were standin' where *she* stood, and then somebody blow out the candle. Then I'll flash a light on you while you move as you moved then, and I'll flash it downstairs so you can imagine exactly what she'd have looked like if she had fallen when somebody pushed her. And, if you should happen to see anything at the bottom of the steps...'

He opened the door a little wider. The draught caught the candle-flame, and it leaped and went out. They heard the door close, so that they were shut up in the dark.

The unseen height was worse than the seen; it was as though the darkness were contracting to force them plunging down from the height. Bennett thought: 'One little shove from anybody—' He felt a movement tremble through the group, and a gasp, just as he discovered that his own heel was on the edge of the chasm.

Far below in the pit, something stirred.

'I can't stand this,' said a voice behind Bennett quietly and quickly. 'Let me out.'

First the voice, which belonged to Louise Carewe, broke and trembled into a hysterical key. Then it began with a rising moan like a woman under an anaesthetic.

'You shan't force me,' she said. 'You won't make me jump over. I know that's what you want to make me do, but I won't. I won't, do you hear? Let me out. Turn on a light. I'm not sorry. I'd push her again. Oh, for God's sake, turn on a light and let me out, let me out of here before—'

Something gave a wild and blind rush. Bennett felt his heel slip off into nowhere, his hand go out over a bottomless gulf. His stomach seemed to rush up as he felt himself falling; but even in that second he knew he must not clutch at anybody or there would be two broken necks. The heel met gritty stone; his hip twisted, and then he crashed backwards into the side of the wall...

He was still there. He had not fallen, for he was pulling himself up with shoulder and leg muscles quivering like jangled strings even as the press elbowed back into the King's Room.

'Lights!' he heard H.M. shout. 'You, over by the door! Emery! Turn those lights on...'

A glare sprang up and filtered out on to the landing. Shaken and still unsteady, Bennett pulled himself upright from a crab-like position against the wall several treads down. Kate Bohun was helping him. They got through into King Charles's Room. The group had scattered back as though they surrounded a bomb. H.M. had just made a fierce gesture to Emery, who stood at the light-switch with a rather more startled expression on his face than the sound of a confession from Louise Carewe would seem to warrant. Through Bennett's mind flashed H.M.'s instructions to Emery. '*Whatever you see or hear, don't speak until*—'

What? What was the damned game, and what was there to be seen?

Bennett stared at Louise, who stood in the middle of

the room with the others round her. Maurice was smiling, and Willard passing a hand over his face in evident bewilderment.

'Don't look at me,' said Louise in a low voice. She was panting, and her hair had been disarranged. She seemed to hold her head low as she looked swiftly round the group. 'Don't you know anything besides cheap tricks? Isn't it cheap and cheap and more cheap? I pushed her. What of it? I'd do it again.'

Maurice help up the brass candlestick as though in salute. 'Thank you, my dear girl,' he said gently. 'That was all Sir Henry and I wished to know. It *was* you who attempted the murder. We know you didn't kill Miss Tait and that Rainger did. We simply wished to complete the picture. That was all Sir Henry and I cared to know.'

'*Was it?*' inquired H.M.

He raised his voice only a little, but it echoed.

'So you told me, I think,' said Maurice. 'It has been a success. She admits having attempted to kill Marcia. Do you doubt it? No. You will be hinting next that she did not go down to the pavilion and return before the snowfall stopped.'

'Quite right,' said H.M. 'She didn't. I tried an experiment, but you don't seem to understand even now what it was. It succeeded, but you don't understand how. I want everybody here to sit down. Uh-huh, that's it. *Sit down.* Lock that door. After we're all nice and comfortable, I intend to tell you what did happen.

'I'll take the girl's word for it that she did what she said. But she never went down to the pavilion, even though she intended to. I don't say she killed Marcia Tait, I don't say she didn't. All I'll say is that she collapsed in the gallery, with too much veronal inside, and didn't go down.'

During the silence Willard said: 'Look here, are you mad? You say she didn't go down to the pavilion, and still you say Louise might be guilty. Good Lord, talk sense! If she didn't go down there, she certainly isn't guilty.'

'Oh, I dunno. That's what I wanted to tell you… Y'see, fatheads, *Marcia Tait was murdered in this room.*'

XIX
THE REFLECTION OF THE MURDERER

'Ho ho,' said H.M., looking round him with something like a leer. 'You think the old man's a ravin' lunatic, hey? His lunacy's goin' to catch a murderer, though, before any one of you leaves this room. Don't anybody move. I suggest you sorta get comfortable, though, because you'll feel better while I'm tellin' you about it.'

Blinking in his near-sighted way, he wandered over to the big chair behind the table and sat down. Then he took out his black pipe.

'That's it, get chairs for the ladies, Jimmy. Miss Carewe needs one. Now, ma'am, take it easy.—You others, shut up!' He turned savagely as Maurice came forward in a cold rage.

'What I'm doin',' he continued almost affably, 'is broadening the whole field again after you'd narrowed it down. I'll let you sorta guess for yourselves, before I prove it, which person in the house came into this room and smashed in Tait's head with... Humph. No; we won't mention the weapon just yet.

'Now we've already heard two very interestin' theories

about how the murderer worked. Both of 'em happened to be wrong. But the interest lay in the occasional glimmer of reason and truth that appeared in each and had just sufficient plausibility to lead the guesser in the wrong direction. I been sittin' and thinkin' about this thing, and, burn me, the longer I sit and think, the more it occurs to me as a miracle that nobody thought of an obvious explanation which would have avoided all the hocus-pocus and camel-swallowin' of the other two.

'So here's what I mean to do. I'm going to hold a little class in what I'll call Imaginative Common Sense. I got another witness besides myself to a certain thing that happened a few minutes ago; so I needn't worry about bein' able to hang the murderer, and I can make this killer squirm a little while I ask my class questions. Ho ho. First, then, I'm goin' simply to state a few clear facts which everybody knows and everybody admits. Second, in case you haven't tumbled to it by that time, I'll state *my* suggested explanation. Third, I'll support it by plagiarizin' the few good wild words of truth from the other two explanations, and complete the pie with a little deduction of my own.

'H'm. Now lemme see.' With the pipe upside down in his mouth, he drowsily held up his blunt fingers and checked them off. 'Quite a little time before midnight last night, Tait began to get nervous and impatient, and began to ask to be taken out to the pavilion. That's admitted, ain't it? She was taken out there at a little past midnight, and was even more impatient. When Willard went out for a sociable chat a bit afterwards, she shooed him out. Point o' fact, as Masters reported it to me, Willard said that she went several times into the drawin'-room of the pavilion and looked out the front windows. Hey?'

'Quite,' said Willard dryly. 'But don't you think this restating of facts has become a bit monotonous by this time?'

'Uh-huh. Burn me, that's what makes me despair of your intellects! I think that at one place John Bohun said his appointment with Canifest was early in the evening, and at another place he said it was at ten o'clock. Now, we won't argue about that. We'll say the appointment (at the newspaper office) was at the rather later instance of ten o'clock. You still don't seem to get it through your heads that, even if it was as late as that, by all rights he should have been back here by midnight at the latest! We're lookin' at it from Tait's viewpoint, who never has been kept waitin' by anybody and don't intend to start it now. We're lookin' at it from the viewpoint of a woman whose life-and-death interests are centred in the news Bohun'll bring back from town, and who ain't likely to be in a patient mood. If you'll admit she was restless at half-past eleven and at midnight, how restless do you think she would have been at half-past twelve? And *another* half-hour passes, until one o'clock, and still he's not appeared. What's her state of mind then?

'But I won't diverge yet from statin' facts. We know, don't we, that you can see the windows of this room—the back windows of this room—' he pointed with his pipe, 'from the pavilion? Uh-huh. We also know that several times, while Willard was with her, she ran into the front room of the pavilion to look out? Quite. Finally, we know that at one o'clock, when she must 'a been a bit furious with impatience, a light went on in this room.'

Maurice, who was sitting bolt upright in a narrow chair, jabbed his stick against the floor. He said gently: 'Most extraordinary. Surely you know that it has no significance? Surely you know that the light was turned on only by Thompson, who put it on for John's return when he set out sandwiches and prepared the room?'

'Sure I know it,' agreed H.M. 'Thompson told me. But how was Tait goin' to know that? Here's a man she's waitin' for, who is already an hour overdue. A light goes on in his room. But does he come down to see her, as he's supposed to do as soon as he returns? No. On the contrary, my lad, this light continues to burn strongly and brightly; and for another half-hour a woman who's already got the wind up pretty thoroughly is *still* required to wait while nobody shows up!

'Now I ain't stretchin' the roseate limits of probability when I picture Tait's mental workings. She knew John wouldn't simply have come home and forgot all about her, when their joint futures rested on the news he was to bring from London. She'd decide it was probably bad news, and John hadn't the nerve to come down and tell her. But whatever she decided, I think you'll agree she had to *know.*

'And, gettin' back to obvious facts, we come to the not very surprisin' information that at half-past one the dog begins barkin' and a mysterious woman is seen runnin' round the lawn.

'As I say, I was sittin' and thinkin', and it struck me that under the circumstances the likeliest person to be goin' on a visit that night was Tait herself. Trouble was, all you lads stared myopically from the house to the pavilion and refused to look the other way. You even refused to look the other way when all the suspected women in this house had an alibi. I don't ask you to *believe* this for a minute, till I offer you proof; but that was the possibility that struck me first off. Because it was a matter of tolerable simplicity, d'ye see, for her to visit this room absolutely unobserved. She could come up the lawn. She could go through the lower stair-case door (which she knew was unlocked, because she'd seen Miss Bohun unlock it for John while they were all here lookin' at the stairs earlier in the night); she could walk up here and confront John. How did she know,' inquired H.M., raising his voice a little, 'that John wasn't here?'

Nobody moved or spoke. H.M. ruffled his hands across his head; scowled, and settled deeper in the chair just after his dull eyes flickered round the motionless group.

'That's simple enough, ain't it? Get out of your heads the collected rubbish of people who were makin' theories merely to hang other people; and consider what the most *natural* course of events must have been. I began to see Tait, crazy with fear or waiting or both, pulling on a fur coat over her négligée—you thought quickly enough of how Miss Carewe could 'a' done the same thing—getting into a pair of galoshes, and slippin' up there secretly for news. But I said to myself, "Here! Would she have wanted to raise a row and maybe get people curious? What about that dog?" Then I discovered, not only that the dog wasn't out at its kennel when she first went to the pavilion, but that it hadn't been loose all afternoon and in fact *she knew nothing about any dog at all*. Why should she? She and the whole party went down there; no dog barked. The rest went back up; Willard, a stranger, came down again and returned; but still no dog barked. Why should she imagine there'd be a rumpus if she sneaked quietly up to see John?

'So I saw her startin' up, and gettin' the fright of a lifetime when half-way up she suddenly hears a big and dangerous Alsatian bust out after her! Children, what would you think if you heard a thing like that; when you didn't know the dog was chained on a runway wire and couldn't get loose, but simply heard it coming after you? That woman must 'a' been petrified, because she don't know which way to go. She don't know whether to run back, or run forward, or stand still. Probably she did a little of all three. And if that don't correspond exactly to the movements of the shape Mrs. Thompson saw, it'll surprise me a whole lot. Well, she still hesitates. Nothin' happens, but she don't dare run back to the pavilion, because the barking's behind her. Then she sees Miss Bohun open the little door to the porch, look out, and go back again. She don't know what that means, but she's got to have sanctuary. So she risks a run up the lawn, while the snow is still failin' thickly, gets inside the door, and creeps up that staircase.'

He pointed. A horrible suspicion was beginning to stir in Bennett's mind; but he forced it back. Somebody in the group jumped a little, because just then there was a sound of somebody's footstep down on the stairs.

'Who's down there now?' Jervis Willard asked quietly.

'There's a dead man down there,' said H.M., 'for one thing. I don't have to tell one of you that. You know who it is? It's Rainger, Carl Rainger. No, don't anybody move!— You're all afraid to, because the innocent ones are thinkin'

I'll think them guilty if they do. Sit quiet, and remember that Rainger was strangled in here this afternoon.

'Last night Tait sneaked up those stairs (this is my theory); like that footstep you hear now, only that's the police waitin' for somebody like Jack Ketch in Punch-and-Judy. She came into this room, and found nobody here. Then she didn't know what to think, and began to realize John mightn't have returned after all. Well, what was she goin' to do? She didn't want anybody to know of her presence here; she was too crafty to advertise any hanky-panky with John. And if she's found in John's room in a fetchin' state of undress at half-past one in the morning...hey?

'But—this is what I want to emphasize—she didn't dare go back. Would *you* go back if you thought a man-eatin' dog was ready to fly out after you; would you walk into that danger again when you'd just got over the shock of encounterin' it a minute ago and thought you'd achieved a miraculous escape? This place was safety; John was bound to come here sometime. She'd take one precaution. I want you to think of what that precaution might be while I go on...

'While I go on to prove that she stayed here,' said H.M., suddenly bringing the palm of his big hand down on the table.

'You've had a look at that pavilion. You've had your attention called to the fires. There were two fires, one in the drawin'-room and one in the bedroom, made by Thompson before twelve o'clock. Everybody agrees, so there'll be no fightin' or dark glares when I repeat it, that she never used the drawin'-room at all last night: each person was entertained in the other room. You don't keep the fire goin' strong

in a room you don't use. Admittin', then, that she used the
bedroom, we know that she hadn't turned in and gone to
sleep. She was killed about a quarter past three.

'So what have we got? We got two very small fires, which
we can prove by the quantity of ash you saw yourself, burning exactly the same length of time—you saw that they were
the same. We're asked to believe that *for three and a half hours*
a very small fire in the bedroom was sufficient to keep comfortable a pampered hot-house orchid like Tait in a literal
ice-house of a pavilion on a snowy December night—while
it was never replenished, but stayed the same as the one in
the other room. We're asked to believe that she was snugly
drinkin' port with the murderer at a quarter past three, sittin' at her ease in négligée before the blaze of a fire which
actually must have been ashes an hour before that time.

'It don't require much brain-rackin' to see that those fires
stayed the same, and went out about the same time, because
she wasn't in the pavilion at all.

'Whereat, before examinin' other things in the room, I
found myself hoppin' back to another fact I'd already heard.
This piece of evidence screamed at you; so loudly that some
fathead did notice it and promptly proceeded to put a far-
fetched meanin' to it when the real one was much handier. I
mean the mysterious figure in the gallery at some time after
three o'clock, who smeared Miss Carewe's hand with blood.
The theorist was quite right in propoundin' the question,
"Why, since there was water at the pavilion, did the fool
murderer come all the way up to the house before washin'
his hands?"

'Then the theorist goes star-gazin' for his answer, with

some complicated tommyrot about the figure being a myth and an even more intricate tale, wholly unsubstantiated, about an attack on Tait with a huntin' crop. Whereas the real answer was, "The murderer didn't come back from the pavilion. He killed Tait here." Which is simple, and true. I said to myself, "Sure, he was goin' out to the bathroom after water; because," I said to myself, "didn't Masters tell me that there wasn't any water in this room, and they hadda send out for a bowl when John Bohun shot himself here this morning?"'

Silence. The vivid memory returned to Bennett. But Maurice was sitting forward now; his shoulders hunched up, and his voice going into a batlike squeak.

'I thank you,' he said, 'for your graceful compliments. But I think I begin to see what you are driving at. You are still accusing—you come back round in the circle, don't you? You accuse my brother John of this murder.'

He struggled to his feet and stood shaking. H.M. leaned forward.

'No,' rumbled H.M., 'I don't. Not necessarily. *But you're getting warm*, Bohun. You're skirtin' near the truth of the impossible situation at last. Speak up! By God, it almost penetrated now. *What happened?*'

The little man moved forward and leaned on the table. His eyes seemed to narrow and contract. Maurice said:

'John returned with his bad news, and found her in this room. He thought he had killed Canifest; he was in a fury and desperate; he did not care what happened to him; and, when she flew out at him as she would, he went fully amok and killed her.

'Then,' Bohun went on, 'he began to realize his position. Nobody had seen him kill Canifest; he might escape that. But if Marcia's body were found in his room, he knew that he had no chance whatever of escaping the rope. The only chance for safety lay in waiting until daylight, in *carrying her body out to the pavilion,* in setting up false evidence at the pavilion to indicate that she had been murdered there, and in finding her body himself... That's it! That's it! He did kill her after all!'

Slowly H.M. pulled himself up out of his chair.

'I said, son, that you were gettin' warm,' he snapped, 'and in that last part of it you ring a crashin' bull's-eye. There, fatheads, is the explanation—part of it—of the impossible situation. Are you beginnin' to see it?

'*Do you understand now why John's nerve completely broke this morning, and he came up here and shot himself?* What broke his nerve? Think back, like Masters told me. John was in the dinin'-room with two or three of you. And he went over to the window. And what did he see? Speak up!'

Again the memory smashed back on Bennett.

'He saw,' said Bennett, in a voice he did not recognize, 'he saw Potter examining and measuring those tracks of his in the snow, because Rainger had said...'

'Because of Rainger's explanation. Uh-huh. And he asked Masters what Potter was doin'. So Masters, with a sinister leer whose effectiveness Masters didn't know even then, replied, "Only making measurements of your tracks in the snow." Why did that break John's nerve? Not because of Rainger's elaborate bunkum of a theory. But because John had carried a dead woman down to the pavilion in early morning, and he thought they were on to him! There you are. No fancy claptrap of playin' pranks with hocussed tracks, that's been makin' your brains dizzy all along. Merely a big and powerful man carryin' a body down to the pavilion through snow that was too shallow to show the deep imprint of two weights. Rainger said one true thing. He said it couldn't have been done without discovery if the snow had been deeper. It couldn't; the tracks would have sunk in too deeply. But with a little plaster of snow… are you beginnin' to see why those tracks were so sharply and heavily printed, like Potter said, and also why they'd dragged a good deal at the toes?'

H.M. had lost his woodenness. His voice smashed across the silent room.

'Didn't I tell you that somebody had smashed a decanter and a couple of glasses on the hearthstone; deliberately smashed 'em, to make it look like there'd been a struggle there? Well, didn't you wonder why? It was to offer proof she'd been killed at the pavilion.

'Now I'm very slowly and painstakingly goin' to tell you what he did. He didn't kill the woman. He found her dead when he got here. And in this tale you'll probably see the dead glarin' evidence that'll tell you who did kill her. Go back to the beginning of it all.

'She left that pavilion, turnin' off the lights; she came up here, as I've told you, and was afraid to go back because of the dog. Now in the tale I'll leave a single cloud of blackness straight in the middle; the cloud of blackness that hides the murderer who finds her here and beats her head in. The murderer leaves her here—maybe on that bed,' he pointed;

'maybe anywhere. We pass the cloud of blackness to the end of the story, when John Bohun comes into it.

'He's driven back from town. He thinks he's killed Canifest, and the only thing that will save him is to lie about the time he reached home. That is, if he can somehow prove that he did reach home at the same time he must have killed Canifest in London; if he can prove an alibi by having somebody swear he was *here* and not in London when Canifest died; that'll save him. That's simple, ain't it? He's got to get that alibi. It's burnin' in his mind all the time he rides hell-for-leather out here. Fix it! Fix it, somehow! So that wild, nervous, irresolute feller who don't know his own mind from one minute to the next—he comes home, walks up here, and finds Marcia Tait dead in his room!

'Look here, do you wonder much at his behaviour this mornin'? Here he was, caught between two hangmen as neat as you please. *Now* if he fakes an alibi, and says he couldn't have been with Canifest because he was here, he's got a dead woman in his room to account for. If he admits the time he got home, they may hang him for Canifest's death. Whichever way he looks, there's a hemp collar swingin' at the end of it. He don't know who killed Tait. He don't even know how she got here, or anything about it. What he does know is that he's in a hell of a mess, and he's got to see a way out so that he won't swing for either crime.

'Could he, for instance, carry her back to her own room and pretend she'd been murdered there? Then he could swear to a faked time at which he got home; and maybe get somebody to back him up. Where was she supposed to sleep? He remembers: the pavilion. Did she go out there?

He's got to find out, and there's nobody awake to tell him. He also remembers: a riding-engagement for this morning.

'The thing to do is find out. Now here's where the grain of truth in Rainger's theory enters. He dresses in riding-clothes, so that if she really has slept at the pavilion (as he believes), he'll have a good excuse for "*finding*" her early in the morning. He wakes up the butler, who tells him she's out there and that horses are ordered for seven o'clock. Good God! There's where the ticklish, dangerous skatin' on ice comes in. The stables are in sight of the pavilion and even the door of the pavilion! If he delays until quite day-light, somebody bringin' those horses out may see him go down with the body... On the other hand, if he can take her in there a few minutes, just a few minutes beforehand; if he can put her in the bedroom, and then walk back to the front door of the pavilion; then stand there until he sees somebody at the stables, whom he'll hail as though he were just goin' in for the first time to "find" her—then he's safe.'

H.M. stabbed out with his finger. 'Do you understand the burnt matches now? He carried her in there and put her on the floor a few minutes before Jim Bennett unexpectedly arrived on the scene: so few minutes that his tracks were still fresh. It was growing daylight, but not quite daylight (I carefully asked that nephew of mine about it) and Bohun had to be able to see clearly to set his stage for the fake murder! Got it now? He didn't dare switch on a light in the room. A large window faced directly towards the stables, where people were already up. *If* a light flashed on in that room, sorta sudden and inexplicable-like, a few minutes *before* Bohun claimed he walked into the pavilion for the first time...why, somebody would have seen it and wondered why.'

'Hold on, sir!' said Bennett. 'There was a blind on that window—a Venetian blind. Couldn't he simply have lowered the blind?'

H.M. blinked at him.

'Do you think, my amiable dotard,' he growled, 'they wouldn't have seen the light just the same? Didn't you and me ourselves see a light, through those slits in the Venetian blind, when Willard turned one on this afternoon in the drawin'-room?—Y'know, it's a funny thing how every one of the answers to all these questions has been repeated before our eyes to sorta help us along. Quit interruptin', will you? Dammit, I'm in full stride and enjoyin' myself...

'He struck matches while he tipped things over, smashed glasses, took off the woman's fur coat and stowed away her galoshes in the closet—where I went lookin' for 'em. He didn't have anything to simulate a weapon with, although he tried to make it seem like the poker. I could tell it wasn't; no blood or hair. He put her on the floor after a couple of minutes of crazy work. Then he went to the door, saw Locker over across the way; hailed him; strolled back, uttered a rather unnecessary yell which didn't sound like Bohun at all and made me suspicious to begin with. Rushin' back to the door, he meets Jim Bennett comin' down the lawn...

'By the way, I hear he had blood on his hands then. Didn't that seem fishy to you, son—sticky blood, although the woman had been murdered some hours before? It didn't mean he'd killed her. It meant he'd heavily yanked or disturbed the body somehow, such as he wouldn't have done merely by examinin' it; he'd disturbed clots and released something, although the heart had stopped pumpin' and it wasn't fresh—'

Somebody cried out. H.M. glanced at them as though he held a whip.

'Then,' he went on heavily, 'he was ready. The feller was clever in everything but one. He forgot about the snow. Do you wonder he was shaken up when Jim Bennett pointed it out; and he yelled out that it didn't mean anything? Do you see why he could afford to laugh when Willard suggested Tait's murder at the pavilion meant an assignation there last night? An assignation, lads, yet the blind wasn't even pulled down on a towerin' window!—hadn't that feature struck anybody's boarding-house mind? Never mind. He thought he'd covered everything up. *Now* he could announce to everybody that he'd arrived home here a good deal earlier than he actually had. He could say he didn't kill Canifest because he was here before the time Canifest was knocked off...'

Maurice Bohun began to laugh; a thin, malicious laughter that convulsed his shoulders.

'Quite, Sir Henry,' he said. 'But I should fancy—in fact I *do* fancy—that's exactly where your theory comes crashing down. Most interesting! You proclaim the spotless innocence of my brother. You say he did all these things for one express purpose. That purpose had two parts: the first, which I concede you readily, was to shift Marcia's body so that he would not be thought guilty by having it found in his room. But the second part—to lie about the time he had actually arrived home—utterly destroys your whole case.

He did *not* lie about the time he arrived home. In fact, what you have done is to build up a brilliant and almost unanswerable case against my poor brother as the murderer. He arrived at shortly after three o'clock. Just a few minutes afterwards, by medical testimony, Marcia was murdered. Well?'

'Exactly,' said H.M. 'That's what makes me absolutely certain, son, that he didn't commit the murder.'

'*What?* I do not think, Sir Henry,' said Maurice, suddenly checking his rage, 'this is precisely the time for talking nonsense...'

'Oh, it ain't nonsense. Just look at it for a minute. Here's a man whose double motive is to prove that he didn't kill Canifest and he didn't kill Tait. Hey? He wants to do the one by makin' his arrival here earlier than it actually was, and the other by movin' the body. H'm. All right. If he really did kill Tait, then he knew when she died: that's not a very far-fetched assumption. Then why the blazes does he want to make the time he says he arrived here so nearly coincide with the time the woman was murdered?—carefully makin' it just a little *earlier* than she was killed? That's an incredibly fatheaded way of bringin' suspicion back to him, especially as after a car-drive from London a matter of twenty minutes or half-an-hour won't matter so much! Why did he say roughly three o'clock? Why didn't he make it earlier, and provide an alibi for both victims?—You instantly reply, "Because Thompson heard him come in, and he couldn't lie." That won't wash. He told his story long before he knew that, by a chance nobody in the world could anticipate, Thompson was awake with the toothache and could check up on him. He told that story deliberately, because...

'Shall I read you a telegram?' inquired H.M.

'A telegram? What telegram?'

'From Canifest. I got it just before dinner. It's interestin.' And this is what it says.' H.M. drew the folded paper from his inside pocket. 'I asked him, as a matter of fact, what time John Bohun had called on him at his home last night.

'"WENT HOME," said Canifest, "JUST AFTER MORN-ING EDITION OF GLOBE-JOURNAL WENT TO PRESS, PRECISELY TWO FORTY-FIVE A.M. FOUND CALLER IN QUESTION WAITING AT SIDE DOOR AND TOOK HIM TO MY DEN. DO NOT KNOW WHAT TIME HE LEFT DUE TO HEART-ATTACK YOU MAY UNDER-STAND, BUT AM CERTAIN NOT EARLIER THAN THREE-THIRTY."'

H.M. tossed the slip of paper on the table.

'He said three o'clock,' snapped H.M., 'because he thought it was a safe time to admit he'd arrived here. As a matter of fact he didn't get here until an hour or two afterwards...'

'But somebody got here!' shouted Willard. 'Somebody drove in at ten minutes past three! Who was it?'

'The murderer,' said H.M. 'He's played in every bit of luck on the globe; he's been shielded by every trick of luck that nature and fate and craziness could invent; he's fooled us in front of our very eyes, but—*grab him, Masters!*'

The voice ripped across the room as somebody flung open the door to the gallery. The door to the staircase banged open at the same time, and Inspector Potter plunged through at the same time that Masters appeared in the other. Masters said with quiet and deadly formality:

'Herbert Timmons Emery, I arrest you for the murder of Marcia Tait and Carl Rainger. I have to warn you that anything—'

The lank sandy-haired figure stared only for a second before it dodged under the hand that had descended on its shoulder. It whirled a chair at Potter's legs; ducked again, while still crying something, and plunged down the staircase door. Potter caught a piece of a coat and then a leg. He should not have tripped the man up. They heard the cry out of the dark, and then the crash. Then there was silence while a white-faced Potter got up shakily on the landing, and they saw him peering down into the dark.

XX

JUNE OVER WHITEHALL

Above the small severe name-plate reading, 'Sir Henry
Merrivale,' the door was inscribed with staggering letters
splashed in white paint. '*Busy! No Admittance!! Keep Out!!*'
And below, in an even angrier script, it added, 'This means
You!' The old hallway was musty and warm at the top of
Whitehall's ancient rabbit-warren; through a crooked
window on the stairs they could see the moving green of
trees.

Katharine looked at the door and hesitated.

'But it *says*—!' she protested.

'Nonsense,' said Bennett. He pushed open the door.

Both windows were open to the lazy June air; there was a
smell of old wood and paper in the dusky room, and a hum
of traffic from the Embankment below. H.M.'s big feet were
on the desk and entangled with the telephone. His big bald
head was hung forward so that the glasses slid down his
nose, and his eyes were closed.

Bennett rapped on the inside of the door. 'I'm sorry to

interrupt, sir,' he said, in the middle of a whistling snore, 'but we thought—'

H.M. opened one eye. He seemed to be galvanized. 'Go 'way! Out! I won't be disturbed, dammit! I sent you that report on the accordion-player yesterday afternoon; and if you wanta know why the key of G had anything to do with Robrett's dyin', then you look in there and you'll see. I'm *busy!* I—who's there, hey?' He sat up a little, and then scowled savagely. 'Oh, it's you two, hey? I might 'a' known it. I might 'a' known somebody like you would interrupt when I'm engaged on a very serious business. What are you grinnin' at, curse you? It *is* serious! It's the Dardanelles matter, only I forget the chief part of it now. It's somethin' to do with the peace of the world.' He sniffed, and looked at them in a disgruntled fashion. 'Humph. You look sorta happy, and that's bad...'

'Happy?' roared Bennett, with an explosive affability. 'Sir, let me tell you—'

'Sh-hh!' said Katharine. 'Be dignified. *Whee!*'

H.M. looked sourly from one to the other. 'You practically light up this office. Gives me a pain, that's what it does. Well, I suppose you'd better come in. You two are goin' to get married, ain't you? Haaah! Just wait till you do; that'll fix you. You see if it don't. Haaah!'

'Are you telling me,' said Bennett, 'that you don't remember we were married a month ago today? I suppose you've also forgotten you gave the bride away? And that Kate stayed with your daughter after good old Uncle Maurice tossed her out of the house?'

'Old Maurice,' grunted H.M. His eye twinkled. 'Sure, I

remember now. Ho ho. Well, now that you're here I suppose you'd better sit down and have a drink. Ho ho. Look
here, I certainly put the wind up you two, didn't I? I bet you
thought old Uncle Maurice was guilty of that funny business down at the White Priory. How's Paris?'

They sat down on the other side of the desk. Bennett
hesitated.

'It's about the funny business,' he admitted, 'that we
wanted to talk to you—in a way. That is...well, we're sailing
for New York in a couple of days, and we've got to take back
some complete account of it, you know. We've never had the
details on account of all the uproar and fuss that happened
after Emery's arrest. We know he died in the hospital two
days after he fell—or threw himself—down those stairs...'

H.M. inspected his fingers.

'Uh-huh. I was hopin' he'd do somethin' like that. He
wasn't a very bad sort, Emery wasn't. Point o' fact, I might
'a' been inclined to let him go after all; I was a bit hesitant
about the thing until he murdered Rainger just because
Rainger had spotted him. That was mucky. The whole thing
was mucky. I didn't hold it much against him for killin' Tait
in hot blood. I didn't want to see him hang for that. But the
nastiness came out in the other thing...'

'Anyhow, sir, what everybody seems to know is that he
killed her with that heavy silvered-steel figure he had on the
radiator-cap of his fancy automobile; that is, the one he *did*
have there the first time I saw the car.[2] When he drove out to
the White Priory next day, he'd changed it for a bronze stork.

---

2 Should there be any doubt of this, it is suggested that the reader consult pages 22
and 181.

I remember noticing that at the time, although it didn't register fully. But what's got everybody up in the air is how you knew all this, how you got on to him in the first place—'

'And,' said Katharine, 'why you put on that little show with us, reconstructing the attempted murder, when all the time you actually suspected *him*—'

H.M. blinked. His dull eyes took in a flushed and radiant couple who had, after all, no tremendous interest in the affairs of the dead.

'So,' said H.M., 'you still don't see it, hey? I hadda trap him, and it was the only way I could prove it on him. I don't like to talk about this kind of thing, much. Funny. Wait a minute. I got Emery's statement, the statement he made before he died, here in the desk somewhere.'

Wheezing, he bent over and ransacked drawers, muttering to himself. Then he produced a blue-bound sheaf of paper; he brushed off some tobacco-ash and weighed it in his hand.

'That's human tragedy. I mean, son, it *was* human tragedy. Now it's File Number Umpty-Umph, so many lines of type, so much "I-did-and-I-suffered" stuck down so formally on a piece of paper that you can hardly believe anybody did suffer. I got stacks of 'em here in the desk. But this man Emery did suffer. Like hell. There were a couple of nights when I kept seein' his face. And I like the chase and the chess-gambits; but I don't like to see anybody take the three-minute-walk to the rope when that man might 'a' been me. Son, that's the last and only argument against capital punishment you'll ever hear. Emery's trouble was that he loved that empty good-lookin' leech Tait far too much.'

He stared blankly at the blue-bound sheets, and then pushed them away.

'What were you askin'? I get kind of absent-minded these days, when it's summer again.

'Oh, yes. I'll let you have the thing as I saw it. I didn't suspect him at first: not at all. I'd have chosen him, when I got to the house at the beginning, as one of the few who didn't kill her. Y'see, I'd heard about that box of poisoned chocolates—I knew he hadn't any intention of killin' her when he sent 'em. He hadn't. It was a press-agent's stunt, exactly what he said and what I thought. That threw me off. I figured him as the nervous, hopping type who, if he had committed a crime, wouldn't rest till he'd told about it and got it off his chest. I was right in that; I figured him to break down in one way or another, and he did. He never meant to kill her (that's what he says, and I believe it) even when he drove to the White Priory that night, until—but I'll tell you that in a minute.

'All the same, I was sittin' and thinkin' about the evidence, and there was two or three things that bothered me.

'I told you, didn't I, my idea about Tait comin' back up to the house to John's room? Uh-huh. And when I outlined that idea, did I say to you that, if she came up and planted herself in John's room, she'd *take one precaution?* Uh, I thought I had. I asked you to think what that would be. Y'see, there I had no evidence at all; not a limpin' ghost of proof; but, if I'd decided she'd done the rest of it, I had to follow my idea through to its psychological conclusion. She's alone in that room, now; John ain't back; but she don't want anybody walkin' in there and findin' her. Well, what would she be likely to do?'

'Lock the door on the inside. I mean, lock the door to the gallery,' said Katharine, after a pause. 'That's what I'd have done.'

'Yes. And that bothered me. She probably wouldn't answer that door, or sing out, or let anybody in, no matter who tried to get in from the gallery. Well, if she did lock the door on the inside, you instantly hadda rule out as possible suspects *everybody* who could come from that direction. That's a sweepin' sort of idea, you see. I couldn't do it just yet. It would force me back on the theory that John *had* come home and killed her, because apparently he was the only one who fitted the facts. Every fact fitted; but, burn me, I wouldn't accept John's guilt!

'There were several reasons why I wouldn't, aside from the pretty thin one I told you when I was sketchin' the theory before. To begin with, the idea that a man who's rushin' home with a murder already on his conscience; puzzlin' frantic plans to escape arrest; full of terror at what he's already done, and shakin' in every joint for fear they'll catch him;— well, is it likely that such a man, near on nervous prostration, will do the murderous job that was done on Tait?

'I doubted that. I also doubted it from this factor: that the murder occurred too *soon* after the time John had apparently got back. Y'see what I mean? He's not in a murderous rage with Tait. On the contrary, he thinks she'll be in a murderous rage with him, and he's nervous about that. Well, the car is heard coming into the drive at ten minutes past three. The murder takes place at fifteen minutes past. Is it reasonable to suppose that he'll rush up and kill her (especially as he hasn't got the slightest idea she's in *his* room) simply off-hand, with no reason, instantly after he returns? Neither of 'em could have had much of a chance to say anything whatever. Does any part of that sound like the conduct of John Bohun, who confessedly thought he had just killed Canifest?'

'Steady, sir,' interposed Bennett. 'Suppose he hadn't known Marcia was married. And Canifest, who had been told by Emery, in turn told him. Mightn't he have been exactly in that rage when he returned?'

H.M. took away the hand with which he was shading his glasses.

'Now!' he said. 'Now you're hittin' on a point that began to strike me pretty strongly. Point is, why should he? He was the woman's lover. There was no talk of marriage between them; never had been. Not only did he accept that status, d'ye see, but he helped her jolly Canifest along in the hope of marriage. If he'd really had any objections to the idea, and didn't know she was already married, wouldn't he have said in either case, "Look here, do you mean business by Canifest?" And if any jealousy of a mere husband came into it, he'd have had a devilish sight more jealousy of a wealthy, powerful man like Canifest than some inconspicuous figure who was always content to keep in the background. Not havin' any aspirations towards bein' her husband, and content to be the preferred stock, why should he flare into a wild fury about a husband at all?—I thought to myself, "Rage, hey? This thing don't sound like the rage of a lover who finds his mistress is married; that's rather thin stuff. It does sound devilish like a husband who's suddenly discovered his wife has a genuine lover."'

'*You mean Emery really didn't know——?*'

'Wait a bit, son. We're only lookin' at the evidence as yet. That's what struck me. As I say, I was sittin' and thinkin', and there jumped up another thing I didn't like. What about this mysterious figure with blood on its hand, blunderin' round in the gallery and runnin' into Louise Carewe? How did they happen to run into each other? You know by this time that little Louise, with too much of a sleeping-drug turned wrong-ways, had put a huntin' crop into her pocket and was goin' down to the pavilion to mess up Tait's face (you could tell it was drug-fog, because she intended to walk straight out through that snow in thin slippers)—she was goin' out there when she collapsed. How did this killer run into her? Surely he could have ducked back somewhere, and would have done that, with that damnin' evidence in his hands; if—if he had known where he was goin'. If, in other words, he hadn't been blunderin' around in the dark in search of a place to wash his hands, and didn't know the house at all.

'That wasn't evidence either, but suddenly I remembered something that was. *Emery was the only person in the whole lot who wouldn't believe Tait had been murdered at the pavilion.* Don't you remember? Rainger had to yell at him over the 'phone, insistently repeatin': "At the pavilion, at the pavilion, I tell you." Even then he thought Rainger was only drunk. And, when he spoke to us, he still said it was non-sense!—In a blindin' afterthought it came to me that of all the dead give-aways I've ever heard mumbled out by a guilty person, that was one of the most blazin'.

'So I thought, "Here, now! What have you got? You've got a lot of indications, and things you think are indications.

You've got a theoretical locked door leadin' to the gallery, so that the murderer came from another direction. But you don't believe it was Bohun. You've got a theoretical man who don't know the house, who came from outside, who had a car. You've got a practical flesh-and-blood man who fulfils these requirements and also declares the woman was *not* murdered at the pavilion."

'Now, what are the objections to that? First objection, which seemed so strong as to put the whole thing out of court, is this: How could Emery, rushing down in the middle of the night to a house he didn't know, unerringly pick out the room where this woman was—especially as she hadn't intended to be in that room at all?

'For a second, that was a poser. And then it struck me that this apparent difficulty might, just *might*, be the answer to the riddle of the whole murder! Here's Tait, waitin' for Bohun up in that room, not darin' to go back to the pavilion. But John had been told to go down to the pavilion when he came back; she supposed he would, and wanted to head him off. Suppose he went down there, discovered she'd disappeared, and maybe raised a row… Well? If you were in her position, what would *you* have done?'

After a long silence Katharine said:

'I suppose I should have waited at the window until I heard his car come in. Then I might have gone down to the side door and called to him that I was in his room…'

She stopped.

'Uh-huh,' said H.M., nodding sombrely. 'And, I think you've noticed, the roof of the *porte-cochère* hides the whole drive except the end of it leadin' down to the stables. I tested that out and looked for myself. From King Charles's Room, you can't see any except a very little of the drive—Hey? You hear a car come in. You're expectin' a car, and you don't suppose that in a lonely community at three o'clock in the mornin' any car *will* come in but the one you're expectin'. Right. So in your fetchin' négligée you either lean out the window and whisper, or sneak down to the staircase-door and whisper to a supposed John Bohun that you're not at the pavilion at all; you're in his room. Listen!'

He flicked open the blue sheets.

'On my oath here, and as I hope to answer for it before God, I never meant to kill her. I never thought Carl was right. I only thought I had to go down to that place and see for myself, or I'd go crazy. It happened like this. When I was in that hospital after I had ate (sic) chocolate with the poison in it, Carl came to me and said, "Well, I've proved to you Canifest is their angel, so now if you got any guts at all you'll walk over and tell him you're married to her. Great Christ," he says, "is everybody going to make a sucker out of you? Are you ever going to act like a man? This guy Bohun," he said, and then he told me all over again what he'd told me before, only I didn't believe it. She swore it wasn't true; she always swore it wasn't true. She said, if I let her alone to have her career, she'd never in the world look at another man except me.

'And Carl said, "Do you know why he's taking her down to this place in the country?" And he said, "Well, if I didn't believe it, all I had to do was go down and *see for myself." He said to go down there late. He said to surprise everybody. He said she'd be in that marble house out at the back, and all I had to do would be walk around the grounds, and I'd see it. Then he said to go down there, and they'd be there; both of them would be there...*

'And I couldn't rest, I couldn't do anything until I did. But I was having a lot of trouble with my car, because the fan-belt was loose and the engine would get so hot; and I think the radiator leaked or something like that...'

'Did you notice,' said H.M., looking up sharply, 'how the bonnet of that car was smoking when we saw it in the drive next day?'

'So I came in the drive, and I noticed my car didn't make any tracks afterwards, because there's trees so close over it that there wasn't much snow at all. And I stopped the car in that driveway under the roof. And I was wondering where this marble-house place was that they were talking about, and I saw the engine shooting up steam again. So I thought I'd get out and stick some snow in to cool it. And I got out and took off that big heavy silver thing that's on top of the radiator cap. It was hotter than hell, but I had my gloves on. And it was dark there, but all of a sudden I heard somebody whisper out behind me, up on the porch...'

'Now use a little imagination,' said H.M. rather curtly:

'Even then she didn't know who it was. I kept my head down. And I didn't know where I was going, but I just followed her. And we went up some steps with her ahead, and everything was dark and she kept talking, until we got up to the bedroom and she turned around and saw who I was.

'I didn't know what I was doing. I hit her, and hit her again with that thing in my hand. I don't know how many times I hit her.

'I don't remember much what I did, because right after she was all quiet and didn't move I knew I shouldn't have done it. I tried to revive her, and talked to her, but she didn't move. And I had to take my gloves off to see what was wrong with her, so when I saw my hands were all over blood I knew she was dead.

'And I don't remember what I did after that, except I had sense enough to see if I could wash my hands. I was afraid that when I drove back to London some cop would stop the car and maybe ask me for my licence or something like that, and I'd have blood on me. So I went out and tried to find a bathroom, but I couldn't because it was dark. And I ran into somebody, and that scared me.

'I think this was a long time afterwards, because just after I hit her all those times I sat down and whispered to her for a while. But after I ran into somebody in the dark I got scared and came back. I had sense enough to stick the gloves and that radiator-cap in my pocket. So I came back and went down those steps to the porch again. And I knew if they heard the engine of

the car they'd come out maybe, because I thought that
woman I'd run into would set up a yell. But the drive
slopes down to the road from there, so all I had to do
was give her a push and let her coast backwards out of
gear till I got to the main road...'

'Which was why,' said H.M., 'a car was heard to go in, and
none come out, which confirmed Thompson's idea that it
was John Bohun. As a matter of fact, John didn't get back—
you know that now—until five o'clock, when Thompson
had dropped off to sleep. You may remember, I asked him
about that...

'But we'll go back again. You've realized by now that the
little piece of silver, the little triangle that's the key to the
whole affair, was broken off that radiator-cap ornament when
Emery used it. John found it; he didn't know what it was, but
it was the only clue he had. When he took Tait's body out to
the pavilion, he thought he was safe. Then he got the wind
up when he saw Potter measuring the tracks, and—'

'He's well enough now,' said Katharine quietly.

'Uh-huh. Well, he still wasn't willing to admit what he'd
done; but in that insane, nervous way of his he put it in his
own hand before he pulled the trigger. D'ye see? He heard the
great Chief Inspector Masters, the all-seeing eye of Scotland
Yard, was there; and he hoped Masters would see through
the brick wall and understand what it was and who had left it.

'Now, then! I had already, when Maurice spun out his
yarn for us, a faint glimmer of suspicion about Emery. But
I didn't know what weapon he'd used; Masters hadn't said
anything about the piece of metal yet. Having absolutely

nothing in the way of evidence against Emery, d'ye see, I couldn't say Boo to him. All I wanted to do was keep him under my eye as long as I could. He was in the house for the moment—but, as Rainger's friend, he'd speedily be shot *out* of the house by Maurice *unless Maurice were kept in a good humour.* And then we'd lost him. He wasn't even on the scene of the crime, apparently, when it was committed; and I couldn't even keep him as a witness for the inquest!

'The only thing to do was to intimate to Maurice, "Give Rainger and Rainger's friend a treat. Keep 'em here, be poisonously pleasant to 'em, and see how they both act when you release your bomb." That struck Maurice as one of the more delectable ideas. I had to pretend to half-believe his theory. Also, I didn't dare risk havin' Rainger get sober again. Because, if he really had an alibi as he said he had, both Rainger and Emery would have been thrown out when Maurice found he couldn't have the pleasure of hangin' Rainger. And in the meantime, son, I had to have a lead; I had to work fast, and either prove or disprove my lurkin' idea about Emery. Son, I was in a bleedin' sweat, and that's a fact; until Masters popped out with that information about the bit of metal.'

H.M. took a deep breath. He reached after Emery's statement again.

'I noticed right away that there was a big piece broken off the radiator-cap, and I knew where it must be. Then when I learned they thought she'd been killed in the pavilion I figured if they found that I might be sunk or I might not be, depending on whether they got wise to her really being killed in that funny room.'

'But I figured I better have a look for it if I could, only I didn't know how I could until that funny old guy comes out and asks me to take care of Carl and says he'll get that Miss Nancy Bohun to invite me to eat dinner there. I knew something was phony about it, but I didn't know what, and he said he didn't have any suspicion of me. And when he says to keep Carl drunk I didn't know what the hell, but I said I'd do it because I was afraid Carl had got wise to me. I gave myself away to him when I talked to him on the 'phone, because I didn't know there'd been funny work about taking her some place else. But I thought maybe Carl was too drunk to remember and I hoped he was.

'But he wasn't, because when I thought he'd passed out, after it was dark, I sneaked down to that big room and tried to look around after the piece off the radiator-cap. And Carl followed me. And I turned around and seen him, and he says, "What are you doing here?" And I said, "Nothing." He said, "You're a liar," and started to shout out that I'd killed her, so I grabbed him by the neck...

'And just after I'd pitched him down the steps, they almost got me. They couldn't hear anything, because there was a lot of reporters coming out of the house and motors back-firing just then. But in comes the old fat guy, and the other cop named Masters, and young Jim Bennett and that good-looking girl. And they come in one door while I was behind the door to the stairs. But I couldn't run down and out the lower door and in the house again, because there was cops and reporters there, and I thought I was caught...'

'And,' growled H.M., suddenly bringing his fist down on the table, 'if I'd had any sense, I'd have caught him then!'

'Caught him? But you didn't know—'

'Oh, yes I did. Now we're comin' to the last of it, and here's what happened. I sat down in that chair, I opened the drawer... And I knew what that piece of silver was. And I was sittin' and thinkin'—hot engine that smoked; I saw his car that afternoon—and it began to sort of swim and twist round in my mind what might have happened. Then was when I saw him.'

'Saw him?'

'His eye at that keyhole. Ain't you noticed how big that keyhole was? I was afraid I gave away that I saw him. How was I to know he'd killed Rainger, or that he could be caught then with his victim? All I saw was somebody behind that door. If I'd opened it and said, "Hey!" I'd have had him in a bad position, only I didn't know it. It'd have looked suspicious, his conduct would (I thought) if I merely found him hanging about on the other side of the door, but what would it have *proved*? Not a blinkin' thing!

'But all of a sudden I got my plan. He was probably, I thought, in that room huntin' the bit of metal I had in my hand. Maybe, maybe not. It was worth a risk. Anyway, I held it up carefully, so's he could see it; I emphasized that I was puttin' it back in the drawer. Meanwhile, I knew he couldn't get away, because Potter and the rest were down on the porch. Even if he left that door, he could hear me because of the big space under the door where the draught comes through.

'Well, I said *I* didn't know what the metal was. But I said I'd put it back in the drawer and take it up to London

tomorrow for a silversmith to tell me. Son, it dawned blazin'
in the old man's mind that that little triangle was the one
piece of evidence I could use against him—but not unless
I could bring it home to him by his own admission. He
could have said it came off *anybody's* radiator-cap. *But, if I
could manoeuvre him into stealin' that piece of silver out of the
drawer;* so he had it on his person when I charged him with
it...how was he goin' to deny *that?*'

Katharine sat up straight.

'Then the whole business,' she said, 'wasn't directed at
us? You didn't need to reproduce that business on the stairs?'

H.M. grinned. 'You got it, my dear. Exactly. All I needed
was an excuse to get everybody into that room, shove 'em
where their attention would be occupied, emphasize to
Emery that their attention would be occupied, and pretend
to let him into my scheme. He had to fall for it, or it wouldn't
work. And, with Rainger's body at the foot of those stairs,
he'd figure that in the confusion *nobody would see him.* That
was what I wanted. After one attempt to find that silver,
he wouldn't try another until he was certain he could do it
safely. And I pretended to play straight into his hands...

'I outlined a part of my plot while he was listenin'
behind the door; pretended I thought the silver was of no
importance; and when he'd got some idea of my scheme
I deliberately opened the window and yelled to Potter to
come upstairs—so he could escape safely.

'He went down, through the side door, and up through
the house again. Beryl Symonds dropped in on him immediately...but, Lord, wasn't the man wild when Masters
walked into that room! Notice his expression, son? Notice

how he acted then? Actually, I'd sent you and Masters down to see whether Emery was there; not Rainger. He burst out, I understand, with some sort of wild story about somebody tappin' at his door. That was obviously hogwash, because he said the gallery was dark; and yet Masters and I had turned on the lights when we came up. He was thinkin' about *himself* turnin' out the lights when he went down to King Charles's Room, and that gave him away. He called on the girl to support him, knowin' perfectly well she was so hysterical she would have agreed to anything.

'I could have cut my own throat,' said H.M. savagely, 'when I found Rainger's body. If I'd had sense enough to challenge him then! But I thought, by God, I *will* get him now... So I came back and deliberately pretended to take him into my scheme. It destroyed his last suspicion. He walked into the trap as neat as you please. Masters—I'd told him Masters was to be downstairs—Masters was actually in the gallery behind, and saw him sneak over and take the silver from the table-drawer when the lights were out. I knew I had him at any time I wanted him. So I called an end to my experiment, and...'

H.M. made a dull gesture. He stared at the blue-bound sheets and put them away in the desk. The drawer closed with a snap.

'That's all,' he said.

For a long time nobody spoke. The honking of traffic floated up in a lazy afternoon. Then H.M. hauled himself to his feet. He waddled over to the iron safe and took out of it a bottle, a syphon, and glasses. His big slovenly bulk showed against the window, high above the green Embankment, the glittering river, and the mighty curve of London.

'So now,' said H.M., 'you can forget it. You've had some nasty times and hours with that family of yours, ma'am; but you're free now, and your husband ain't a half bad feller. If ever you need the old man to break any more curses, sing out. In the meantime...'

'In the meantime?'

H.M. peered at the glasses. He looked round at the ancient room with its stuffings of crazy books and crooked pictures; of dust and the trophies of one man's deadly brain. He glanced down at the scattered lead soldiers on one table where a problem of human beings was being worked out...

'Oh, I dunno,' he said, and made a vague gesture. 'I'll go on, I suppose. Sittin' and thinkin'...'

If you've enjoyed

THE WHITE PRIORY MURDERS,

you won't want to miss

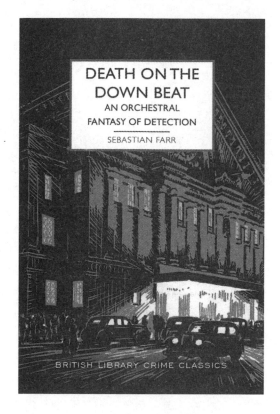

DEATH ON THE
DOWN BEAT
AN ORCHESTRAL
FANTASY OF DETECTION
─────────
SEBASTIAN FARR

BRITISH LIBRARY CRIME CLASSICS

the most recent
BRITISH LIBRARY CRIME CLASSIC
published by Poisoned Pen Press,
an imprint of Sourcebooks.

Mystery in the Channel
by Freeman Wills Crofts

Mystery in White
by J. Jefferson Farjeon

Portrait of a Murderer
by Anne Meredith

Santa Klaus Murder
by Mavis Doriel Hay

Secret of High Eldersham
by Miles Burton

Serpents in Eden
edited by Martin Edwards

Silent Nights
edited by Martin Edwards

Smallbone Deceased
by Michael Gilbert

Sussex Downs Murder
by John Bude

Thirteen Guests
by J. Jefferson Farjeon

Weekend at Thrackley
by Alan Melville

Z Murders
by J. Jefferson Farjeon

Praise for the
British Library Crime Classics

"Carr is at the top of his game in this taut whodunit... The British Library Crime Classics series has unearthed another worthy golden age puzzle."
—*Publishers Weekly*, STARRED Review,
for *The Lost Gallows*

"A wonderful rediscovery."
—*Booklist*, STARRED Review, for *The Sussex Downs Murder*

"First-rate mystery and an engrossing view into a vanished world."
—*Booklist*, STARRED Review, for *Death of an Airman*

"A cunningly concocted locked-room mystery, a staple of Golden Age detective fiction."
—*Booklist*, STARRED Review, for *Murder of a Lady*

"The book is both utterly of its time and utterly ahead of it."
—*New York Times Book Review* for *The Notting Hill Mystery*

"As with the best of such compilations, readers of classic mysteries will relish discovering unfamiliar authors, along with old favorites such as Arthur Conan Doyle and G.K. Chesterton."
—*Publishers Weekly*, STARRED Review, for *Continental Crimes*

"In this imaginative anthology, Edwards—president of Britain's Detection Club—has gathered together overlooked criminous gems."
—*Washington Post* for *Crimson Snow*

"The degree of suspense Crofts achieves by showing the

growing obsession and planning is worthy of Hitchcock. Another first-rate reissue from the British Library Crime Classics series."
—*Booklist*, STARRED Review, for *The 12.30 from Croydon*

"Not only is this a first-rate puzzler, but Crofts's outrage over the financial firm's betrayal of the public trust should resonate with today's readers."
—*Booklist*, STARRED Review, for *Mystery in the Channel*

"This reissue exemplifies the mission of the British Library Crime Classics series in making an outstanding and original mystery accessible to a modern audience."
—*Publishers Weekly*, STARRED Review, for *Excellent Intentions*

"A book to delight every puzzle-suspense enthusiast"
—*New York Times* for *The Colour of Murder*

"Edwards's outstanding third winter-themed anthology showcases uniformly clever and entertaining stories, mostly from lesser known authors, providing further evidence of the editor's expertise…This entry in the British Library Crime Classics series will be a welcome holiday gift for fans of the golden age of detection."
—*Publishers Weekly*, STARRED Review, for *The Christmas Card Crime and Other Stories*

Poisoned Pen
PRESS

poisonedpenpress.com